The woman who loved to dance

Anne Ousby

ISBN: 9781095874844

THE WOMAN WHO LOVED TO DANCE

To Carolyn

Anne Ousby

All love

Anne.

x x

Dedication

This book is dedicated to the women who love to dance. Too many to mention them all but top of the list comes Virginia, my friend and our inspiration — who just happens to be a Dance Master.

'Dance me to your beauty with a burning violin
Dance me through the panic till I'm safely gathered in '

Acknowledgments

Heartfelt thanks to everyone who has supported and encouraged me throughout the writing of this novel.

Especial thanks to Maureen for her editing. For Ali for her invaluable help in publishing this book. For Anne and Erica, Cath and Rachel, for their encouragement and insightfulness. For my family, as always, excellent blurbers and amazing book- cover makers.

And for Hazel and Chris for sharing their passion and knowledge for historical dance..

The woman who loved to dance

Prologue

The sun is rising as we close our door and set out. There are few people abroad, but those we see greet us, wishing us good day. It has rained in the night making everything fresh and clean. Even the rubbish, floating in the rii, sparkles with bright morning dew. Sunlight polishes the cobbles into burnished gold and jet, while fingers of light probe into the narrowest dark calli. Birds sing from every rooftop and brightly coloured butterflies wreath the lemon trees, which droop over high walls.

I hate it all.

We walk in silence towards the Rialto, where we must cross into San Polo. The famous Rialto markets attract merchants and traders from all corners of the empire and, as we near the bridge, it grows busier and louder. Everyone is shouting , the men's foreign tongues clashing with the shrill voices of women, bartering with stallholders. Barges and skiffs jostle for position on the rio, waiting their turn to unload cargoes into the huge warehouses. Normally I relish the vivacity of this place but today I keep my eyes lowered. Forcing my way through

1

the crowds I ignore the traders as they chase away little beggar children, and the boatmen, who hawk long skeins of spittle into the rio, as they wait for passengers.

Nonna grips my arm tightly. 'Stay close...' she warns, as she has a hundred times before, '...and don't talk to anyone. There are bad people here.' But this is daytime and the place holds no fears for me. It is what lies ahead that terrifies me.

Just before we cross the bridge Nonna leads me into the ancient church of Giocomo di Rialto. We are to light candles. Sitting a few rows back I watch as Nonna kneels to say her rosary. I wait until I am certain that she isn't watching, then I creep outside.

There is a statue on the Bridge of a little hunchback. His name is Il Gobbo di Rialto. He carries a stone slab on his crooked shoulders. Legend has it that The Hunchback brings good fortune to those who pat his rough head and wish him good health as they pass by. People write down their wishes and leave the messages on the slab. I run my hand over his bent head and whisper, 'Good health, sweet little,, Gobbo,' then I wish that my friend is in Paradise with her mother and brothers and that she will always have enough to eat and there will be music and dancing and sunlight, all day long. When I am finished I make the sign of the cross. At that exact moment Nonna comes out of the church and sees what I am doing. She grasps my arm, fingers pinching into my flesh, and hobbles away, dragging me along behind her.

'Why do you venerate the pagan statue, Veronica?' she hisses. 'It is sacrilege. We are not heathens. We are Christians. Now come."

2

She had never understood my love of Venice's pagan past, but how to explain to such a saintly person? I had grown up amongst the poor and destitute of San Marco and I was repulsed by their dirty, deformed bodies. I saw them mirrored again in the churches. They were the saints and martyrs, with their broken limbs and tortured flesh. They were the Christ in agony on the cross, abandoned by everyone, all hope gone. I couldn't bear the pain and anguish of Christianity. Little Gobbo made me smile, even though he had a bent back, and today I needed to smile.

We hurry on in silence, both caught up in our own thoughts. Halfway down a narrow calle we hear a cart coming up fast behind us and scramble into a doorway to allow its passage. The cart is rickety and drawn by an old nag, driven by two grim-faced men. As it rattles past I see there are shrouded corpses in the back. Each time the wheels strike a cobble the bodies shift and jostle against one another in some sort of obscene dance. A small group of wretched women with their heads covered, shuffle along behind the cart. One is carrying a wailing infant.

If Nonna had turned for home then I would have gone with her but she walks on and my pride will not allow me to take the coward's way out.

By the time we get to the pit the men are unloading the bodies. There are no prayers or reverence or dignity. I would have cried then, but I could think of nothing but the stench of decomposing flesh. Nonna pulls her scarf up to cover her mouth and nose and motions for me to do the same. The smell of vinegar is strong but the stench from the pit is overpowering, I feel bile rising in my throat.

I want to look away but I cannot, my gaze keeps returning to that hole, where a shifting black veil of flies rise and fall over what remains of the corpses. We watch in silence, except for the crying of the child. It is such a forlorn sound. I don't think you should take a baby to a funeral. It's not proper.

As the men hurry to finish their task I'm sure I catch a flash of red as they take the last, smaller body from the cart and heave it into the pit. Nonna must have seen it too because her grip on my hand tightens.

'No, no.' I sob, ' It can't be her. She was bigger than this, Nonna. It's a mistake ...it's someone else. See? The body? It's so thin. It isn't her.'

Nonna looks away but I see her lips moving in prayer.

The woman carrying the baby is weeping silently, her body shaking with grief, she uses the edge of her shawl to wipe away her tears. Another woman steps forward and throws a branch of apple blossom into the pit. I wish I had brought something but it's too late, everything's too late.

When it is over the women turn to walk away and the one with the baby looks straight at me. She is tall and bent and her face is streaked with tears and dirt but there is something about her, something so familiar, and that's when I see the jagged scar running down her cheek. 'Wait'. I call. 'Is it you?' She stares at me for a long moment, then turns her back and hurries away. The others follow. 'Please wait.' She must hear me but she keeps walking.

Nonna squeezes my hand and leads me gently away. 'Come, my Veronica, leave them to their sorrow. There is nothing you can do.'

And I allow her to take me away, back to my life – my blessed life.

Today

1576

There is that moment between sleeping and waking when the mind floats free − no pain, no sadness, just random images and memories, tumbling, tumbling, and I see Ginevra.

She is dancing. Her faded, patched dress flares about her skinny knees as she turns and spins like a bud about to open. She is younger than me, with green eyes and hair the colour of the sour little plums that grow on a crooked tree in our campiello wall. I am jealous of her hair.

I mark the rhythm with a stick on an old metal pot, while the little blackamoor plays a tin whistle. He lacks talent but Nonna says I must be kind and allow him to play for us. Maybe he will improve. I call him Boy. He has another name, but it's not important. He doesn't live in our campiello and he stinks of the rio. He knows he mustn't sit too close to me. I asked him once why he smelt like dead dogs and he says his father made him swim in the rii.

'How disgusting,' I sneer. 'Christian boys wash in clean water.'

6

'I am Christian,' he answers softly, looking up at me. his large brown eyes full of sorrow. 'My papa says I must learn to swim because I'm a boatman.'

Boys aren't supposed to cry so I turn my back on him.

As Ginevra pirouettes, her hair streams out behind her like a banner of the rising sun. Some of us in the campiello have dark hair, like me, with brown eyes. Others have golden hair and blue eyes, and there are a few with tight, curly black hair like Boy. Ginevra is the only one with red hair. Nonna says she is a Cypriot. I am jealous of that too. I am just an ordinary Venetian and my name is Veronica Maria Bracci.

Dancing is my passion, even without music. What need of music when I have the rhythms in my body? When I dance I feel a sort of power, too grown up to explain. It takes hold of me and I have to go where it leads. I forget the men watching and the women's voices, I forget everything but the dance.   Sometimes Nonna takes my hand when I am done and leads me away, whispering. 'Veronica, Veronica. Modestia.' But when I look up into her face I see the smile hiding in the corner of her eye.

Once, she told me such a strange thing. She said that bodies have memories. I laughed out loud at that. Little Nonna was being silly. But she shook her head and put her finger to her lips, so that I knew to listen carefully.

'This is our secret, piccolo. You were a dancer in a past life.'

7

Past Life? What was that? I knew about the next life, about Hell and Purgatory and Paradise, where all good little girls went, but, past life?

However, Nonna wasn't finished. 'You have forgotten who you once were and where you came from but the steps and rhythms you possess have always been part of your soul.'

My soul? That belonged to God — didn't it? Nonna must have seen my confusion because she pulled me into her embrace and I felt her powerful heartbeat against me. 'Do not be afraid, Veronica. The Good Lord has given you a gift—a precious gift. You must use it well.'

I always remembered her words and I wasn't afraid. When I couldn't sleep at night I created new dances in my head. I danced to the storm winds rushing through the calli, or whistling down the chimneys. I danced to bird song and people's laughter, to children playing and babies crying. I danced for sadness, for joy, for every sound, and for every emotion.

I tried to teach Ginevra to see and hear what I did but ,when I tried, she wrinkled her nose at me and tapped her head with one finger. I didn't mind. I was proud I was a little crazy. I have a precious gift.

While Ginevra performs, mothers lean over the balconies, laughing and calling out to each other. 'Hey, Sofia. leave your work. Come watch your Ginevra dance. She has talent.'

'Where are you, Nonna? Put down your scrubbing brush. The child's dress is washed by now.'

8

Ginevra skips in and out of the billowing bed linen, strung on lines from balcony to balcony. Men lounge in the doorways, their eyes never leaving her. She is giggling and waving at them and loses the beat. My friend is so easily distracted. 'Ginevra,' I hiss, 'concentrate.'

We often perform plays for the mothers and their men and I lead the Dance. The men promise us sweetmeats and pretty trinkets if we will perform for them alone, but Nonna forbids it. Sometimes Ginevra dances for them. I tell her not to but she looks at me, in that way I don't understand, and shrugs. 'They give me coins and food.'

I have decided that I don't like men.

Ginevra couldn't create dances like me but she was very good at finding things to use in our dances. She picked up all sorts of discarded objects on the tow paths, or floating in the rii. Once she found a beautiful velvet mask. Someone must have dropped it during the Carnevale. We took turns in wearing it. She had a collection of hats, cloaks and remnants of colourful cloth. Most of it was old and torn but we could still swish the material about us and pretend to be nobili. The best thing she ever found was when she was begging at the market. All the stall holders knew Ginevra and she usually returned with a basket full of old vegetables, bits of meat, and sometimes eggs.

On that particular day I was sitting waiting impatiently for her to return, and, when she'd taken the basket to her mother, she squatted beside me, munching a very old carrot. I knew before she spoke, that she'd found something special. Ginevra's face was never good at lies. I was feeling kind that day and I didn't want to spoil her moment of

9

glory, so I pretended I hadn't noticed one of her hands hidden behind her back.

When she was finished eating she got up and curtsied low before me, then she went, 'la la,' did a twirl and produced the most beautiful crimson ostrich feather I had ever seen.

'But, where did you get it, Ginevra?' Fear clutched at me and I lowered my voice. 'You...you didn't steal it, did you?' We both knew what happened to thieves in our Glorious Republic.

'No, course not, Nica', she always called me that. 'I'm not stupid. I found it, honest. It was sticking out of the water, like someone was holding it out to me. I just leant over and grabbed it. Isn't it the best feather in the world?'

And it was. If I balanced the quill on my palm, the plume reached so high it tickled my nose. Ginevra and I competed with each other to see who could balance it for the longest. A group of younger children made a circle around us and they counted off on their fingers until the feather decided to jump away from us. After we grew tired of that, I said, 'Let's see where it takes us', because I had already felt the pulse of the feather and I knew it wanted to be free.

'No.' Ginevra insisted. 'I'm taking it where I want it to go.' but she didn't, she couldn't. It allowed her to think she had it tamed but then it would suddenly shoot off to the side, or collapse against her chest and slide down her body to the paving. It would rear up high and then low, it would turn quickly or stay immobile. It was like it was alive and the more Ginevra tried to make it do what she wanted, the more it refused. In the end she got frustrated and threw it at me. I still

10

had difficulty but I followed where the feather led me, instead of the other way round. There were still times when it tricked me but I was laughing and shouting to Ginevra. 'See? This is the way to do it, Ginevra. It's a dance and we must forget everything and go where we're led.'

But Ginevra charged after me and tore the feather out of my hand. Her face was as crimson as the feather. I'd never seen her so angry. 'No, I decide where I go, not some stupid feather,' she shouted. Then she broke it into pieces and tossed it at my feet. 'I decide,' she shrieked as she ran into the house. 'I decide.'

It was only later that I realised how carefree my early childhood had been. Our campiello was a secret place without a proper name. A stranger might walk past unaware that the crooked gap in the wall, where some old stonework had collapsed, was the entrance to our world. This narrow space led to a yard behind a crumbling old house, where mothers, children and 'sometimes' fathers lived.

I lived there with my Nonna. We had a bed each and food every day. Ginevra lived in the room above us, with her mother and four brothers. Those boys were very noisy. I often saved food for Ginevra. We were free to run wild, exploring San Marco and playing games on long summer's evenings, when the cobbles warmed our behinds and the orange shafts of dying sun made our faces glow.

I was twelve when this idyllic life ended. One by one my friends disappeared from the campiello. They were there one day and gone the next. It was the older ones first, like Pazienza. who took the boy's

11

part in my dances. She was tall and graceful but had an ugly scar stumbling across her forehead and down one cheek. Nonna said it was rude to stare or ask questions, so I never found out what had happened to her. After she disappeared from our campiello I asked her mother where she was but she refused to answer me, and, when I pestered her, she said a very ugly word.

All this made me uneasy but as long as I had my Ginevra I felt secure, that was until the terrible day when she vanished too. I ran to Nonna screaming. 'Where is Ginevra? I can't find her anywhere and she didn't come for her breakfast. Is she ill, Nonna? Is she dead?' People died all the time in our part of San Marco but it could never happen to me and Ginevra. We had sworn to be friends forever.

Nonna hugged me and wiped away my tears. 'Caro figlio, Ginevra is not dead. She is grown up now and has to work.'

'But I am older than she is. I want to work too.' Nonna had those bright red spots on her cheeks but I still spoke. 'She doesn't have muscles like me and I can run faster than her. She coughs if she runs. I'd be better at a job than her. It's not fair. I will make her Mamma tell me where she is, then I shall bring her home.' I was hysterical by then, my eyes screwed up in fury.

Women had come out into the square hearing the commotion and I spotted Ginevra's mother, standing behind the others. A boy clung to her skirt and another straddled her hip. Before I could move, Nonna caught my arm and marched me indoors. I screeched and struggled to get free but she wouldn't let go. Inside, she swung me

12

around to face her. 'You will not go anywhere near that poor woman. She has enough sorrow to bear. D'you hear me?'

I didn't reply and she shook me hard. 'I'm waiting, Veronica.'

'Nonna, you're hurting.'

'Say it, Veronica. Say you'll leave her alone.'

I mumbled 'yes' and she let me go. 'But who will dance with me now?' I whined. ' I hate her, she's never going to be my friend again.'

Nonna sighed and patted my head. 'Always remember, Veronica, that you are blessed. Each day get down on your knees and give thanks to the blessed Madonna for your good fortune. Now come, we must hurry. Your Mamma will be here and you must put on a clean dress and brush your hair.'

It was a long time before I realised that this mamma – the beautiful, fierce woman, who swept in and out of my life like a hard, yard brush – was my mother.

This is no dream

And then my eyes snap open. Some noise has woken me. The room where I lie is in darkness and, at first, I am disoriented, but then I hear the pounding of blood in my ears, reminding me of what I have become, and the feeling of dread returns. How many days is it since my Nonna died? Two, three? I have lost count. Each moment is like a day. The pestilencia is a cruel death but the suffering is brief, they say. May God be praised. I should have left this place before, but I wasn't sure then, I'm still not sure.

From somewhere nearby comes a sudden crash and thud of an axe in wood. The looters are getting closer but what do I care? I'm not frightened. What can they take from me that hasn't already been lost? Another splintering crack, then the shouts of angry men and feet pounding along the path beneath my window. A dog barks frantically close by, a door slams, then silence, except for the drip, drip of water. It rained again last night and rivulets of moisture worm their way down behind my once beautiful silken, wall-hangings. Venice is sinking into the sea. People are deserting the city, abandoning the old and the dying. Our Most Serene Republic is reduced to foul, flooded rii and collapsing buildings. The stench of decay and death grows stronger with every passing hour.

14

I lie there watching as the first fingers of morning light probe the darkest recesses of my chamber, bouncing off the mirror and sending a kaleidoscope of colour across the walls and ceiling. The light drills into my aching eyes and I attempt to turn away but the heavy covers pin me to the bed like a crucified butterfly.

How many times have I lain here at dawn and heard the gondoliers' songs drifting up from beneath my window and the 'slap, slap' of water as the boats slid gently along the canal? Once I loved the morning clamour, the ringing of voices, like metal striking metal, as the tradesmen tied up on mooring posts and unloaded their goods onto the towpaths. Then came the haggling, the raised voices, the oaths, the laughter and the smell of freshly baked bread and ripe cheeses. The good natured ribaldry of the boatmen, the vitality, the life force.

'Ciao, bella Signora', some youth would call. 'I have sweet oranges from Tovioli, honey from the slopes of Mt Etna, wine from Modena, Sweetmeats from Arabia. Whatever you desire we can supply.'

I would lie awake, my arms cradling my wondrous sleeping boy, and watch the sun's reflection in this same mirror, like a liquid golden sundial, tracing the sun's path, as it crept up his naked body, lighting on the gold chain lying on his chest and the small delicate key hanging from it. Carlo never took this chain off and, when we were first married I asked him what the key was for and he would change the subject. I used to say the key unlocked his heart but he would smile and shake his head. I don't think I'm any more inquisitive than most

15

women but the mystery of the key began to prey on my mind. I imagined it was the key to some precious gift given to him by some lover. Yes, I was jealous. Carlo was mine, and mine alone. So I began to hate that key and wanted it gone.

One morning, as I lay impatiently, waiting for him to wake, it seemed the perfect opportunity to take the chain from around his neck. I had no thought beyond this. I had the key in my fingers and was lifting the chain carefully over his head when he woke and leapt from the bed grasping my fingers hard, crushing them into the chain, so that I cried out in pain. He was like a mad man and I thought for one terrible moment that he was going to murder me. His hand clutched at my throat but then he saw it was me and let go. I didn't recognise this Carlo. His blue, blue, eyes had turned almost black with passion and he was shaking uncontrollably. Pulling me into his arms, he covered my face with kisses. 'Mia, Veronica. I'm so sorry, my darling, I'm so sorry. Please forgive me. Please, please forgive me'. He was crying now in great gulping spasms like an abandoned child. 'Please don't hate me, my darling.'

I looked up at him. 'I could never hate you. But what ails you, my Carlo? Are you ill?'

'No, no. But you must promise never to do that again.'

'But why?' I was getting my courage back. My love had returned. 'It's only a key.'

'No, Veronica, this key is my life, your life...our unborn children's lives. Without this, Bertrames is nothing. Do you

16

understand? This key,' and he lifted it up to the light. 'This key unlocks our 'treasure.'

My fingers reach automatically to the blue phial on the chain, hanging about my neck. Uncorking the bottle, I drink a few fetid drops but my mouth is dry and the vile potion pools in my mouth. I force myself to swallow. The after-taste is rank.

I am trying to have faith, my love.

The ferryman will be here soon. I must dress. I have a dread of dying alone in this room, a feast for the flies. The pestilencia vendors pass beneath my window each morning, bringing me provisions. When I have need of something I leave a note and money in the basket, which is tied with a length of rope. They put food and water inside and I wind it up to my room. I have done this since Nonna's death but I have not the strength nor the appetite any longer. The basket and rope lie abandoned beside my window – the food untouched, the un-stoppered flagon of water on its side beside the basket, its precious liquid seeping onto the tiles. I am so thirsty.

I have no news of Alfonso or the child. Before the maid abandoned me she took theriac to La Guidecca, and to Giada and my sisters on the Rialto.

The hammering starts up again but this time it is different. I know this sound, this is the rhythmic, organised pounding of workmen as they knock wooden staves into the ground. They are closing off the bridge on my rio, my only escape route. The vendor called up to me yesterday, or was it the day before? He said it was rumoured that the

17

Doge has ordered that all rii in San Marco be closed to water traffic, entering or leaving.

Struggling to the edge of my bed, and, with what little strength I have, I push away the remaining bed covers. The effort leaves me gasping, like a dying fish and the stench of my unwashed flesh rises. There is no one to bathe me now, or hold a wet rag to my burning skin. The servants are dead or fled. And my little Nonna? I miss her so much. The street children called her, 'fat toad', but I only saw the kindness in the lines about her eyes and felt the softness of her touch. I lie back down again and close my eyes. Blessed sleep.

Blame

After Ginevra's disappearance I needed to blame someone for my loss, so, at first I hated her mother for making her go to work, then it was Nonna's turn for not caring enough and finally I blamed the unknown people Ginevra was working for. But deep down I knew who was really to blame. It was me and it was a punishment from God for my vanity and immodesty. So, I made a solemn promise to be good and devote and never to dance again until my friend returned.

With no Ginevra, or music, or dance, the campiello became a foreign land and for the first time I saw the squalor, hopelessness and ugliness that surrounded me. How could I have thought this place so magical? There were no children of my age to play with now, no one to dance or sing with, no laughter, just screaming infants and long, long days and nights. Nonna saw my misery and tried her best to entertain me by singing peasant folk songs in her deep, cracked voice and clapping her hands in time to the beat. She had no sense of rhythm and once it would have made me smile but no longer. I had no joy in my heart.

Boy still came each day, hanging about until I could stand it no longer, so I shoved him hard and screamed at him to go away. 'Where is she?' he begged, his little voice quavering. 'When is she coming back?'

I glared at him. 'What's it got to do with you?' My voice came out all ugly, but I was Ginevra's best friend, not some smelly little Moor from Africa. I was the only one allowed to be sad. I chased him off that day but he was there again the next and the next until I lost my temper and threw stones at him. I hurt him on purpose. He didn't come back after that and I was glad.

There was a huge block of fallen masonry in the centre of our courtyard, made from black bubbly stone, rough to the touch, and spiked with wild flowers, growing in the cracks. Green, soft moss sprouted like cool velvet on the sides, where the sun never reached.

Ginevra and I loved that stone and used to climb onto its top and pretend to be emperors and empresses, lifting our arms to the sun and jumping off, high into the air. Sometimes we held hands and leapt together. We would scream out our names, as loud as we could, as we fell together in a laughing heap. Our knees were always covered in scabs, where we had tumbled on the broken paving stones.

No one else was allowed on our stone. The boys tried to steal it off us once but we fought them. I was strong and could hit really hard and I knew how to hurt boys. Nonna had shown me once − just in case I was ever attacked, she said. Ginevra was quite weak but she was good at throwing stones. After the battle we had injuries but the boys had more cuts and bruises than us and they never tried it again.

After she went away I spent a lot of time sitting on that block of stone and thinking about her. I had to believe she would come home

20

one day and everything would be as it was. But that never happens does it? Not in real life.

I roamed the canal paths picking bunches of wild flowers and leaving them for her on the stone, along with crusts of bread. I imagined her happiness as she ate the bread and held the flowers to her nose, breathing in their fragrance. I only had to shut my eyes and there she was again, grinning at me, with the gap between her front teeth and her hair shining in the sunlight, like a glittering helmet.

On waking each morning I prayed it would be the day I found her. San Marco was my entire universe and I reasoned that Ginevra must still be here, somewhere. Her mother and brothers had left the campiello shortly after her disappearance, so Nonna was the only person I could ask. I badgered her day and night to tell me until I wore her out and she would sink into her chair and hide her head in her hands. 'No more, my Veronica, please, I beg of you, no more.'

That's when Nonna started to take me on long explorations of our Most Serene Republic. We walked the rii and crossed many crooked, forgotten pontis. I memorised the names of churches, monuments and the six areas of the city − the siestri. I made up a song about them. There was Cannaregio, San Polo, then Dorsoduro, including the isla Guidecca. There was San Marco, where I lived, which included San Giorgio Maggiore and lastly there was Castello, including San Pietro di Castello and Sant'Elena. There were all the islands too but they weren't as important as the six and my brain was already full with the other names.

One day Nonna pointed to a gondola as it swept past us. 'See. Veronica. On the bow of that boat there is a metal ferro? See? It has six fingers. That is to remind us of our six siestri, lest we forget.'

Nonna's eyes sparkled when she talked about our city. She called it Serenissima as if it were a favourite child. Serenissima? A lovely word to remember. And bit by bit I began to see the beauty of my world through her eyes and it eased the ache in my heart. She took me into the Basilica of San Pietro Castello, and showed me the ancient stone seat, they call St Peter's throne, that the Byzantines had given to Venice as a gift for something we'd done for his country − I can't remember what. I saw the magnificent gilt, bronze horses that stood proudly outside St Marco's Basilica, and the famous Winged Lion. We visited the Campiello dei Mori, where statues of four Muslim men stood, dressed in flowing robes. We walked beside the boarding houses where pilgrims lodged before journeying to the Holy Land. Nonna hurried me through the calli of the Ghetto, where the buildings rose five or six storeys high on either side. She warned me not to look at the Jews in their yellow caps and badges. I asked her why they wore the yellow and she whispered that they had killed our Lord and ate Christian babies. The people looked like ordinary people to me but I walked very fast, just in case.

I loved it all, but one of my most favourite outings was to the busy fish and food markets lining the waterways. There were all sort of stalls, where we loitered amongst crowds of strangers dressed in costumes of saffron, indigo, crimson and gold. The cacophony of clashing languages and dialects as they bought and sold goods made

22

my ears ring, and the aromas of spicy, strange food made my eyes water and my tummy rumble. There were Muslims in flowing robes, Turks with their strange shaped zami hats and their white horned judicial turbans, and one morning I even saw a Moor gondolier, rowing a beautiful patriciate gondola. The feize, hiding the noble occupants, was covered by a shimmering blue satin curtain, decorated with intricate lace work. A barefoot child guided the aft rudder and I thought for a moment he might have been my Boy but the gondola had disappeared into a smaller waterway, before I could ask Nonna.

The rii fascinated me and I never tired of watching the hustle and bustle of water traffic. It didn't matter that the water was full of filth and stank, because, even as a child, I knew these waterways were the lifeblood of my universe. In the early mornings, before the river mist cleared, huge, flat-bottomed water barges lumbered out of the mists, like great beasts. These barchi, carried fresh water for sale to the Republic from TerraFerma. After them came the heavily laden cargo boats piled high with all manner of goods — wine, cheese, fresh fruit and vegetables. Smaller barges ducked in and out of the larger vessels, carrying precious cargoes of Moreno glass, Turkish carpets, silks and exotic spices from the Orient, while fleets of public gondolas, painted black, buzzed in and around the others, carrying citizens to their work places. Nonna said that Our Excellent Prince — the Serene Doge, had passed a law that gondolas be undecorated because he believed that ostentatious displays of wealth were ungodly. It took me a while to master ostentatious. Heavy fines were levied on anyone breaking the law. Of course the wealthy didn't care about this, they could afford the

23

fines, and their privately owned patriciate gondolas were covered in ornamentation and had brightly coloured satin and velvet seats and fittings concealed within their feizes. I especially liked the small gondolas called puparin, used by messengers, or small parties of patriciates, carrying crossbows and dressed in hunting clothes, on their way to the lagoon to shoot wildfowl. But if I had to choose my favourite boats, these were the public ferries. I would hurry to the slipways when they docked, dragging Nonna along behind me to watch, as the passengers streamed off. I wanted to know where they were going, what they were doing. Why was that woman smacking her child? Why did that old man make a strange sign to another one? Look at that old woman nearly bent double. How does she not fall over? Where does she live? What lives do they lead?

Nonna held my hand tightly at these times, as if she sensed my desire to go where these people led, and she would say 'It's time for Mass, Veronica.' Whether it was or not, but for Nonna it was always time for Mass. She was very holy and fasted four times a week. She could never pass a church, however insignificant, without entering and praying in the Lady chapel or lighting a votive candle for the poor and destitute. I would sit in a side pew waiting for her, pretending to pray. I loved the drama of those holy places and had a terrible urge to jump up onto the benches and dance across from one side of the church to the other, arms reaching up to the ornate vaulted ceilings, covered in grinning golden cupids and angels. I loved the heady smell of incense, hot in my throat, and the hushed voices of worshippers as they passed softly beneath the exquisite stained glass windows. I was stunned by the sheer beauty of it all, as sunlight flared through the windows and illuminated the darkest recesses of the church, revealing the frescoes painted by our famous Venetian artists. What a dance I could have created for God. I still believed in Him back then.

Nonna worked very hard to make me forget my sadness and I was truly grateful to her, but beneath all the sensory stimulation she lay before me, there was always that one hope, getting smaller and smaller as time went by, that this might be the day when I found my friend and we would run into each other's arms and swear that we would never be parted again. For those hours of hopeful anticipation I shook off my melancholy but the moment I set foot in the campiello again, the black cloud of misery and loneliness descended once more.

I don't know how long this state of affairs lasted but there came the day when the inevitable happened. I was sitting on our block of stone, with my usual offerings, waiting for Nonna to take me exploring, but when I tried to picture my friend's face and her delight in the flowers and bread, she refused to appear for me. Try as I might, I couldn't see her face or hear her voice. She had abandoned me. And that was when I decided who was the real person I should hate. It was Ginevra. She was treacherous and didn't love me, she never had, or she would have come back to me. I tore her flowers into shreds and stamped on them, until they were an ugly green smear on the paving stones, then I broke the crust of bread into tiny pieces and threw them high in the air. After a moment a blackbird flew down and pecked at the crumbs and when I raised my hand, to frighten him away, he put his head on one side and stared at me. I flapped my hands and he took off lazily, with some bread in his beak. He flew to the other side of the campiello, settling on a ledge, where he ate the bread slowly, his beady eyes never leaving mine. I had the strangest feeling that I had no business being there, in his world. I was trespassing. Who was I? I was nothing but an interloper in his kingdom. He was lord of the square and the offerings were for him. But I was so much bigger than he, so why wasn't he afraid? Because you're a lump, a big lump. that moves about slowly and flaps its wings, but cannot fly.

And he was right. I couldn't fly. I was stuck in this place with Nonna, amongst people I didn't understand or like. All I knew was that I was different from them. Why wasn't I working? Where did our food come from? Who paid for our needs? Compared to the others I think we must have been rich. The mothers had reason to mistrust us but they didn't treat us unkindly. Perhaps they were just too exhausted to care? But if they accepted us, what must they have made of Mamma, who visited us like some exotic creature from across the seas. I always

26

knew when she was coming because the women would gather at the windows to watch as this wealthy, confident woman stepped daintily amongst the filth and street garbage, side-stepping the sprawling drunks at our door – a 'kerchief clutched delicately to her nose.

So began the season of questioning and Nonna bore the brunt of it. Why didn't we live with Mamma and who was my father and did I have brothers and sisters and who was she and why wasn't I sent to work, and, and....but then Nonna's face would flush and she would shake her head as though she was overwhelmed by it all. 'I am your Nonna,' she would repeat, over and over again. 'And you are my Veronica.'

'I know you're Nonna,' I'd screech back at her. 'But who is Veronica?'

Matters were made worse by my mother's sudden and inexplicable interest in me. Her monthly visits became weekly, and then, almost daily. It left Nonna in a perpetual state of anxiety.

'Your Mamma's coming, Veronica.' I can still hear the panic in her voice. 'Please try to smile. Your Mamma will like that.'

But I wasn't going to smile for anyone, least of all this stranger called Mamma. I knew she didn't like me. I was an inconvenience to be dealt with as quickly as possible. She was always in a hurry, on her way somewhere else – somewhere much more interesting. I didn't love her, how could I?

There was, however, something about her that I admired. It was the way she dressed. I preferred to wear jerkins and breeches back then but some of Mamma's dresses took my breath away. She dressed

27

like a noble woman, and never more so than on the day she changed my life forever. That day her gown was made from many-layers of whispering silk, covered with embroidered flowers in gold thread. The material changed colour as her body moved. One moment it was purple, then lilac, then pink. I wanted to touch that dress so badly, it was like a pain in my side. Here was someone who knew who she was and what she was worth. I had a sudden impulse to ask her all the questions that needed answers, but she never gave me the opportunity to speak. She was complaining as soon as she caught sight of me.

'Are you determined to have perpetual frown lines, girl? Stand up straight. Shoulders back. You're not a child, Veronica, so stop behaving like one. There are going to be big changes around here.'

She left in a frenzy of rustling skirts and determination and, within days, had hired a tutor for me, an old man who smelt of fish – very old fish. I was told to call him il proffesore. I didn't. He came each morning for two hours.

At first I proved an obstinate pupil, but then he taught me to read. He told Mamma I had aptitude and brought me religious tracts about Catholic morality. But I didn't care what the subject matter was, it was the shape of the letters and the sounds that fascinated me. I trailed my fingers around the curves of the letters and drew them in the sky. I practised writing chastity, silence, modesty, reticence, sobriety and obedience with a stick, on the rii paths. People passing by must have thought I was crazy. I knew what modestia meant but the rest of the words were a mystery. I asked the old man and he said, 'They are

28

the attributes that all Christian girls should aspire to, in order to attain eternal life.'

Writing was an extension of reading for me and I was soon copying words down, that I admired. I drank up each syllable, rejoicing in their sounds. I also scribbled little stories about girls – not unlike myself – who vanquished devils and ventured to the Orient. I took passage aboard wooden galleys or majestic round bellied cogs – five storeys high – that lumbered into the Lagoon, like monstrous, sea monsters.

Nonna warned me that it was unnatural for girls to write words down and would rush around picking up scraps of my stories and hiding them before Mamma saw. But fear of this Mamma never stopped me doing anything I wanted and I began to write poetry too. My desire for knowledge outweighed every other thought. Nonna said I made her brain hurt but at least she was able to relax a little because I had something else to think about. There was no time to waste on Ginevra, my once upon a time friend. She was an old enemy now, deep down in my bad heart And the Dance? Oh, the Dance was still there, waiting patiently, just out of sight, around a corner.

The next stage

My education continued but Mamma was never satisfied with my progress. She was never 'pleased' with anything I did and I knew she was planning something else. There was never any discussion about my wishes and the first I knew of the next stage was when three of Mamma's men arrived and ordered us to pack our belongings. They didn't tell us where we were going, and it was only after I screamed at one of them that he said we were to be moved into rooms, adjacent to Madam's, and to hurry up. I told him I wasn't going to be ordered about by servants, particularly ugly servants with no manners, so he thrust me rudely aside and set to work. I saw the contempt on their faces as they tossed our few meagre possessions into panniers. Grabbing my few precious books I stood with my back to the door glaring at them. Meanwhile. Nonna had retreated to her favourite rickety, old chair, refusing to move and was wailing like a strangled cat.

'But this is my home,' she kept shrieking, 'I'm never leaving. This is my home. I shall die here.'

If I'm honest I was quite enjoying this new experience. At least something exciting was happening in my life and I had always wanted to see where Mamma lived.

When the men had moved everything outside, apart from Nonna, they grabbed one arm each and attempted to pull her out of her chair. She tore her arms away and punched and scratched and kicked out at them. One of them raised his fist to her, but I jumped in front of the chair. 'You touch her, you big bastard, and I'll tell Mamma.' The man backed off, cursing me, and after a hurried conversation two of them picked Nonna and the chair up and carried her out into the campiello. It was difficult getting her through the crumbling entrance, but they pushed and heaved until she and the chair came through, like the stopper out of a flagon. I followed. A gondola awaited us on the rio.

A few women came and stood in the entrance calling goodbye to Nonna, but no one spoke to me. I saw the blackbird out of the corner of my eye, watching me, head on one side. He looked...amused.

Nonna is a small woman but it took two big strong men and a lot of bad words to get her into that gondola. I sat beside her, my arms wrapped around her, shushing her, but she cried all the way to our new lodgings. 'It's all right, Nonna,' I said, 'it might be exciting.' For some reason this made her cry even more.

Mamma's house fronted the Big Canal and we entered our rooms from the lower balcony. It was so different to our campiello.

As soon as Nonna stepped into our new home she stopped crying and hobbled about the luxurious apartment, her eyes wide, like a small child's. 'This is too good for me, Veronica. I'm not worthy.' she whispered, as if she were frightened her peasant dialect might break something. It took her a whole day before I could persuade her to sit down on one of the fancy chairs. She allowed the men to dispose of her old chair without a moment's hesitation.

So? Nonna was happy but I wasn't. I loathed the place on sight. It was a prison – a well-appointed prison, but a prison nonetheless. There were no children playing outside, no street sounds, no shouts from the rio, no laughter, no music, no crying babies, no smells, good or bad, all there was, was silence. And that sort of silence is cold. It was like living in a marble, airless box – with rules. I had never had rules before but, from that moment onwards, Mamma controlled every minute of my life. She chose my clothes, criticised how I talked and walked and even how I breathed. She had this way of peering at me as if she were inspecting some inferior made garment.

'You speak like a scullery maid,' she complained constantly. 'Don't gabble. A Lady never rushes her words, she speaks slowly, distinctly, and never, ever uses dialect.'

The only thing that made this new life bearable was that as long as I had a book and could write I would survive. Over the next three long years Mamma hired several more tutors. One was a pale-faced youth, with a sing-song voice, who attempted to teach me French and poetry. He made no impression on me whatsoever. I couldn't even be bothered to remember his name. I was sure that if I had wanted I could have pushed my fingers right through his chest and out the other side. I liked poetry but not the sort of dry, boring classical myths, that he favoured, written in incomprehensible, old-fashioned language. I knew he assumed that the reason I didn't like the 'great works' was because I was an ignorant girl, so he suggested I try to write some 'little' verse of my own. He looked down his long nose at me and smirked, so sure that I would be unable to write anything of merit.

I was fifteen with no experience of love or lust apart from what I had seen and heard in our campiello but I was beginning to understand my power. I knew I was pretty, maybe even beautiful. Nonna said there was a strong resemblance between me and my mother, which I wouldn't have admitted to anyone, but I began to notice the way boys stared at me. My tutor, for example, never looked me in the eyes but I often caught him staring at my breasts.

Did I say? I hated my breasts. They were determined to grow and grow, even when I attempted to squash them into submission. I was used to the rough boys on the streets, who shouted and fought and laughed and sometimes tried to touch me, but then I had been one of them. I dressed like they did and tucked my long black hair into a cap. In the old days, the only time I wore dresses was when Mamma came, but now I was forced to wear them every day. I kept my old things and as soon as she'd made her daily visit, I would strip off and be one of the boys again.

So? Back to this poem. I decided to write something about real life, even though I hadn't really experienced 'real life' yet. Nonna had protected me from the rough street life all around us, I was never allowed out at night but after Nonna bade me goodnight I would get out of bed and peer out of my window. On warm summer's evenings the campiello would be crowded with rowdy men and women from our building. There was music, drunken laughter and shrieks and sometimes fights. I saw someone knifed once and a woman with her dress all torn, showing her breasts. It didn't frighten me because I was safe, I was in another world, where nothing could harm me. I was a watcher.

I might not have actually experienced what was happening outside my window but I had a very good imagination. By now I knew what Ginevra's fate had been and I dedicated my poem to her, to the young girl with plum red hair and a gap between her front teeth. By the end I was satisfied with my description. I had made her live again. She was there watching those scenes of drunken debauchery, where men rode naked women, she heard the screams and shouts of fear and passion in the night. She smelt the stench of unwashed bodies and experienced the agony of women in childbirth. She was the young girl fondled by horrible old men and parted from her best friend when she was just a child.

I was pleased with the results. Writing the poem had brought me closer to my one-time friend again. When I asked my tutor if I might read my verse out loud to him I was very humble. He sat, while I stood in front of him like a little girl and I made my fingers tremble a little as I held the paper so that he would think I was nervous. Finally I took a long shuddering breath and began.

As I read I watched for the boy's reaction. After a few lines his prim mouth hung slackly open in shock and there was a look of horror

34

in his small pale eyes. He seemed attracted and repelled by me in equal measure. When I was finished I smiled and curtsied. He got unsteadily to his feet, backed away from me, and ran from the room. I never saw him again.

I don't know what he told Mamma but within days a new tutor arrived. His name was Monsieur Bonnert, my Dance and Singing Master. He spoke with an exaggerated French accent. At that time anything from France was thought to be fashionable in our Serene Republic. I heard Mamma say that to Nonna once, but if a girl of fifteen knew this man was a fraud, why couldn't she? I nicknamed him Monsieur le Porc, because his nose was squashed in and his nostrils flared, just like a prize pig. He snuffled when he spoke as if he were rooting in the garbage cans for turnip tops. He wore rouge and his high-stacked shoes had red satin bows on them. How was I expected to take this man seriously?

Mamma ignored my complaints and insisted that I learn the proscribed dances of the day. Every step and move was written down in Monsieur le Porc's Holy Book and in this weighty tome, with its printed pages, copied straight from the work of famous dance masters, there was no place for any interpretation of the music. If I strayed from the 'proper' steps he would scream 'Non, non, petite bête'. He spent weeks teaching me how to skip and curtsey prettily, and always the obedient child, I would skip like a drunken sailor and fall over when I curtsied, just to see his nostril's flare. But there was one thing I thanked Monsieur le Porc for, his attempts to teach me to dance had awakened my old passion. When I was alone I created dances again, writing the steps down in a special book, accompanied by sketches of the moves. This was my Holy Book, Amore per la danza.

No one needed to teach me to dance, Monsieur le Porc, least of all, but he always reported my disobedience to Mamma, who would punish me by not letting me leave the house for days, sometimes weeks. She knew how to hurt me. It wasn't so bad during the day because I had Nonna with me and my books, but the nights were torture. I had always been a poor sleeper and prowled about the house while everyone slept. Even as a baby I preferred darkness. I think my body had a different clock to everyone else's. I was often wide awake at night and then dormouse-sleepy in the day. Nonna told me that when I was an infant I refused to lie down in my crib until she had sat me on her lap at the window, so I could watch the planets dancing in the sky. The moon and stars dance was one of my favourite creations. Nonna made star hats for me and Ginevra, and the mothers and the men shouted and cheered us, so that we did it over and over.

As I grew older I begged to be allowed outside at night but I was made to feel guilty at such unnatural desires and experienced the thorny lash of doom-laden prophesies. Maybe I should have listened to them.

'There are wicked, godless men, lurking in the shadows my Veronica', warned Little Nonna, her sweet face broken into a thousand worry lines.

'God made the night for the godly to take their ease, before the travails of the morrow,' the priest lectured me in a throaty whisper. I often lingered in the confessional, making up sins, just for the sheer delight of being in the black night of that box.

And from Mamma. 'Only whores, criminals and beggars inhabit the night, my girl. Stop fidgeting, stand still. This hair, Nonna? Do you never brush the child's hair?'

During a particularly long episode of house-arrest, my desire for freedom grew so strong I knew that if I didn't escape soon I would do something terrible. Nonna's worried gaze followed me as I raved and kicked out at the furniture.

'Please, Nonna, just let me go outside for a few moments, Mamma will never know. '

But Nonna was frightened of the dark and even more terrified of Mamma. So, I made a plan. I waited for an inky black, starless night and went to bed early, lying itchy-eyed awake until I heard Nonna snoring. Then I dressed in my old breeches and boots, scraped my hair up into a cap and wrapped a tattered cloak about my shoulders. Then, opening my door quietly, I crept down the backstairs, tiptoed past the sleeping night watchman and then out into the cool, quiet night. I was free.

Night Walking

On that first night of freedom I was terrified and only ventured a short distance from my house. I remember my heart pounding so loudly I was sure someone would hear it. Every shadow hid a murderer carrying a knife or a wild dog or a drowned ghost with dead white fingers clutching at my legs as I ran over the bridges. Sounds became maniacal laughter or heavy footsteps following me. Safe home again in my bed that night, I vowed I would never do it again, but in the bright light of day I laughed away my fears. So what if it was dangerous? I could run fast. So, I went out the next night and the night after, and as my confidence grew I went further and further afield. I explored the backwaters of San Marco until I knew them like the back of my hand, and gradually, my area of exploration widened. But I was still very careful and mainly kept to the narrow little side calli. When I ventured further afield I used the wider, paved salizadi and hid in the shadows, as groups of night revellers passed close by. If anything happened to frighten me I ran home.

I became a street child and glory of glories, I dance once again. I run and jump and twirl until my body is exhausted and I creep back to my bed, waking in the morning refreshed, with the sound of sweet music still rippling in my ears. The melody is familiar yet I know I have never heard it before. It is the music of my soul.

In the daytime I suffer the dead dances that Monsieur le Porc allows, but at night I am Veronica, Queen of the Dance. I think I may be happy. But happiness is like an overripe peach, one succulent, delicious bite and then the noxious after-taste of the black, tainted flesh, surrounding the stone.

I came across the Rialto by accident on one of my night time adventures. It was a magical, starlit evening and I let my feet take me where they would. I ran and jumped with sheer joy along unknown calli and across strange little crooked pontis until I was totally lost. I wasn't frightened, because as long as I knew where the Lagoon was, I could always find my way home. However, when the time came to retrace my steps I must have taken a wrong turn because, as I rounded a corner, I emerged into a wide open piazza, full of bustling, busy walkways and crowds of people surging across it into another broad salizada. I didn't know where the people were going but I was taken up by the throng and swept along in their midst. There was music and dancing. It felt like a fiesta and I wondered, once again why the adults in my life were so afraid of the night. There were flaming braziers placed at intervals and torches lighting the stalls which lined the piazza, selling food and drink and trinkets. It was thrilling and different and I allowed myself to be carried onwards. As we shuffled slowly forward a small gap appeared between the people in front of me and I stood on tiptoe and saw the Rialto Bridge straight ahead of us. It looked so different at night. It was the biggest wooden ponti I had ever seen, made from two huge inclined ramps, which met at a moveable central section. In our journeys around the Republic Nonna and I had once watched in awe as this central part had risen, allowing the passage of a tall masted ship. Nonna told me a story of how this bridge had once collapsed when too many people crowded on the bridge watching a boat parade..The crowds of people milling around and on the bridge looked like an army of ants on the march and I was one of them.

New crowds of revellers from other streets converged with ours and we were all funnelled into a single stream of humanity, winding inexorably towards the bridge. Bodies pressed in on me from all sides. People pushed against those in front of them, whilst they in turn were pressed from behind by those who followed. I was squashed so tightly I could hardly breathe. Suddenly it wasn't fun anymore. My chest was tightening and I panicked and pushed wildly at the bodies penning me in. I tried to scream but I couldn't make a sound. Someone collided with me and punched me hard in the back. I stumbled forwards losing my balance and fell forwards. Instantly the spaces my feet and body had been inhabiting were filled with other feet, other bodies, and I was left dangling. I threw my arms around the shoulders of the person in front, trying to get my balance, but hands ripped my fingers away and I was falling. I hit the ground hard and rolled into a ball covering my head with my hands. Heavy boots trampled on me and over me. Several people stumbled and fell on top of me, cursing and kicking out. I was being crushed into the cobbles and there was nothing I could do about it. I thought I would die there amongst those monstrous legs but I found strength from somewhere and crawled towards where I thought the edge of the crowd might be. Suddenly I felt someone grasp my hair, then strong arms forced me to my feet and I was pushed forwards, 'fight, fight, 'a voice shouted in my ear. 'Fight. Fight.' And I did, I punched and scratched and screamed until miraculously I found myself in a calmer part of the melee. At last I managed to escape the crowd and scrambled into a dark doorway where I remained until my breathing became more regular and my head stopped spinning. I got unsteadily to my feet and leant back against the door for support, waiting for a gap in the crowd so that I could run homeward.

As I waited, bands of men lurched past me on their way to the bridge and taverns and the Carampane on San Polo − the most wicked place in Christendom according to my Nonna. One group of sailors passed close and I shrank back into the shadows. They were drunk and loud and one saw me and grasped my shoulder, swinging me out into the light. 'Well, well, pretty boy,' he slurred, holding my arm tight. 'What have we got here, eh?' I could smell his foul breath and I squirmed out of his grasp and kicked him hard in his pants. He doubled up in pain and as he rolled away from me, I jumped over him and took to my heels. I could hear his friends laughing as I fled. I didn't stop running until I reached home and I thanked the good Lord that my frightened feet knew the way.

The French Disease

We had been living in the house beside Mamma for some time and I had grown accustomed to the daily routine. I had my secret night-dancing but there were still the tedious days to be endured. I am marking time until I can escape. I suppose in many ways my life is better than it was in the campiello but I don't know whether this is a good life. I have little to compare it with, except for my previous existence – which seems like a life imagined by someone else. What do I miss? I miss noise, people's voices but most of all, I miss freedom.

One morning, as I came up the stairs to our apartment, I overheard Nonna and the maid talking. They were whispering, so I stood out of sight in the stairwell and listened. There wasn't much excitement in my life except gossip and our maid knew everything that was going on in all the sinestri and what she didn't know she made up.

'But is it true?' Nonna's voice. 'You know how these common women love to prattle?' I had noticed lately that Nonna spoke rather haughtily to the servants. My perfect Nonna was a snob.

'Cross my heart, Mistress,' the maid continued. 'They were full of it in the market, saying what a terrible shame it was, her not having her mother alive or any family left to bury her.'

'So? It will be a pauper's burial?'

'Yes, tomorrow. I know she was a whore but she doesn't deserve that, does she? No one deserves that.'

Nonna sighed and I heard the chair creak as she got to her feet. I turned to run back down the stairs but the maid hadn't finished.

'Signorina Veronica used to know her, didn't she, when you lived... down there?'

I froze.

Nonna was quiet for a moment and when she spoke again her voice was sharp. 'That'll be all for now, thank you. Madam will be here presently and I don't want to find a speck of dust anywhere.'

I heard the door open and shut and waited a moment before stepping out of my hiding place. When Nonna saw me she clutched her hands together and her voice shook as she spoke. 'Ah, Veronica. There you are. It's almost time for your mamma's visit.'

But I wasn't going to be side-tracked. 'Who were you talking about?'

She pretended to be busy tidying my books away.

'Was it Ginevra?'

She looked at me for a long moment, as if she was working out what to say, finally she stepped towards me and tried to touch my hand. Her eyes were full of pity.

I took a step backwards. 'She's dead?'

She nodded.

'Ginevra's dead?'

'You don't have to worry about it, Veronica. It happens. These girls are...dirty, they don't wash properly, they catch diseases.'

43

I could feel my anger rising. 'Ginevra washed every day in our fountain, Nonna, you know that. She was never dirty.'

Nonna stared at me, lost for words.

'You must remember how I used to tease her. I told her that she'd wash herself away but she said she was trying to scrub away her freckles. She thought they were ugly.' I could feel the tears coming but I managed to keep my voice steady. 'But they weren't ugly, they were beautiful.'

Nonna looked away from me.

'How did she die?'

'You wouldn't understand."

'I'm not a child, Nonna, and I need to know. Please, tell me.'

She sank down into her chair and sat there for a moment staring at me. When she finally spoke, her voice was full of sorrow. 'She had the French Disease, Veronica. It's...it's a terrible thing.'

'But what is it?'

She shook her head sadly. 'I pray you will never have the need to find out.'

I couldn't breathe. It was like there was a metal band tightening about my chest, crushing me. 'But she's just a young girl. It's not right.' I was gasping for air and crying all at once. Nonna got up and held her arms out to me but I backed away, then turned and fled. She caught up with me at the bottom of the stairs. My fingers were struggling with the key in the lock, grief making me clumsy. She pushed me aside and got between me and the door. I tried to get past but she stood her ground. I'm much taller than her now but she can be strong when she

44

wants. I was desperate to get outside and I lifted my fist, but then I saw her face. She looked so frail and sad and I dropped my hands to my sides and whispered. 'I just want to breathe the fresh air, Nonna. I need to know I'm alive, not dead like...'

'...Oh, my Veronica.' she said, unlocking the door and leading me out onto the sunlit pavement at the back of the house, from where I could see people walking by, at the far end of our campo. My legs were trembling so much I thought I might fall and I leant back against the wall for support. 'And it's true?' I pleaded. 'You're sure it's true?'

She nodded. 'The child has been ill for some time.'

'You knew? But why didn't you tell me?'

'What good would it have done? You would have been upset and there was nothing we could do. No one recovers when they have the French Disease.'

'But I could have looked after her, taken her food, I could have told her I loved her, paid for a proper doctor.'

'Paid? What with? You have no ducats, Veronica, and your Mamma would never allow you to go. Come, kneel with me, we must pray for Ginevra's immortal soul. The good Lord is merciful...'

'...Merciful? No...not merciful. Cruel. I hate Him."

'You don't mean that, child.'

'I do,' I screeched, thrusting myself away from the wall. I was already running before Nonna realised what I was doing. She called after me, pleading with me to stop, but I ran blindly on. I don't know where I went, I just ran, legs pumping, arms flailing. I charged through groups of people, knocking children over and spilling barrels of food. I

45

lurched across bridges while dogs snapped and snarled at my heels. Trades people shouted angrily at me and street boys threw stones after me. I felt one graze my head and the warm spurt of blood on my skin. Finally, when I could run no further, I sank down on my knees in a deserted calle of whispering, leaning houses and wept until there was nothing left in me but a jagged aching hole.

Light was fading when I dragged myself back to the house. Nonna was where I had left her. A small stooped figure holding a cloak in her arms and peering worriedly up and down the darkening street. When she saw me she hurried to me and wrapped the cloak about us both. She hugged me so tightly. 'Thank God, thank God ' she moaned. 'I was sure I had lost you. I thought you had thrown yourself from a building or drowned in the rio.' Then she led me into the house and up the stairs. Sitting me down on my bed she rocked me in her arms and her warm familiar scent wrapped itself around me.

'It was Ginevra's time,' she whispered. 'We never know the hour of our passing.'

The tears were coming again.

Nonna took my hand and kissed it. 'Don't be sad. Tonight your Ginevra will be in Paradise. '

I pulled my hand away as if she'd burnt me. She didn't understand. I wasn't crying because I was grieving, I was crying because of my shame, my guilt. Why hadn't I found Ginevra and helped her? We had promised that we would always be together and I had failed her.

Nonna got painfully down onto her knees beside me and waited, expecting me to join her, but I couldn't. What good would the prayers of a faithless person be for my Ginevra? I curled up on the bed, my back towards Nonna and after a while I heard my door shut.

She kept away until it was late, then she came to me with some broth and a candle and sat on the bed saying her rosary. The clicking of the beads and her soft monotone grew louder and louder until I thought my head might burst. When she was finished she wrapped the beads around her fingers, held them to her lips and kissed them. She saw me watching her and smiled. 'The good Lord loves sinners, Veronica. HE has infinite mercy and Ginevra's time in purgatory will be brief. Her sins will be forgiven'.

I jumped off the bed spilling soup everywhere. '...Sins? What sins? Ginevra never chose to be a whore, Nonna. She was a child when they took her. No need to look at me like that. I'm not stupid, I know what happens to girls like her. I grew up amongst whores, Nonna, do you imagine for one minute that I don't know about such things? '

She struggled to her feet. 'What are you saying, child? Who's been gossiping? Is it the maid? I will speak to your Mamma about her.'

'Mamma? But she's a whore too.'

'Your mother is not a whore. Veronica.' I saw her searching about for the correct words no doubt words that Mamma had schooled her in, for such an occasion. 'Your Mamma is a highly respected cortigiana onesta and her status allows her to mix with the cream of Venetian society.'

I wasn't interested in Mamma's status. 'I'm going to Ginevra's funeral tomorrow, Nonna, with or without you.'

'Put that idea right out of your head. The pauper's burial sites are evil-smelling pits of contagion. The corpses are flung in, like so much trash. and quick lime thrown on them. Your Mamma will never allow it.'

'Mamma, Mamma! What has she to do with it? She never even knew Ginevra. She doesn't know me. I will live my life as I see fit...'

'...But she...'

'...Yes, I know, she pays the bills, but that doesn't mean she owns me. If you're frightened I'll go on my own.'

The Rialto

But I did go, we both went and I will never forget that day and the paupers' pit. I only had to close my eyes to see poor Ginevra's thin, wasted body once more and hear the lonely wailing of that child.

As we walked home from San Polo that day, neither of us spoke, but I felt Nonna's eyes on me, watching, always watching. I went straight to my room when we got back and sat staring out of the window, seeing nothing but that pathetic little body being tossed into the pit. There was a book open on my knee and when Nonna poked her head around the door, I turned a page, so that she'd think I was reading.

'You must be hungry, Veronica?'

'No, I don't feel hungry, thank you, Nonna.'

'I'm going to the market. Can I bring you something special?'

I shook my head.

'What about some of those peaches, you know, the little ones that look like babies' dimpled bottoms...' She was trying so hard to be kind and it made me want to weep. '...or, maybe, you'd like to come with me? You know how you enjoy the market. It's a Feast day, maybe there will be acrobats.'

49

I shook my head again. 'I'd like to stay here and read, if you don't mind.'

'And you'll be all right?'

'Of course.'

'I won't be long.'

After she left I lay on my bed and closed my eyes. I wanted to sleep, to forget what I'd seen – to wash those images from my mind forever, but most of all I wanted Ginevra beside me. I needed one last chance to make things right between us. Surely there was something I could do? It was too late for my friend but I remembered the look on Pazienza's pinched face and the forlorn sound of that wailing infant. Jumping up from my bed I ran to the storeroom, found an old sack and searched our rooms, stuffing it full with old clothes, raggy blankets and what food I could take, without Nonna noticing.

When I was finished I hid the sack beneath my bed and waited for Nonna's return. Later I joined her for supper and made myself smile and talk, as if everything was well with me. I could see Nonna's relief and we both retired early. She gave me a blessing and kissed me on my head. 'Try to remember that Ginevra is in a better place, Veronica. You will meet again in Paradise.' She must have felt me stiffen because she took her leave quickly without uttering another word.

After that first terrifying night experience on the Rialto I had vowed I would never return, even if all the devils in hell pursued me. However, that was before Ginevra's cruel death and, while I waited for Nonna's snuffling, sleep sounds, I attempted to build up my courage.

50

I wasn't a silly little girl any more. I had improved my street skills and knew which places to avoid, what bridges were dangerous, where the beggars and thieves lived. I had learnt to use bad words in various languages. I found this most useful. I didn't know what most of the profanities meant but it seemed to have the desired effect. I would rub dirt on my face and smear foul smelling waste on my clothes. I even had a knife. I had found it one night on a small bridge spanning a stinking rio. It had shone brightly up at me in the moonlight. It had a short, sharp blade and ever since that night on the Bridge I had tucked it down my boot when I went exploring.

The knife gave me extra courage. I was determined to succeed come what may. This time I would not hesitate on the Bridge, but run quickly over and into the squalid buildings, where the meritrici lived.

I was nearly sixteen, a grown woman. I could do it, I must do it, and before I could talk myself out of it I jumped out of bed, dressed quickly in my boys' clothes, then stole out of the house, clutching the sack.

Thank goodness the weather had changed and it was a wet, dark, moonless night. There would be no dancing tonight. Darting from shadow to deeper shadow. I slunk through the streets like the feral cats that haunted the winding paths and slipped through deserted calli, as groups of drunken, fighting men passed on the main vias. There were less people about than usual because of the weather but I knew the contigiana di lume would be working as always. I would find Pazienza quickly, give her the sack and leave – even more quickly.

51

I reached the Rialto without mishap, determined to stay relaxed, but I still felt my heartbeat, drumming loudly in my ears. The women I sought lived in a warren of dilapidated buildings near the bridge on the San Polo side. I had worried that I wouldn't be able to find them but I soon realised that all I had to do was follow the gangs of men headed over the bridge. I took a deep breath as I stepped up onto the boardwalk but there was no time to look about me before the mass of people crossing caught me up in its maw. I knew it was useless to struggle against this force. The bridge is humped backed like a turtle and I allowed myself to stumble upwards, pushed from behind, and in my turn pushing those in front of me. I was managing to stay upright and began to relax a little , but when I was almost at the middle there was a terrifying scream. The crowd parted as people shoved their way to the railings to see what was happening. I went with them and found myself against the edge of the bridge, looking directly down over the canal. The woman beside me pointed her finger and we saw a small figure running. It was a young girl I think, from the way she moved. Once or twice she fell but then she struggled to her feet and ran on again. Her scream had turned into a wail. It was impossible to tell her age from where I stood, but young. I willed her to run as fast as she could to her mother, away from whatever was pursuing her.

The people around me soon lost interest and rejoined the throng . I was on my own and about to turn away too when I saw why the child was running. Two burly men came into view behind her on the path. As they lumbered along they were bellowing at her to stop.

And they were laughing. She was desperate and I caught a glimpse of her white exhausted little face as she fled into a pool of torch light. I ran headlong back into the crowd, desperate to get to the San Polo side. I had no idea what I would do once I was over the bridge but I knew I had to do something. I lost sight of her as I dodged through the crowd, desperately pushing and shoving my way forward.

When I reached the other side I slipped down onto the towpath and saw the child, still running. For one moment it looked as if she would escape, but then a crowd of men and women burst out from a nearby tavern and one of the men scooped the fleeing child up and presented her to the two men, as if she were a gift. 'This yours?' I heard him shout. He held the struggling, frantic child at arm's length. 'God, she stinks. Best get her cleaned up before you have her.' And then he walked to the edge of the rio and tossed her into the water. I swear my heart stopped.

I was running and screaming. 'Help her, someone, help her.' But no one took any notice. The men had lost interest and were already walking away, the child forgotten. Her head broke the surface once...twice, her arms flailing as she fought to keep afloat. She went under again and I flung myself down on the tow path, as close to the edge as I dared. I waited for the next time her head broke the surface and then I stretched out one hand as far as it could go. 'Take my hand.' I screamed. Her eyes locked with mine and I think she tried to say something. 'Please,' I begged. 'Please, try, take my hand.' Her small mouth was opening and closing, gasping for air, but she couldn't reach my hand and then she was going under again.

I couldn't swim, I was frightened of the weed that clutched at your legs and the dead bodies reaching out to pull you down into the water. The rii are full of human shit and terrible diseases. Only boatmen learnt to swim. The boy's face lurched into my mind and for one moment I looked about me desperately, hoping he might be there, but there were no boatmen, or boats, just the stinking, black water. The child had stopped struggling now, she was too exhausted, and I saw resignation clouding her eyes as the water closed over her head. 'No, please. Please, someone, anyone, a child is drowning. For the love of God help her.' But no one came and I watched as a great bubble of air broke the surface of the water. The child's last breath. It slowly dispersed and then the water resumed on its turgid way. Getting to my feet I stood looking down into the water. I was holding my breath too, counting to see how long she could last under the water, before she needed to breathe again. I stayed there for a long time after I knew for certain that she was drowned.

As I waited I saw her pursuers going into the tavern with the man who had thrown the child into the rio. They were shouting and slapping each other on their backs. The child was forgotten, like some discarded, broken toy.

I searched the faces of the people hurrying past on the tow path and not one of them looked at me. Surely I wasn't the only one who had seen it happen? It was impossible. Had I imagined it? Please God let it be my imagination. Because then the child wasn't dead, not really, she was just in my head. It was because I was so fearful. My mind often plays tricks on me. Nonna says I have too much imagination. Yes, that was it. Too much imagination.

I hoist the sack onto my shoulders , preparing to join the throng. I must do what I came to do. I take one last look at the rio. No, nothing there, just the usual floating debris, empty casks, rotting vegetables, tangled old nets and bits of rope, covered in slicks of black filth. I was turning away when I caught sight of something in the corner of my eye. I thought I might be dreaming this too, so I blinked a few times to clear my eyes. But no, there was something floating on top of the scum − something that looked very much like a small shoe...a child's shoe.

And that's when I did something very stupid. Pulling the knife from my boot I set off after the retreating backs of the men. I was walking fast, then I was running, forcing my legs to go faster and faster, my lungs burning with the effort. 'Murderers ,' I shriek. 'Cowardly murderers. You will rot in Hell for all eternity.'

The men must have heard me because they turned to face me. They were still laughing. I wasn't scared. I didn't feel anything but cold hatred for these vile, odious men. I didn't care if I died, I wasn't going to let them get away with it. The knife was in my hand and I was going to use it. One of the men was pointing at me and held his arms out as if inviting the first cut. Well, his wish would come true.

I could hear his mocking laughter as I ran at him, the knife slashing through the air, but then, suddenly, I was falling and I felt hands grabbing at me, then my world went dark.

Pazienza

'Ragazza stupida,' a woman's rough voice. Warm hands on my face. Water on my tongue and then the overpowering urge to be sick.

Blackness again until I wake, lying face down in my vomit. I try to turn my head from the stinking mess but I can't move. The urge to wipe the putrid bile from my lips is overwhelming but my hands refuse to obey me. None of me works. I am paralysed. like those beggars on the bridge. Oh God, I am paralysed. 'No, no', I sob, but the woman's arms hold me and she raises me up, steadying me.

'Keep still, stupida,' she orders, 'You will be well. Your body? It is too hurt.' She cleans my face, then she holds a cup to my mouth and I gulp down the liquid.

When I have had enough she lies me back down again and her fingers probe my forehead. I yelp with pain as she gently bathes the bruises. All of me hurts but my head feels the worst. My eyesight is blurred but I begin to see the room I am in. I stare around as she works on me.

'I thought you might have had your fill of pain after that last time, but no, Veronica the Dancer never learns. Veronica stupida more like.'

She knows my name? This woman knows my name. I try to see her face in the dim light, but her hair hangs loosely, covering her features.

'Who are you?'

She brushes the back of her hand across her face, pushing her hair behind her ears. 'How many whores do you know with a face like mine?'

'Pazienza?'

There must have been other women in the room because I could hear their laughter. And there is a baby crying.

'Pazienza, is it really you? I came to see you.' Suddenly I am shivering. I can't stop. I am so cold. She puts her arms about me, rocking me.

'And you have found me,' she says. I breathe in her rankness. She reeks of wine and sweat and dirt but she is so warm. I must sleep now. My eyes close and as I drift away Pazienza's voice is like a lullaby. I don't understand the words. They are not proper words but they comfort me and I feel safe.

It is still night when I open my eyes again and see I am lying on a pallet. There is no light except for a guttering candle, burning on a nearby table. Pazienza sits beside the bed watching me. She is holding a sleeping baby in her arms. Seeing me stir she puts the infant down on an old blanket and helps me up into a sitting position. Then she puts the cup to my lips. I automatically put my hand out to take the cup and my fingers curl around the handle. I wriggle my toes, I stretch my arms and turn my head this way and that. I can move. I must have sighed then because Pazienza leans closer.

'I told you, you will be well. You have been fortunate. The good Lord was watching over you.'

'But I don't understand. Where am I? And how did I come here?' There are some things I am beginning to remember. There was Ginevra's funeral and then my plan to bring things for Pazienza, and then, the child... Oh my God, the child. I clutch at Pazienza's hand. 'Did it really happen' Did the child drown?' I want her to lie to me but she squeezes my hand and nods.

'Do you remember what happened after that?' she asks. ' The man? '

'That bastard. I wanted to kill him. Did I hurt him?'

She shook her head, 'Sadly no, Veronica. There are many of us who wish you had, but you fell before you reached him. You were like a mad woman, running and screaming, slashing the air with that little blade. I was there, I was with one of them and I saw it all . But I couldn't help you. If I had, they would have ... Well it doesn't matter what they would have done. The murderer you sought has the blackest heart on the Rialto. Even the strongest of us avoid him. But God was watching over you and he placed that broken cobblestone in your path to save you, or, by now, you would have been as lifeless as that drowned child, drifting in the weeds at the bottom of the canal.'

'You saw it?' I sobbed 'You saw him throw that defenceless little girl into the canal and you did nothing? '

I saw the anger in her eyes. 'What did you do?'

58

'I couldn't do anything, I can't swim.'

'Neither can I. None of us can. So, if I had jumped in the canal and tried to save that child I would have died too and then what would have happened to this little mite?' Pazienza looked down at the baby at her feet, who whimpered in her sleep, like a puppy missing its mother. She covered my hands with hers. 'When you fell you hit your head and knocked yourself out. We all thought you were dead, and so did they, so they allowed us to carry you away. Someone shouted that the Signori dell notte had been summoned and they didn't want to have to explain away another dead body. So, like all cowards, they left us and ran, to save their black hides.'

'But they murdered that little girl. They must be brought to justice.'

She laughed. It wasn't a pleasant sound. 'This is the Rialto, Veronica. There is no justice here, unless you are a noble or have powerful friends. Welcome to Our Most Serene Republic,' she said, waving her arms around the squalid little room. 'May they all rot in Hell.' She stood up and I saw her face in the dim candlelight. The jagged scar running across her forehead and down one cheek was lit like a bolt of lightning. 'Now, come. No more talk. I must get you away from here.' She grasped my hand and put her other arm around my waist, dragging me to my feet.

'But you said the Watch were coming? That's good. There will be witnesses. They will find him guilty and he will be executed.'

59

Pazienza shook her head. 'As for the witnesses, Veronica, no one will speak against that man and, besides, the Watch aren't coming. It was me. I lied and I hope to God he never finds out.'

'But you could be a witness and so could I.'

She shook her head. 'We are poor women, Veronica. They wouldn't take our word against any man.'

'But what about justice.'

She laughed.

'Wherever and however we live, Pazienza, there is right and wrong. If we ignore that we are no better than animals.'

'Don't preach to me, girl, I can't afford to be good.' She grasped my arm and pulled me towards the door.

Suddenly dizzy, I grasped her arm. ' I don't think I can find my way on my own.'

'I will take you.' She was already throwing her shawl about her shoulders.

'But you don't know where I live.'

' I know everything about you, Veronica Maria Bracci .'

I noticed several other women in the room, gathered around the sack I had brought. They were searching through the contents and one woman was clutching an old red blanket that I had used as a child. 'That would be warm for your baby, Pazienza. ' I said, and the woman tossed the blanket to Pazienza, who picked up the sleeping infant and wrapped the blanket tightly about her.

'She's not my child, Veronica.'

It was cold in the room and the thin little brazier gave out little warmth. I put out a hand to stroke the child's silky hair. 'Is her mother dead?' I asked. A piece of dying wood spat one last defiant gobbet of light into the darkness before it too was extinguished and I saw a sudden flash of colour. The baby's hair was red, like the first bright fruit on the plum tree that grew in my old campiello wall. Pazienza saw me looking and squeezed my hand. 'She is the mirror of Ginevra, no?'

'Ginevra's child?'

She nodded. 'You saw me carry this infant with me today − to her mother's burial, so that one day I can tell the child that she was with her mother when she was laid to rest −that there is a link. It's important to have a link, Veronica. We all need one, however lowly.'

'Ginevra had a baby?' I was trying to absorb what Pazienza was telling me but my brain refused to accept it. 'But she was only a child herself.' I couldn't take my eyes from the child. I wanted to hold that baby so badly and talk about Ginevra. I needed to feel goodness and love again and block out all those other terrible images. This was Ginevra's child. .'Please let me stay a little while longer, Pazienza.'

But she wasn't listening. She thrust the child into another woman's arms, put an arm around my waist and opened the door. Without her strength I would have collapsed. I was so weak and faint. 'I don't think I have the strength to walk.'

'It will be daybreak soon, you will be missed and your old woman will squawk like a rooster. You must not be found here, or we will all suffer.'

61

'I can deal with Nonna. You remember her? She would never tell. She is too frightened of Mamma.'

'She has reason. Your mother is under the protection of the Duke and he, and his sort, would like nothing better than to send us all to the fires of the Inquisition.'

I think my mouth fell open. 'You are witches? '

She laughed out loud at that. 'If I was a witch do you think I would be living here in this hell-hole? No, we are only witches when it pleases them to think so. When we are too old or ill to service them. When they want someone to blame, for something, anything, then we are all witches — you too.' She was pushing my arms into my coat and my hair into my cap as she talked. 'Now come, I am strong. You may lean on me.' And bidding the others farewell she hurried me out onto the grey, predawn streets.

All I remembered of that journey home was the dampness in the air and the chill clutching at my bones. Fingers of mist curled about my legs as I stumbled along and there was ice on the cobbles. I would have fallen if not for Pazienza's arm, strong about me, as she hustled me through the deserted calli. When we reached my campo she led me to my door and I stood there swaying as she unlatched the door and pushed me gently inside. I took a tottering step forward and nearly fell but she caught me in her arms. 'Goodnight, Veronica ,' she whispered, and kissed my head.

I mumbled something in return and she turned to go, but after a few steps she looked back at me and whispered. 'Is it beautiful in your rooms?'

I was too tired to answer but she didn't seem to need a response.

 'I have often followed you here through the calli.'

'You came here?' I stuttered. 'But why didn't you speak?'

She shrugged. 'Would you have noticed the poor whore, staggering in the gutter? Your servants would have beaten me.'

I was so ashamed, because what she said was true.

'I have been watching you for years and wondering if you would ever find us.'

'I'm so sorry, Pazienza, I wanted to but...'

'...I helped you once.'

'What?'

'I rescued you on the Bridge. You were in a crowd of people. Do you not remember?'

I couldn't believe it. 'Fight, fight. Was that you? Thank you, thank you.'

'It was nothing. Ginevra was happy when I told her. She was ill then, but when she knew I had saved you she smiled. Do you remember her smile?'

I couldn't speak

'She missed you so much, Veronica. Do you still dance? She used to dance for those bastards. They all wanted her, even the nobili. but then she became infected and no one would touch her.'

I sank down on the step, covering my face with my hands. She came and stood before me, her hand resting on my head, like a blessing. 'Now you have found us, Veronica, don't forget us. Little Ginevra will have need of friends like you.'

'You call her Ginevra?'

Pazienza nodded.

I wanted to thank her for saving me, for caring for me, for not hating me, but the words wouldn't come.

She took a step away and I felt the loss of her.

'Do you remember our dances?' She said wistfully, turning her face to mine.

'Of course.'

'Ginevra remembered and promised that she would teach her little daughter to do the same one day, but...'

My heart was breaking. '.You must go,' I stammered. 'Look, it's getting light.'.

She was still standing there, watching me, as I shut the door.

A new life

I don't remember taking my clothes off or getting into bed that morning but the next thing I knew I was waking up to a feeling of warmth on my face, as the bright, midday sun streamed in through my windows. My body ached and my head still throbbed but I felt stronger and very hungry. I sat on the edge of the bed and gazed at my cast-off filthy clothes and boots.

What had Pazienza asked me? Was my room beautiful? I looked around, trying to see it through her eyes. It was large and full of light and the quality of the furniture and rich colours of the fabrics and wall hangings were perfect. It was tasteful and expensive. Turkish carpets covered the floor. Yes, it was beautiful, very beautiful, and I thought back to that dark little hovel I had lain in the night before.

At that moment Nonna hurried into my room and scurried about picking up my things and taking them away. She was breathing heavily as if she'd been running, She didn't look at me.

'Nonna, sit down,' I pleaded. 'It's not good for you to rush around. I'll do that.'

But she took no notice of me, so I got out of bed, put my robe on and went to the door. I was going to find something to eat. Nonna grasped my arm. I could feel her trembling. 'Please, Veronica, go back to bed. I will bring you something to eat as soon as I've dealt with all this. Please,' she begged, ' do as I say.'

So I hopped back into bed. I hated to see her so upset. 'Mamma will never know about last night, Nonna, I promise. I will never tell anyone but you.'

But Nonna was on her knees, scrubbing at the dirty stains on the carpet as if her very life depended on it.

'Nonna?'

She ignored me.

'Ginevra had a baby...a little girl, Nonna. She has hair, just like her mother's...remember the baby at the funeral? That was her, Ginevra's child.'

Silence except for the sound of Nonna's scrubbing brush and her laboured breathing.

I got out of bed and grabbed the brush out of her hand, hurling it away, then I crouched down in front of her and cupped her face so that she had no option but to look at me. 'I have seen such terrible things, Nonna. This man, he...he drowned a little girl. Threw her into the rio and turned his back on her. He was laughing, Nonna, I wanted to kill him, so badly...but she saved me, Pazienza saved me. Oh, Nonna. How they live. How those poor wretched women live. I never imagined such poverty.'

I let my hands drop and Nonna struggled to get up. Grabbing her around the waist I lifted her off her knees. My arms were around her, hugging her, but she moved out of my embrace and stood with her back to me.

'Get back to bed, Veronica.' Her voice was flat, emotionless but I saw her clenched fists. 'You must go back to bed.'

'Oh Nonna, I so wanted to hold that beautiful little girl'....

'....No,no,no, no...' Nonna moaned. She sat down on the bed, hands covering her ears and rocking backwards and forwards. She was making that high keening sound like old women do at funerals.

'Nonna, stop, you're frightening me.' I touched her hand but she snatched it away, as if I'd burnt her. 'Alright, alright. I'll get back into bed if you promise to stop that noise.'

As soon as I was safely in bed she scuttled away to bring me breakfast. Neither of us spoke as I ate. She seemed to have calmed down a bit. When I was finished she brought a bowl of hot water and gently bathed the bruises on my forehead and body, then she washed my face and hands and brushed my hair. Finally when she was satisfied I asked her to bring me clean clothes, so that I could get dressed, but she shook her head.

'You aren't well, I have already spoken with your Mamma and told her you have a fever. She says you must stay in your room until you are well. She wanted to send for her physician but I told her I would care for you.'

We both knew that Mamma had a horror of illness and would leave me alone. Nonna picked up my breakfast tray. 'She asked me to give you her blessing and says she will send you fruit and whatever

67

you need. Now sleep.' She hesitated at the door. 'She must never know... that I allowed you to roam the streets alone at night ...'

'...But you didn't 'allow' me, Nonna.' I interrupted.

Ignoring me she went to my bedside table and brought the bible to me, then she took my hand and placed it firmly on top of the book. I tried to take it away but she pinned it down. 'Now swear. Say you promise not to tell your mamma what happened '

'I won't tell her, Nonna. I'm not stupid.'

'Swear it.' So, I did, what else could I do? Afterwards she took a long, shuddering breath. ' If she found out that you had been to that place at night, while under my care, she would send me away.... I would never see you again and...my life would be over. '

Later that day I heard Nonna and Mamma outside my door discussing me and then my mother's footsteps as she hurried away. Nonna saw to it that my bruises faded long before I was 'better' again.

My external injuries healed quickly but the unspeakable savagery I had witnessed that night, and the things that Pazienza had told me about Ginevra and her baby, would always stay with me. Nonna continued to pretend nothing had happened and maybe that was the best way for her but it wasn't for me. I was going mad with the need to tell someone about that terrible night. I longed to make people understand the injustices of Venetian society against these poor wretched women. But there was no one to listen to my story, so I decided the only thing I could do was to keep a journal. I wrote it every day, describing everything that had happened and adding any further injustices to women that I encountered. Sometimes I wrote impassioned 'speeches' and I would read them out aloud, as if I had an audience. Once, after a particularly strident lecture, Nonna came into my room, a worried look on her face, searching the room with her eyes.

'Who were you talking to, Veronica?' she asked.

I looked puzzled and shook my head. 'You must have been hearing things, Nonna, there's no one here. I'm all alone, as usual.'

'But I heard raised voices like you were arguing with someone,' she insisted.

Shrugging, I touched her arm, as if I were consoling her for her bad hearing. I know it was cruel of me but I was protecting her.

Writing it all down helped my feelings of impotence a little, but one thing I knew for certain was that I would never be able to live happily in a society where such cruelty and hypocrisy existed side by side. I was determined that somehow I would make a difference in those women's lives. There would come the day when I was powerful and courageous and then nothing would stop me from fighting their cause. I was still such an innocent but I was learning fast. However hard I tried I couldn't imagine what it must be like to live in constant fear like that little girl. Was this what Ginevra and the others had to suffer every night, while I was tucked up safely in my own bed, with clean linen and food in my belly?

I consoled myself that, although unable to protect Pazienza and the child as I would have liked, I might help them a little. I began to save every ducat Mamma gave me for birthdays, or new dresses, and when I had a reasonable amount I would take the money and any old clothes to Pazienza on the Rialto. I always visited her during the daytime − the women's rest time. I didn't hide what I was doing from Nonna and neither did I ask for permission, or for her to come with me. I wasn't a child, those days were behind me.

To begin with Nonna left the room without a word when she saw me preparing to visit Pazienza. I was sad but not surprised. She had to do what she thought was right. But then the day came when I was about to set off and she appeared with her arms full of old clothes and blankets. On top of the pile was her doll. It was made from an old scrubbing brush carved into a head and body and dressed in worn fabric. The hair and face were painted on. It had always sat on Nonna's bed and I knew how much she loved it.

'These things are for Pazienza and the others,' then she touched the doll gently. 'And this is for Little Ginevra.'

She didn't come with me that day but she was waiting, with her shawl on, the next time. She was very subdued on the way there and for once it was me holding her hand, looking after her. I worried a little that she might say something to offend the women, chastity and purity were very important to my God-fearing Nonna. However, I needn't have worried because as soon as she saw the child, she was in love. I'll never forget the look on her face as she held the baby in her arms and stared down at her, her mouth slightly open, as if she wanted to say something but it wouldn't come.

After that visit Nonna always came with me and sometimes, if one of my tutors was there or Mamma wanted me to attend her, she would go on her own. Pazienza thought that Nonna was obsessed with

70

the child and, maybe she was, but all I knew was that I'd never seen her so happy. The years dropped away from her when she was with the child. Looking back I think Nonna and Mamma must have been similar ages but I had always thought of Nonna as an old Lady. She spent hours taking care of Little Ginevra and walking her around the Rialto. It was such a joy to both of us to see the baby growing up. She truly was the mirror of Ginevra.

Pazienza had no children of her own, so Little Ginevra became hers. It was Nonna who persuaded Pazienza that the child should be baptised. and take Pazienza's family name, Bagnio, and Elizabetta after Pazienza's mother. Nonna and I were to be the child's godmothers. We went to the small church close to the Bridge. I learnt something else that day. The priest needed my and Nonna's names to write in his parish ledger. Nonna couldn't write so I asked if I might write her name for her. The priest shrugged, so I wrote my name in the book then looked at Nonna.

'Nonna?'

She looked worried.

'What is your name?'

She looked frightened now and whispered. 'Will I be in trouble if I don't have a name?'

'You must have a name. Everyone has a name. What were you called when you were a child?'

She looked away. 'I can't say in front of him,' and she glanced to where the priest waited impatiently. Then she whispered in my ear. 'They were bad names, Veronica.'

71

Pazienza raised her eyebrows at me. 'Just think of a name, any name,' I tried to think up a good name for my friend, but she shook her head at every suggestion.

Then suddenly she whispered, ' Carlotta.'

I wrote it down quickly before she could change her mind and added Bracci, my name. after all she was my nonna. While the priest waited he held the child in his arms and she reached up a chubby finger to touch his nose and his stern priestly face softened. He beamed down at her, and gently touched her glorious hair. 'Bellisima, Ginevra Elizabetta Bagnio.' Then he baptised her. I was glad she had a name.

Afterwards we emerged into a bright, sparkling Venetian day and the church bells were ringing. I patted Gobbo's rough head as we passed and wished him well.

Nonna carried the child back to Pazienza's room. I heard her whisper to the baby. 'My name is Nonna, piccolo. And I am your Nonna.'

There were twenty women at Little Ginevra's party. They had given up their sleep for their friend and Ginevra's little girl. We ate the almond pastries that Nonna had prepared and drank some sweet wine tasting of honey. There was much laughter and happiness. Nonna didn't say much in front of the women. Maybe she was shocked to be in the presence of so many whores. She held Ginevra close and fussed over her while the child clutched Nonna's doll. She hated to be parted from it.

I watched them together, this child who was born from an immoral act. This child with no father and a mother dead from the French Disease. This child with no future other than that of following her mother's trade. But I was her godmother now and whatever it took I would make sure she never had to sell her body. And yes, the irony of the situation wasn't wasted on me. Nonna had held me once like she was holding Little Ginevra. I was the child born from an immoral act. I was the child with no father.

Nonna had impressed on me, all my life, that I must be pure and modest in order that a man might wish to wed me. But these same husbands, who demanded virgin brides, were the very ones who bought the whores on the Rialto. And it wasn't just in the Rialto where women were used and abused. Even in the fashionable quarters where Mamma and I lived I had seen girls, younger than myself, being dragged along by men and forced up against walls, their flimsy dresses pushed up and the coarse cloth of sailors, traders and nobles alike, chaffing their little girl skin. Thanks to Nonna I had avoided the grasping hands and leering faces on those putrid streets but it was a game for me and so far I had never been caught. I didn't need to sell myself to strangers, because my mother had money and status. I would have that one day and I would do good with my wealth or die in the attempt.

One last mouthful

Awake again. The thudding in my head is one with the noise of the workmen toiling outside.

I am so thirsty. The after-taste of the theriac still burns the back of my throat and my tongue sticks to the roof of my mouth. The upturned flagon may still contain some water if I can only reach it. It is so tantalisingly close. Dragging myself to the edge of the bed, my bare feet graze the blessedly cool, tiled floor. I sit for a moment, gathering my strength, then I push myself upwards and stand there swaying, one hand on the bed to steady myself. Only four steps to the flagon but it might as well be four leagues. Taking one trembling step, then another I make a lunge and manage to grasp the edge of my dressing table and lean down to grasp the handle of the water bottle. The room spins but I cling on and very slowly straighten up and pull the flagon up onto the table. Still holding on with one hand I use the other to pull the flagon close and angle it towards my mouth. The water spills out but I catch some precious drops. The liquid is old and fly-strewn, but no matter. I drink, and when it is gone I prop myself up onto my elbows and catch a glimpse of my reflection in the mirror.

The wretched creature staring back at me, mimics my incredulity. My once lustrous black hair sticks to my scalp like a smoke-dirty spider's web. My skin is waxen and stretched taut across my cheek-bones and my eyes are slits in pools of red and purple.

'Help me, someone...anyone.' I whisper, but no one answers. I am alone. No sound but for the drone of a biting-fly and the tolling of bells. Once I would make my Carlo hunt and kill every fly before I could sleep. He would laugh and say how silly I was but he always did it for me. I screamed if they came near and complained when I was bitten and my flesh broke out in red lumps. Carlo was never bitten. It doesn't matter now, none of it. Come biting fly, feast on my rotting flesh, but the fly is too wise, he will find a healthier host.

The bells toll, day and night, calling the people to prayer for the deliverance of Venice from the pestilencia. The Serene Prince, our Doge, has pledged a magnificent new church for San Stefano if Venice is spared. The foundations are dug. Much good may it do them. I have no faith in a God who slaughters men, women and children as if they were corn for the reaping. Even if I was able I would not be attending the Mass.

All those people rotting in the plague pits on the island – their corpses slotted like chrysalides, row upon row. But God may spare me yet. See what a hypocrite I am? I pray to God when it suits me. I have no great desire to live, except for the girl. I won't think about her, I can't. I should have used the last of my money to send her with Mamma to Terra Ferma. But I was too frightened for her. I didn't trust Mamma. Ginevra is such a beauty –but what if she caught the pestilencia here in Venice? It would be my fault. Which 'death' is worse? I'm not God, I can't decide. I pray she is under Alfonso's

75

protection and he will keep her close, whatever happens to me. I have to believe this.

Glancing out onto the canal I see that the workmen have almost finished erecting huge iron gates to block the bridge exit on my rio. There are two gondolas on the water still making their way under the bridge but soon there will be armed guards stopping any craft attempting to flee San Marco.

There is so little time left for me. The criers came last evening, patrolling the tow paths, proclaiming that the Magistrati alla sanita say the infected and their families will be transported by public ferries to the Lazzaretto Vecchio. Maybe I could hide when they come for me? But where would I hide? Cannaregio and Guidecca are infected now. Most of my theriac was taken by the inquisition. They say the Doge is dying too, so maybe there is some justice in this miserable world, after all.

I must dress but before this there is one ritual to observe. Holding onto the dressing table with one hand I run the other slowly down my body, trying not to tense as my fingers gently probe under my arms. The acrid stench of unwashed flesh makes my gorge rise and a dribble of putrid liquid spills out of my mouth. It chokes me with its vileness. I run a shaking finger across my jaw-line, nothing, and lastly I press the flesh between my legs. My hand stops there, frozen. Is it? I am not sure, maybe it isn't what I fear. Maybe, there is still hope? Stumbling backwards towards my bed, something hard and painful digs into the bottom of my foot and looking down I see the pearl

76

necklace, each large pearl's opalescence glowing up at me. Mamma's necklace. The one for women like us.

Women like us

Today it will be impossible to visit my friends because it is my sixteenth birthday and Nonna and I have been ordered to attend Mamma for my 'celebration'. It has become a tradition − a horrible tradition.

On the morning of my birthday I wake with bad stomach cramps. I always get these pains when it is time for my menses. Nonna brings me a bowl of milk, bread and honey and while I eat she rubs my lower back with her strong, warm hands. Her touch is firm and healing and I close my eyes and breathe in and out slowly, until the cramp lessens.

When the blood first showed I was scared but Nonna told me that it happens to all girls and is normal. 'We are all Eve's daughters,' she says, ' we must atone for her sins in the Garden of Eden.' That doesn't seem fair. She also says the bleeding means I am a woman now, and I should be proud. I love Nonna dearly but sometimes she contradicts herself and I don't know what I'm supposed to think, so, I have decided not to worry about it. All I know is that I don't want to be a woman and I hate my body. I am becoming someone else, some stranger. I don't even recognise my smell any more. I didn't like this new Veronica one little bit, however Mamma seems very interested in her. She had her dressmaker create me women's dresses with plunging necklines and tight bodices. My ugly breasts are forced into them and I am worried about leaning over, in case they roll out.

As soon as I feel better Nonna urges me to get up. 'Your Mamma's maid will be here very soon.'

Once I had loved my birthdays. When I was very small in the campiello, we children got to be queen or king for the day when it was our birthday, and we got to wear a special 'crown' that Nonna had found floating on the canal. It was just an old black cap but we stuck flowers in it and bird's feathers. Everyone had to bow before us and do our bidding. I loved my birthdays then, but not anymore, not since Mamma had taken charge.

Now I was dressed up in some hideous gown that she had had specially made for me, then she sent her maid to do my hair in the latest stupid fashion and at midday I would be admitted to her apartment and paraded down a long, fidgeting line of servants, who clapped and sang 'Happy Birthday' and made rude gestures at me behind Mamma's back. It was so humiliating, but my embarrassment didn't end there because Mamma would be seated at the end of the long line with my present, which I had to open in front of everyone and given a round of applause. I'm glad Mamma enjoyed it because no one else did, but at least I could go to my own home afterwards.

In my small experience children lived with their mothers, but it had never bothered me that I didn't. I never thought it odd. When I lived in the campiello I didn't even know where her house was, but now everything was different. It made me uneasy. Why had she moved

79

us to live beside her and expect me to act like she was my mother? Why would I have feelings for someone who had made it obvious from the start that she didn't like me? But I had heard the rumours, even back then, it was hard not to when we lived so close to so many people.

'It's the Duke...what's is name? She won't like him finding out she's got a kid.'

'Wants him to think she's younger than she is. '

'Na, worried he'll take a liking to the child — more like. Pretty little thing like that.'

'Dirty old devil.'

Did I not say? Mamma is a famous courtesan and her lovers are amongst the greatest patricians and nobles of the Republic. The Duke di Vasallo has been her benefactor for years. Her house, our rooms, the money, her gowns and jewels, everything, comes from this Duke— 'The dirty old devil.' Before this I had only ever caught glimpses of him as he visited Mamma or they left together for balls and entertainment. He was old but he strutted about in striped breeches, pretending he was a much younger man. Ludicrous. He and Monsieur le Porc had a lot in common, except that Mamma's Duke was rich.

If what the gossips said was true, why Mamma's change of heart? Why was I suddenly welcomed into her household like the favourite child? Didn't she care what the Duke thought anymore? Something was going on that I didn't understand. It made me uneasy and when I asked Nonna about it, she changed the subject.

80

And here I was again at 12 o'clock precisely, waiting to enter the long gallery. I was scrubbed and trussed-up like a roasting fowl. The corset thing, Mamma insisted I wore, dug into my ribs. I creaked as I walked. The sooner this was over the better. As the doors swung open I took a deep breath and stepped inside, but, to my huge relief, the gallery was empty. A footman led us down the length of the richly carpeted room and into a small anti-chamber at the far end. Mamma was seated on a sofa and smiled as we entered. I was so relieved I almost embraced her − I didn't, of course. She bade me to sit beside her, then she patted my knee and complimented me on my hair. 'Happy Birthday, Veronica, ' she gushed, leaning towards me as if she might kiss me. I was so surprised I turned my head the wrong way and our noses clashed. Sighing heavily she thrust a black velvet box into my hands. 'This is for you. Well? Open it.'

My fingers were trembling as I lifted the box lid, disclosing a necklace of large, glowing, cream pearls, held in place by an inner circle of smaller gems. Mamma had always worn this necklace and even as a small child I remembered watching the pearls shining out, as she moved about me. I wanted to touch that necklace so badly but I never did, and now it was mine. I held it to my face, the pearls warm against my skin. It was so beautiful. 'For me?' I managed, at last, amazed at her generosity.

She nodded.

I didn't know what to say.

'Well, fasten it for her, woman.'

I could feel Nonna's hands trembling as she tried to do up the clasp but her fingers were too bent and painful.

'I'll do it, Nonna,' I said.

But Mamma pushed Nonna aside and scowled at her. 'Sometimes I wonder why I keep you on.'

Mamma did the necklace up as I watched my poor Nonna's face crumple. 'Pearls are a rite of passage,' Mamma said, her smile switching back on as she looked at me. 'You are a woman now, and women, like us, wear pearls.'

I had been prepared to love this gift. It was truly exquisite but Mamma had spoilt it, like she spoilt everything. I jumped up, unclasped the necklace and threw it at her feet. 'I don't want your necklace, nor do I want to be a woman, like you.'

Mamma didn't speak she just picked up the necklace and put it back in the box as if nothing had happened. When she had the box firmly closed she turned to me. "Sit down, Veronica, we have business to discuss.' I glared at her before seating myself as far away from her as possible.

She was silent for a moment and then she looked me straight in the eyes. 'You are to be betrothed.'

I heard Nonna's intake of breath, or was it mine?

'His name is Carlo Bertrame,' she continued. 'The only son of the illustrious apothecary, Vincenti Bertrame.'

I looked blankly at her. Was this a joke?

'The Bertrames are an up and coming family. Not of the patriciate yet but in another generation or so, who knows? '

I didn't understand a word she was saying. Betrothal? Didn't that mean marriage? I was to be married? I shook my head and muttered. 'No, I won't.'

Mamma ignored me. 'Bertrame is one of the fifty licensed Guild apothecaries in the Republic of Venice and is immensely rich. The Bertrames trade all over the Holy Roman Empire and the father has died leaving everything to his son Carlo. I was exceedingly fortunate to broker such a good match for you.'

Nonna was smiling and squeezed my hand. 'Congratulations, Veronica.'

I looked from her smiling face to my mother's and knew they had been planning this behind my back. I was stung by Nonna's treachery and shook my head. 'No. I will not marry this ...apothecary, were he the richest man in Christendom. I will not be sold off to the highest bidder. I am not a whore, even if you are.'

Mamma shrank away from me for a moment but then she drew back her hand and struck me hard across the mouth. I felt a sharp pain as her rings cut into my lip. Wiping my hand across my mouth, I stared down at the blood. I wouldn't cry.

'Oh, Madam.' Nonna moved towards me, arms outstretched to comfort me, but Mamma pushed her away. 'Keep your mouth shut, you old fool,' she hissed. 'You've always been too soft with her. Well, all that is about to change. She will do as she's told or she will regret it – you will both regret it. D'you understand?'

Nonna nodded.

'And you?' Mamma's face was white with rage. 'You will apologise to me immediately, or you can pack your bags and go on the street, where you belong.'

I stood up, facing her. My heart was racing but I wouldn't let her see my fear. 'Why should I apologise. It's the truth. I know all about the Duke and the others before him. None of this belongs to you. He owns you. You're no better than my poor sisters on the Rialto but they sell their bodies because they have to.'

'The Rialto? What do you know of the Rialto?' Mamma was watching me closely.

'Nothing,' I said quickly, avoiding the look of panic on Nonna's face. 'I've heard about it, that's all.'

'Huh.' Mamma glared at me. 'You carry on like this and you'll find out all about your 'poor sisters'. Now, I need an apology. Well? I'm waiting.'

'I'm sorry,' I lied.

Mamma's voice was soft when she finally spoke again. 'Do you think I live like this because I want to, Veronica? Where do you imagine the money for your upbringing has come from, or your education, or the clothes on your back or the food in your belly?' She thrust a hand towards Nonna, 'Who pays for this old fool? And, who has scrimped and saved for years to provide you with a dowry? Well? Every ducat of your good fortune and charmed life has come from me. From your whore of a mother.'

I couldn't look at her. I was ashamed. 'I'm sorry, Mamma,' I said, meaning it this time. 'I shouldn't have insulted you. I'm not

84

judging you, but you've brought me up to have a different life than yours. Why throw away all your effort and self sacrifice only to give me to a common potion-maker? He'll be old and fat and smell of cough linctus. I will never marry this...whatever his name is. I'd rather go on the streets. '

'You have no idea do you? I blame myself. All these years I have sought to protect you but those days are over. Now you face the real world for women like us. It's not nice but we have to learn how to survive in it.' She covered her face with her hands for a moment, pressing her fingertips into her temple. ' If you knew how much I envy you.' When she looked at me again her eyes were bright with tears. She was silent for a moment, then, taking my hand she pulled me down beside her on the chair. 'These are enlightened times, Veronica. You are fortunate to be living in them. As the daughter of a courtesan you have some status. But you must still obey the rules. You may dress like nobili women, you can do your hair like them, you can speak and dance like them, but you must never wear jewels like diamonds or rubies, only pearls. Even your choice of textiles must match your status. But, most importantly of all, you must always, always remember your place in society. The nobili of Our Most Serene Republic. be they ugly, stupid, cruel and not fit to lick your boots, will always be your superiors. I am giving you the chance to marry well and, then perhaps one day you may be accepted by the patriciate and your children and their children.'

She stopped speaking, then she squared her shoulders and sat up straight. 'But for now, Veronica, you will do as I say.'

'But why this Bertrame creature, Mamma? Why can't I choose my own husband?'

Mamma sighed. 'I have no more patience, Veronica. You have two choices. You either marry the apothecary or I cut you off and you earn your own living. I will not waste another ducat on you.' And with that she called the servant to show me out. When we were back in our rooms Nonna bathed my lip and held my face between her hands. 'Maybe this man will be kind, piccolina? He will surely adore you. What man could resist my little one?'

Poor Nonna, who thought that kindness was the most any woman could expect from a man. She, who had been abused by the brute who owned her and sold to my mother for a bottle of brandy. How could she understand that I wanted more, much more. This Carlo Bertrame was thirty years old, almost twice my age, and I would have to take my clothes off before him and let him do things to me. I'd seen and heard the mothers with their men and I wanted none of it. Making love is what they called it. I'd seen the men like beasts, sweating and straining, as if they would kill their woman, there was no love there. Was this what I had been educated for? It was ludicrous. I excelled in the arts. I read and wrote poetry. I sang and above all else I created dances which, one day will make me famous. I was beautiful and had a mind of my own. I would never marry this Bertrame. Never.

The next day Mamma sent a short note with the pearl necklace, informing me that I was to be introduced to Carlo Bertrame, at the forthcoming Grand Guild Ball. She ended by saying that I must attend her every day from now until the ball so that she could educate me in the etiquette of the Dance.

The Guild Ball

I dealt with the horror of my forthcoming betrothal to the loathsome Bertrame by not thinking about it. I reasoned that all I had to do was be as objectionable as I could be, when we met, and he would decide he didn't want me after all. This was plan A.

In the weeks leading up to the Ball I didn't have a moment to myself. If I wasn't with Mamma, learning the etiquette of the dance, I was being measured and fussed over by her dressmakers. Fortunately Nonna was only too willing to visit Little Ginevra and the women in my place.

Mamma made it clear from the beginning that she would have preferred a more prestigious introduction into society for me, but she was determined to make the best of it. So...each afternoon, between two and three, I attended her in the small salon with a group of musicians. She taught me all the latest imported French dances. There was the sedate Pavana, the athletic Goglianda and a daring new dance, La Volta, which Mamma seemed especially excited about. She told me that at the climax of this dance the man lifts his partner high and swings her around, and if the woman is unable to keep her skirt under control then her partner might catch a glimpse of her knees. Really? This was exciting?

I had never seen Mamma dance before and I was surprised and not a little envious of her grace. True she was a little stiff but that was because of the clothes she wore. She taught me to keep my gaze modestly lowered and not to make eye contact with my partner or other dancers. She showed me how to stand and make deep curtsies. She taught me to sit with one hand draped on the arm of my chair while the other rested on my breast, clasping a flower, or a fan. We studied the hierarchy of Venetian society over and over and how deep the obeisance should be for each ranking and sex. If my attention wandered Mamma tapped me with the hard edge of her fan − on parts of me that didn't show. So? That's why fans were so important? When the sun shone I was only allowed outside in huge ugly hats. She insisted that my skin should be a milky-white.

My mother puzzled me. I wished I knew what went on in her head. She was a strong woman and must have been frustrated and angry about her position in society. Surely she questioned the subservience of women, particularly women like her. All I knew was that I would rather die than be like her. It was only later that I understood that in order to think freely, you had to be free.

On the day of the ball Mamma's maid arrived ,very early, to prepare me. First, she and Nonna laced me into a new corset. This one was more stiffly boned, in front and back, than my old one and dug painfully into my ribs. When it was secured I was unable to bend, twist, or lift my arms above my shoulders. 'How am I supposed to dance like this?' I complained, but they ignored me and helped me into a chemise and then a heavy orange and brown brocade gown. The puffed sleeves were slashed with velvet and filled with bombast, which kept my arms away from my body. The material was covered in gold embroidered flowers and the tight bodice and neckline were studded with pearls nestling amongst creamy lace. I tried to hate that dress but I couldn't. It was exquisite.

Next came the shoes. 'What are they supposed to be?' I asked, as the maid helped me to sit down so that she could attach the strange orange satin slippers to my feet.

'These are chopines,' Nonna said. 'Your Mamma says they are the latest fashion. All the fine ladies on the continent wear these for the Dance.'

My feet weren't used to any sort of shoes, let alone these ridiculously uncomfortable high, hard-heeled things. When I was shod and the satin ribbons tied securely about my ankles, I attempted to stand. Impossible. Nonna and the maid took an arm each and pulled me upright, and then they led me around the room until I could stand unaided. I took a tentative step on my own. 'Small steps, Veronica'. Nonna urged, 'not great strides.' I tried another smaller step by sliding the shoe over the floor. The heels made a very satisfying clumping sound. I repeated this several times, more and more energetically, until the maid and Nonna put their hands over their ears.

'No, no, Veronica. You must not bang your foot on the ground you must lift your toe before you step, no sliding, don't slide.' I could see the maid smirking.

At least the dress had a modest neckline but the bodice was close fitting and I could feel my breasts fighting to escape. Nonna prophesised that those unruly mounds of flesh were going to be like Mamma's. She had smiled as she said this as if I should be pleased. I had taken to walking with my arms clamped across my chest, so that they wouldn't bounce about. 'Shoulders back,' Mamma screeched each time she caught sight of me slouching past.

When they were satisfied Nonna angled the mirror, so that I could see myself. I took one look and burst into tears. Nonna assumed I was crying with joy. 'You are so beautiful, Veronica. Your Carlo Bertrame is the luckiest man in all the Republic.' But I didn't care what the odious apothecary might think of me. In fact I wished, more than anything, to be as ugly as a pox ridden old crone with no teeth and breath that smelt like dog shit.

This stranger, staring belligerently back at me from the mirror, was a woman and I hated being a woman. I wanted to be dressed in my old breeches, running and playing freely in the campiello, my feet bare, my hair jammed into a cap. I didn't want to be a woman like Mamma, because if I was like her, I would have to act like her. That thought made me bawl even louder and Nonna rushed to dry my eyes before the tears stained my dress's delicate fabric.

To cap it all Mamma had insisted that I wore her odious necklace and I scowled at Nonna as she did up the clasp for me. When Nonna was finished she and the maid took a hair brush each and tamed my long hair. The maid wanted to do something fashionable with it but

I had had enough and insisted that I had my usual centre parting with the hair drawn back from my face and pinned up at the back.

When the time came to leave, a man-servant carried me to the gondola and set me down beside Mamma and Nonna. I felt like a trussed up hen bound for the market. On the journey Mamma tested me on etiquette. I punished her by pretending to have forgotten everything and she became more and more agitated. I had never seen her nervous before and relished her discomfort. Nonna kept squeezing my hand until I relented and told Mamma I knew it all and I would behave. She frowned, suspecting my sudden acquiescence, but I smiled reassuring]y at her. I could afford to be magnanimous because I had made a plan, another plan, in case the other one didn't work. This was plan B. I was rather good at plan-making. So this is it.

It was Monsieur le Porc who first told me about Caroso and Negri – the famous Italian dance masters. Negri was a great favourite at the court of the French Dauphin, the Duke of Brittany. So...to my plan. Before the wedding Nonna and I would run away from Mamma and the apothecary and Venice, and travel to France, where I would meet Negri. We would create beautiful dances together and he would fall madly in love with me and eventually, when I was very old, we would marry. So? What could go wrong?

Mamma had grown quiet at last, lost in thought, and I took the opportunity to enjoy the late afternoon sun on my face. It was a beautiful day. There was no wind and the gondola slid effortlessly towards our destination like a skater on ice. I was relaxed and enjoying the young gondoliers eyes on me. I rearranged my heavy skirts, so that

92

he got a glimpse of my legs. Practice for La Volta? This might be more fun than I had bargained for.

Liveried servants lined the steps at our destination, waiting to help us disembark. Nonna whispered a blessing before disappearing, to wait for us in the servants' quarters. I hardly registered her departure because all my concentration was focussed on the building that rose majestically out of the water in front of us. The Ca D'ora. We had arrived just as the sun was setting and golden suffused light bathed the palazzo's loggias, its elegant pointed arches, oriental windows and lacy caps of delicate tracery. All this splendour was reflected in the canal, making it seem as if the palazzo was set adrift in a lake of shifting liquid gold.

Mamma must have seen my face because she touched my arm. 'This is the most lavish Palazzo in all of Venice, Veronica. You are fortunate to attend your first ball here.' Everyone in Venice talked about this place, but nothing could have prepared me for its full glory. It was like a Persian Palace out of one of the stories I had read and decorated in gold leaf and coloured with turquoise Moorish pinnacles. I had seen a painting of this palazzo once but no painting could do justice to the reality. Nonna had taken me to all the churches and the cathedrals in San Marco but none compared to this.

'Close your mouth, Veronica.' Mamma instructed, as the servants prepared to help us from the gondola. We were carried up the steps to the entrance and then escorted inside. The servants lit the way with torches. It was dark, after the blazing light on the Big Canal, but as my eyes adjusted I saw the magnificence of the room we entered.

93

The opulence of the furnishings, the colours of the women's gowns, their perfumes, the scents of the towering vases of heavenly lilac, the mellow, flickering light of candelabras, all of it, left me struck dumb. ' Shoulders back, Veronica,' warned Mamma as we moved slowly forwards in a line of people, waiting to be announced. It was no good, I didn't want to be, but I was excited. I seemed to be getting used to my heels, although I was still very cautious.

Mamma had timed our arrival to perfection. We were neither early nor late and our entrance was noted by the assembly. I could feel their eyes on us and I saw some of them murmuring to each other as we passed. Mamma swept onwards, relishing every moment. She was still a beautiful woman. I trailed after her, concentrating on not falling over and once I stumbled and almost fell. I caught sight of a woman saying something behind her fan to her escort and laughing, while looking directly at me. Did she know, did they all know, that I was there for this Bertrame creature? I felt my cheeks flaming and suddenly the excitement and lavishness of the place tasted like sour cherries in my mouth. The clamour of hundreds of people laughing and talking all at once was deafening. There was too much false jollity, too many prancing and primping young men running around like little ponies. If I could have laughed it would have made me feel better but Mamma caught my eye, as if she were reading my mind, and scowled. I looked down and walked on, dutifully curtseying deeply and painfully, because of my steel corset, to the hostess and then her husband and then the guest of honour and so on.

We were seated not far from the musicians, between a group of animated young men on one side and giggling chaperoned young women on the other. Not long after this the musicians struck up with tabors, flutes and a lute. They were dressed like Arabians, with brightly coloured baggy pantaloons, waistcoats and turbans decorated with sparkling gems. Their leader, the lute player, was a tall young Moor, who was fighting a losing battle with his over-large turban, that kept slipping down over his nose. I had no idea how he managed to concentrate on his instrument as well as control his wayward headgear, but he did. I had never heard such beautiful music and I ached to dance.

I must have been swaying to the wonderful rhythms because Mamma trod heavily on my foot. Many of the men and women on either side of us joined the dance and I was so envious, but I contented myself by watching the musicians. I had never been this close to real musicians before. Once Nonna had taken me to watch a street performance by a group of travelling players, but I couldn't see the musicians from where we stood at the back of the crowd.

I had never realised that musicians danced while they played. The lute player, especially, seemed lost in the power of the music he played. One day I would like to create a musician's dance.

But even the magic of the music wore thin as the Ball ground on and I was forced to watch yet another clumsy couple attempting the dance. Mamma sat erect and forbidding beside me. I also sat erect, it was hard to do anything else while those bones stuck into my ribs. There was no one there who danced as well as I, and it was torture to watch these ungainly men and women with their stiff bodies and stupid faces, trying to be graceful. I could see their mouths moving as they counted the steps – imbeciles.

Was I to sit here all night? Maybe Bertrame was too fat to dance? Perhaps he was one of that group of old men over there playing cards and drinking excessively, or the ones standing by themselves with disdainful looks on their faces. Maybe he detested dancing?

I tried to concentrate on my escape plan.

Then, just as another dance came to an end and the couples returned to their places, Mamma raised her fan to hide her mouth and said, 'The man there, with the black velvet tunic? See him?'

I nodded. He was hard to miss.

'You may approach him for the next dance.'

I looked at her in surprise. The man she indicated was very handsome. I'm sure that every woman in the room had noticed him. I certainly had and I knew he was aware of me. I had felt his eyes on me, while he pretended to be interested in what his friends were saying. His black hair fell across his eyes and he kept absentmindedly pushing it away as he laughed and joked with the men. I was confused. I thought I was there for the apothecary, but I am nothing if not obedient and rose immediately before Mamma could change her mind.

I took careful, small steps and my hips began to sway as if they had a will of their own. Was this what being a woman meant? Your body moving to a new foreign rhythm? I quite liked the feeling but would I be able to dance? When I arrived in front of the man he was still engrossed with his companions, apparently oblivious to me. I

96

didn't like being ignored and I could feel my anger rising. If he didn't look at me shortly I would turn my back on him, and approach the ugliest man in the room. However, I could feel my mother's glare in the middle of my shoulder blades so, I continued my vigil. He made me wait for another long minute before he looked up, as if in surprise, at my being there. I had decided to be cool and aloof to this rude person but this was proving to be difficult because when he finally deigned to look at me I saw his eyes. They were the most incredible deep blue, almost black. I stared at him for a moment longer than was necessary, before remembering to look away. I curtseyed and offered my hand, palm up, while my other hand clasped the flower to my breast. Then I looked him straight in the eyes, daring him to laugh at this ridiculous posing. But he didn't laugh, he put his head to one side and grinned. Yes, it was a grin. There was nothing about grins in Mamma's etiquette book. This was becoming intolerable, to be ignored was one thing, but to be an object of ridicule was quite another. How dare he. I glared at him but he chose not to see my anger and uncurled from his chair in one fluid movement, never taking his eyes off me. Then he slowly unpeeled one of his gloves and kissed his fingertips, before offering me his hand. I bounced my fingers off my lips and thrust my hand at him. I could be uncouth too. He gripped my hand and walked me quickly towards the dance floor. I couldn't do 'quick' in those ridiculous shoes and if he hadn't steadied me around the waist I would have probably broken both ankles. He held me close for a moment then gently unwound his arms from me and held his hand out, which I took. I needed him to safely escort me onto the ballo.

97

His touch was light but I felt the strength in his fingers and I allowed my hand to relax against his. I had never let a man hold my hand before and the sudden ripple of pleasure I felt, journeyed through my body, like the shock of icy water on a winter's day. He pressed my fingers gently, as if he felt the excitement too and in that moment I forgave him his rudeness. I forgave him everything. And my resolve to escape Carlo Bertrame increased. How could I marry someone else when this man had captured my heart by simply holding my hand?

On the way to the dance floor my partner stopped beside the musicians and rested his hand on the lute player's shoulder. The young boy looked up very slowly, so as not to lose his headgear, and our eyes met.

My partner smiled broadly. 'I think you two have met before? But allow me to introduce you properly. This is my good friend Alfonso Ortha.'

'Of course,' I laughed. 'It's you, my 'boy', my little Moor.'

He smiled shyly, got carefully to his feet and, holding onto his turban, ducked his head in greeting. 'Signorina, Veronica.' He was a head taller than me now.

'Alfonso Ortha? Not so little now.' I was truly delighted to see him. 'You have given up the tin whistle I see?'

'I have practiced every day, like you told me, and now...'

'...And now he is a maestro,' my partner finished for him.

'I am not worthy, Signore.'

I was busy remembering all the dreadful things I had done and said to this boy. 'I think I was very cruel to you, but I was a silly little girl. Forgive me? I so wanted to tell you how sorry I was but you stopped coming to the campiello. You disappeared just like Ginevra. Just like them all ' I saw the boy's reaction at the mention of her name. 'I'm sorry, Alfonso, but she is dead.'

He shook his head, sadly.

I couldn't bear the look on his face. 'So? Why didn't you come back?'

'You threw rocks at me. See?' he said, pointing to a thin scar on his temple. 'I still bear the mark of your displeasure.'

My partner laughed out loud at that.

'Oh dear, I had forgotten I was so nasty to you.'

'It was no matter, Signorina. I had to go to work for my father at that time. I am the oldest son. My father needed help in the traghetto.'

'But you were a baby.'

'I was nine. My childhood was over, like it was for...your friend, but I never forgot you, or the Dance. You had a passion, as did I…' he trailed off, unable to say more.

Seeing the boy's embarrassment my partner turned to me. 'Alfonso is the most accomplished lute player in the Republic, and also the best gondolier. We've known each other since he was a child. His father owns the famous Ortha traghetto on the Guidecca and runs a fleet of gondolas for transporting cargoes of pharmacological products from the ships that anchor in the Lagoon. Alfonso's father worked for my father and now Alfonso works for me. I owe him much.'

'And I you, Signore.'

99

I must have made some sound then, because both of them turned to stare at me. 'Bertrame? You are Carlo Bertrame?' I stammered. 'The ...renowned apothecary?'

He gave me a mock bow. 'The very same. And you are Signorina Veronica Maria Bracci ... the renowned...?'

My head was spinning. ' and we...you and I...'

'...Renowned apothecary and renowned... beauty,' he added, mischief dancing in those deep blue eyes.

But I wasn't going to be embarrassed into simpering silence. If he thought I was that sort of silly girl he had a lot to learn about me. 'We,' I said, a little too loudly, so that several people close by looked at us with interest. 'We,' I lowered my voice. 'We are to be betrothed?'

'Apparently so.' For a moment he seemed to lose some of his composure. 'Have you some objection to this arrangement?'

I shook my head so hard it hurt my neck. 'No, no, it's just that I wasn't expecting ...I was expecting a ...'

'...A what? An old man stinking of potions and salves. I can assure you, Signorina, I never miss my yearly bath and smell quite sweet,' he raised one arm and fanned the air towards me. I couldn't help laughing out loud at this, which intrigued onlookers even more.

The boy's smile spread from ear to ear. 'Do you still dance, Signorina Veronica?'

But Carlo Bertrame spoke before I could answer. 'That remains to be seen, Alfonso.' Then he turned to face me. 'And now we will show you how good we are. And maybe,' he added, 'How good you are. Alfonso has told me many stories about you and your creations.'

'Maybe you disapprove of women like me?'

'I have never met 'women like you' before, Signorina. I will tell you what I think of you when I know you better. Now, to the Dance.'

I saw the conspiratorial look pass between them and then the boy inclined his head to me and took up his lute. I curtseyed and we walked on. Once on the floor Carlo swept me around him in an arc until we were facing one another. Alfonso struck the first chords and then he and his fellow musicians began. The tempo was slow and languid, interwoven with the new Arabian rhythms, that I had heard but never danced to. Carlo's eyes never left mine and all the lessons, all the do's and don'ts flew out of my head. I knew I was blushing but I couldn't look away. My whole body tingled with anticipation. I felt so light I thought I might drift away, up into the golden vaulted ceiling of the Ca D'ora. Alfonso was playing the music of my soul.

The dance begins. I follow my partner's lead effortlessly and as the tempo increases, so our moves became more provocative. I see the married women in the company hiding their faces behind their fans. I dare not look at Mamma. But I see courtesans applauding our daring as their consorts move closer to them, hungry to share the passion of our dance. Some young, single men stand on the edge of the dance floor and ape my partner's leaps and spins.

The lute plays sweetly as we step, pause, glance to the left, slide the right foot to the instep of the left, pause, look right, incline

101

the head,. mark the rhythm. This is the first time since my childhood, that I am allowed to dance to the music, instead of the other way round. In all of Monsieur le Porc's dances the steps were never changed, whether they fitted the music or not. But now the music and movements were one. My partner is laughing, showing his shapely calves and buttocks to the women, his tunic glitters with semi-precious stones. We are the golden couple. I nearly lose my composure at this thought but manage to flatten my smiling mouth before it betrays me. I take my lead from him and our moves shadow each other's perfectly. My new swaying walk suits this dance and for the first time I am glad I have a woman's body.

When the music ends we leave the dance floor, side by side. The company is standing and applauding, even Mamma. Carlo's arm encircles my waist as we return to our places, but this time he seats me beside him. He smiles a long lazy smile and murmurs, 'La mia, bella ragazza, La mia, Veronica. I think I can love a 'woman like you.''

Negri ? Who is Negri?

Marriage

And so, I am to marry Carlo Bertrame.

I wake each morning with such a feeling of joy in me that it would take a moment or two before I remembered why I was so happy. I still couldn't quite believe it. Carlo Bertrame, the famed apothecary, wanted to marry me? The most handsome, kind, funny man in the whole Republic and probably the world, wanted me, the daughter of a courtesan, dragged up in the poor, back streets of San Marco? It was like a fairy story and I was a beggar princess. It was a miracle.

And amidst all this excitement another miracle occurred.— Mamma was happy too. I couldn't remember when I'd last seen her smile, but now she positively beamed at everyone, including me. If I'm honest it was a little disconcerting. My marriage might not have nobili status but Mamma was determined that my wedding nuptials would be the best Venice had seen for a long time. She threw herself into organising countless social events that Carlo and myself must attend, and spent her time drawing up lists of likely people to invite to the wedding feast, including high ranking guild members, merchant traders, artists, poets and the few lower ranking Patriciates — who might deign to accept her invitation.

103

She rushed into my room one morning — she still never knocked — waving a gold-edged invitation card at me. I'd never seen her lost for words before but she thrust the card into my hands and waited impatiently whilst I read it. It was from Anna del Vasallo — wife to the oily duke — Mamma's lover. Venice can be a very confusing place to live in sometimes. I could see Mamma wanted a response, so I said, 'That's nice.'

'Nice, nice?' she said, staring at me as if I'd lost my reason.

'The Duke is one of the Ten, Veronica. Don't you understand? To be invited to the Del Vasallo palazzo as part of your wedding nuptials is nothing short of a miracle.'

There you are, another miracle.

'His Excellency is one of the most powerful men in the Republic. They do us much honour.'

As it happened the Duke couldn't attend his wife's soiree to celebrate my betrothal. I was mightily relieved. It all sounded extremely dull to me and slightly embarrassing but Mamma was so excited I couldn't refuse to go. She made me swear I would conduct myself with decorum and I complied. As expected, it was a very boring affair, where a pale, young woman read poetry — very badly, about some Greek youth whose lover was ravished by a bull, who was really the king or something. I lost the gist after the first three pages. I almost wished I'd kept the poem I'd written all those years ago for that anaemic youth. That would have livened up the evening. But at least Mamma enjoyed herself.

She arranged interminable gatherings where Carlo and I were introduced to people I didn't know, nor wished to know, except for the lovely Jacopo Tintoretto and his family, who were close friends of the Bertrames. His daughter Marietta was a few years older than me and we got on very well. I think I can make a friend of her. She is an artist.

Carlo had no other family except an uncle and aunt, but he had a lot of friends and business acquaintances, so he knew most of the people we met. He had just been made chairman of the new Venetian College of Apothecaries — a great honour and Mamma was very excited about our future. She was convinced that our children might be elevated to Patriciate status in their lifetimes.

I teased Carlo that he was only marrying me for my dowry, but he assured me that he was only a little influenced by the money and gems. He said this with a wide grin on his face and then he kissed me hard and passionately and wouldn't let me go, even when my outraged Nonna took a hair brush and hit him hard on his backside. She pretended to be shocked but she loved him too and if I'd been a jealous woman I would have had to kill her.

Mamma ordered Nonna, on pain of instant dismissal, to never leave Carlo and myself alone. Apparently my virginity must be guarded like a precious jewel — Mamma's words not mine. It was fortunate that the wedding was going to be very soon because I don't think either Carlo or I could have waited too long.

Nonna instructed me about my wifely duties in the bedroom. Poor Nonna. Her cheeks were bright pink as she spoke and she couldn't look me in the face. I tried very hard not to laugh. Her sexual experience would have covered a grain of rice and, even with my lack of experience I knew that Carlo's and my loving would be very different from her dire warnings.

I had never known what sexual arousal felt like until now. Carlo only had to walk into my room and I burned with desire for him. He was so beautiful. Everything about him thrilled me. There was a smoothness to his neck that I longed to kiss; and his head — the shape of his head — and his full sensuous lips and his long muscular legs and, above all else, his smell. I would take his hands in mine and press his fingers against my nose, breathing him in. He said he was frightened I would eat him. So was I.

All I wanted was for the wedding to be over, so that I could have Carlo to myself. I desired him so keenly it was like a very painful stomach cramp that refused to go away. I was jealous of anyone or anything that took him away from me. Why could he not leave Alfonso and his assistants in charge of the farmacia? Why did he have to attend guild meetings that went on all night? Why did he have to visit his nobili and patriciate clientele in their homes?

I had created a very special dance for our nuptials, but when Carlo discovered what was entailed, he shook his head and wagged a finger at me. 'No, no, my sweet,' he scolded. 'The only place you can perform that dance is behind my bedroom's locked doors.' I pretended wide-eyed innocence but he shook his head at me in mock horror. ' Veronica, Veronica, what am I to do with you?' I had several ideas.

Carlo was having a wedding dress made for me as part of his wedding gift but I worried when it hadn't arrived and there were only a few days left before the wedding. What if the gown needed altering, or, heaven forbid, I hated it? Mamma was calm and smiled at me reassuringly telling me not to worry and, at last, with only two days to go, it was finally delivered. As I waited impatiently for the dressmaker to peel away the protective outer covering on the dress Nonna and Mamma stood beside me, watching. They were smiling but how could they be so certain I would like it? I steeled myself to look pleased, however awful it was. I swore I would wear it, even if it was hideous. I couldn't hurt Carlo.

At last the dressmaker was ready and shook out the gown so that I could see it in all its glory. I was speechless.

Mamma wrinkled her brow at me. 'Well, child, aren't you going to say something?'

'I...it's...oh, Mamma, it's so beautiful.' It was the most glorious gown I had ever seen, made from heavy purple brocade with inserts and slashes of rich creamy Venetian lace and covered with exquisitely embroidered flowers and birds, sewn with golden thread and small pearls. The dressmaker helped me into it and it fitted me perfectly, thanks, no doubt, to Mamma's dressmaker who had taken my measurements so accurately.

There was also a purple brocade caul edged in gold for my head and ribbons of the same colour to braid my long black hair. Finally there was a velvet pouch containing amethyst earrings and necklace. Nonna kept touching the fabric reverently, crossing herself and sighing, 'ah, bellissimo.'

107

We were to be married very simply in the nearby ancient church of San Nicolo dei Mendicoli, accompanied by a few family members and close friends. Mamma would have preferred us to make our vows in San Pietro Castalto Cathedral, with its throne dedicated to St Peter, and its glorious frescoes but Carlo didn't mind where we were married, as long as it was soon. As for me, wedding ring or not, I would have given myself willingly to my love.

After the wedding we would return to Mamma's to welcome our guests for the wedding feast and celebration. There would be music and dancing. Alfonso came every night, after the shop closed, to play for us while we practiced the dances. The boy was so solemn but I grew to love him. He was like a younger brother to me. His family lived on La Guidecca too, and he had the sweetest little sister called Sofia.

It was traditional for the groom to walk to his bride's house and escort her to the church, so, Nonna, Mamma and Jacopo's daughter Marietta, stood beside me as we waited for Carlo on our wedding morn. It was one of those bright early summer's mornings when the rising sun promised a glorious day. Neighbours and servants clustered in the campo and outside in the via, waiting to wish us good fortune. Some held flowers to strew in our path. I was so excited I thought I might faint. Nonna hid her nerves by fussing about me, smoothing down my skirts and pushing tendrils of my hair back under my caul.

As Carlo entered the campo with his uncle, Alfonso and Jacopo beside him, the sun crested the surrounding buildings and bathed my lovely boy in golden light. He looked like an angel. I swear I am not

108

imagining this. His beauty took my breath away. He was dressed in a jerkin and breeches of deep, almost black, blue, with a pure white shirt and silk stockings. On his head was a rich blue and white velvet cap, and when we looked at each other I saw his bright eyes full of tears. I was crying too.

'My, Veronica,' he whispered, as he took my hand in his and kissed it. 'Mia ragazza. Come. Let us be married.'

The small church was a hushed world of diffused light and muted colours rippling across the tiled floors, like gentle waves. Our priest had an angelic round face like a baby gargoyle and his smile was wide and his clasp warm as he joined our hands together as man and wife. When my husband kissed me for the first time as a married woman, I wanted to run and dance and clap my hands in joy.

It's hard to remember all the details of that day. It was like a dream, a blissful dream. One thing I do recall however, is that, at some point, I embraced Mamma and whispered, 'thank you.' She was as surprised as I by my spontaneous show of affection and looked as if she might cry. She had given me the most precious gift – a man I could love forever.

Alfonso and his musicians played all night and Carlo and I led every dance. Some were my creations and some were the proscribed dances of the day with small bits added or taken away, all set to Alfonso's music. Finally we fell exhausted into our chairs. and looked at each other. Carlo gave a slight nod of his head. It was time.

The wedding festivities would continue but we were going to slip away without anyone knowing. There was a tradition that the newly wedded couple should be accompanied to their bridal bed by the wedding guests with much noise and laughter, but I wanted none of that. Mamma talked of a flotilla of gondolas, hung about with lanterns and guests in their finery, seeing us across the lagoon to Bertrame's spezerie on La Guidecca, where we were to sleep that night, in the apartment above the shop.

When I first told Carlo my plan, he was surprised. 'You don't like tradition?' he asked.

'Not much,' I said.' You?'

He shook his head, 'But you surprise me. I thought all women liked that sort of thing.'

I patted his hand, kindly. 'Poor Carlo. You have much to learn about women.'

He patted my hand in turn. 'And you, my dear one, have a lot to learn about men.'

Only Nonna and Alfonso knew of our plan and after we crept away we separated. I went to my rooms and Nonna helped me undress down to my chemise. It was heaven to take off the boned corset and the tight stomacher. I threw the chopines across the room, then I dressed quickly in my old street clothes. They were clean this time. Then I jammed my hair into the cap, pulled on my boots and stood up, taking a deep breath. It felt so good to be free.

Carlo and I were to meet at the servant's door behind the house, then take his old gondola and make our way to the Island. Alfonso would ferry Nonna and my belongings to us the next day. When I was

110

ready Nonna whispered a blessing in my ear and kissed my cheek. 'Please don't cry,' I murmured in my dear friend's ear. 'You will always be with me. I promise.' Then I ran down the stairs, through the now deserted kitchen, and out through the back door.

Carlo was waiting for me in his work clothes, but still wearing his wedding cap. He didn't recognise me. Why should he? He had never seen me as a street urchin before. 'Well, boy.' he said ' What's your hurry?'

'Mind your own business,' I said.

He caught my arm and swung me around to face him. 'Hey, no reason for that. Have you been stealing?'

I wriggled out of his grasp and grabbed his cap.

'No, give that back now.'

I backed away from him and he made a grab and pulled me towards him, reaching for the cap. I hid it behind my back and his arms came around me. His face was very close to mine and then I was kissing him, on his mouth, his face, his neck. He took a step backwards, his eyes wide with astonishment, and then, he saw it was me. 'Veronica, Veronica,' he murmured. 'What have you done to me?' And he gently removed my cap, cupped my face in his hands and found my lips.

And that's where we consummated our love. Not in the bridal bed covered with flowers, nor between the pure linen sheets that Nonna had laundered so lovingly, but there in an alleyway. When we were finished, Carlo picked me up in his arms and we giggled our way through the darkened alleyways, to where our gondola was moored on the Lagoon.

When he lifted me into the gondola it rocked dangerously and he pretended he might drop me, but I laughed and wrapped my legs about him. If I fell so would he. He set me down on cushions beside the oarlock and, with one final flourish, took off his cap and tossed it high into the night sky.

We glided through the black, black water, leaving trails of green sparkling phosphorescence in our wake. Carlo was singing softly as we slowly drifted out into the Lagoon and I stood up beside him, my arms about his waist and we watched together as the stars danced about our heads.

Money of my own

After a few days Nonna joined us in Carlo's quarters. It was only later that we moved back to San Marco and bought the house I live in now. Nonna told us that Mamma had not been pleased when she discovered that we had robbed her of her flotilla of gondolas, but she never mentioned it.

Being married to Carlo was the best thing that had ever happened to me. We were so happy. We loved and laughed and, joy of joy, we danced. Carlo had music in his soul too. And, as if all these blessings weren't enough, now I was a woman of means. Carlo gave me a more than generous allowance and never asked how I spent it, so at long last I was able to fulfil my promises to Pazienza and Little Ginevra.

Nonna was a woman of means too because my generous husband insisted that she be paid a proper wage. At first she shook her head furiously. 'No, no. I am Signora del Bertrame's Nonna, what need have I of money?'

But Carlo ignored her objections and presented Nonna with a beautiful little wage bag, embroidered with silver threads. Every Monday morning he would call her to his office, where he placed a coin inside her bag. She couldn't sign Carlo's ledger so he wrote

Carlotta Nonna in big bold letters and she would trace around the letters with her finger. She kept the bag attached to her belt and slept with it under her pillow. She never spent any of it and when the bag was full, she hid the money beneath the floorboards in her bedroom. I tried to encourage her to spend some of it on herself – to get some luxury or little trinket but she said it was to pay for her funeral and the priest and above all else, now she could leave something for Little Ginevra, too.

When Carlo was at the farmacia, my days were my own, and I was able to visit the Rialto whenever I chose. The destitute women and their children lived in the Carampane, a squalid warren of tenements, close to the Big Canal on a side-rio – an evil smelling, putrid dribble of water, in which human excreta and dead animals floated. It took a long time for Nonna and myself to get used to the stench but now we are accustomed to it, just like we accept the ever-present misery and hopelessness that we see every day on the faces of the women and their children.

Ginevra has begun to inhabit my dreams again. She is always there, on the periphery of my vision, standing in the shadows. I never see her clearly but I know it is her and I know what she wants.

This was my opportunity to put my grandiose schemes into practise. First of all I would need to hire a doctor for the women and children, before Ferocious Summer brought the hot, disease-laden winds that funnelled down the rii, dragging the Coughing Disease and worse, in its wake. I was determined that Ginevra's child and the others would learn to read and write and I searched for appropriate

114

rooms and teachers, so that the children could be educated. I intended that the women would be taught useful skills so that they could earn a living and not have to sell their bodies. I had so many ideas, so many plans. And I couldn't wait to share my dreams with Pazienza.

It was an early summer's day and the sun danced on the water as Pazienza and I sat in companionable silence watching Nonna, as she hummed some old song and rocked the child to sleep. The child had been fretful. Her little head felt hot and her cheeks were flushed. Nonna had made a poultice for her chest, from pigs' fat and herbs. The smell brought back the memories of my own childhood. I had hated Nonna's cure but it had always worked. This seemed the perfect moment to tell Pazienza my news. I had managed to hire a doctor willing to care for the women and children. As well as this I was looking to rent a room where the women might shelter from the rain and sun while they waited for their men. It wasn't much but it was a start.

After I stopped talking I looked at Pazienza, waiting for a reaction but she was silent, lost in thought, as if she hadn't heard me. Her face was raised to the sun and her eyes were closed. She looked old and weary.

Suddenly her eyes snapped open and she scrambled to her feet. 'Time to go, Veronica. It is late.'

I jumped up beside her. 'But what do you think?'

She shrugged.

' Have you nothing to say? I thought you'd be pleased. '

115

She stared at me. She had always had a hard stare. Even when I was little, if I got too bossy or cross, she would fix me with that look and walk away from me until I ran after her to apologise for something stupid I had done or said.

'You thought I'd be pleased?' she asked. 'Why? Because you've paid some old quack, who probably isn't a doctor at all, to care for us? Because you've spent a fortune for some leaky awning?' She frowned at me. 'You don't want to know what I think, not really, you just want me to smile and say thank you, thank you.'

I was astonished. Couldn't she see how life-changing my help could be? 'But I'm doing this for you, Pazienza,' I sounded like a spoilt child.

'Are you? Or are you just bored with living in your beautiful house with servants and a wealthy husband, and mixing with the nobili? You were always easily bored. You have food in your belly and warmth and a future. That's why Ginevra loved you. She thought she might be someone else, with you as her friend, but....' she looked away. 'But it didn't happen, did it? It never does.' And there it was again. The guilt. It was my fault my friend had died. My fault. I was angry now. 'And what's wrong in wanting to help?'

'Nothing.' She said. 'As long as you don't promise things you can't deliver. Because the worst thing for us is having our hopes raised then dashed, time and time again.'

I grabbed her hand and held it tight. 'I'm not that Veronica any more, Pazienza. I promise.'

'Big dreams,' she said. 'Always big dreams.'

116

'And what's wrong in dreaming?'

I think she almost smiled then. 'So? What makes you think we'd be interested in what you plan for us? Have you asked anyone's opinion? Or are we too stupid to discuss it? '

'Of course they'd be interested,' I snapped. 'My help could change their lives.'

'Ahh. You have a magic potion for us? Something to turn us into respectable married women and our children into those little angels who sing in the church choirs and have never watched their mothers being used by men ?'

I was quiet for a moment. 'No magic. Just hope, Pazienza. These things take time.'

'However many lifetimes we live, Veronica, we will always be whores, and our children, the children of whores. '

I turned my back on her then, determined to keep my temper, but the sad thing was that I knew what she said was true. Women had three roles in our Most Serene Republic. Wife, Nun or Whore, and we had no choice about which lot we drew. I had indeed been very lucky.

Before I left the Rialto that day Pazienza rested a hand on my shoulder and squeezed it. I looked at her and she smiled. 'I know you mean well, my friend, but just one piece of advice. Get to know us before you tell us what we want. Who knows? Maybe some of us might have better ideas? But before all that, show us that we can trust you, and more importantly, believe you.'

117

I was cross at first, that she had thrown my ideas back in my face, but after a few days I realised she was right. So, I took her advice and began to visit their campo, once a week for several months, without saying a word to anyone about my plans. We continued to look after little Ginevra and to feed and clothe the women and children – nothing more, except now I talked to them and heard their stories. Some of the women I remembered from my childhood, but many were strangers and suspicious of me, in my fine clothes and obvious wealth. It was only after they discovered I had once lived in the campiello and was Pazienza 's friend, that they opened up to me. Most of their stories were heart-breaking and Nonna and I would often walk home in tears.

The Speech

Nonna and I always timed our visits for the late morning, after the women had managed a few hours sleep. We stayed for an hour, leaving before they had to patrol the streets once more. Bit by bit I felt their trust in me growing until eventually they greeted me like one of their own, and the day came when I thought they were ready to hear what I had to say. Up till then I had always talked to one woman at a time but now I gathered them all about me, in front of the tenement. Pazienza came out and stood beside her door, watching me, her arms folded. Nonna was beside her with the struggling child, who wanted to join the older children, who shouted and played tag amongst the women. I had to shout over the racket but as the women began to pick up what I was saying they shushed their children. None of them interrupted as I talked, but I saw their heads nodding in agreement as I spoke about their being taught a trade, so they might earn a living. They murmured their approval when I promised to provide their children with an education and one or two clapped when I said I was employing a doctor to look after them. I was acutely aware of Pazienza as I spoke and watched for a reaction, but she gave nothing away. Her expression was inscrutable. I still had to prove myself to her.

When at last I was done the women cheered and clapped, shouting encouragement, wanting more. Some of them were nursing quiet listless babies in their arms. Older children clung to their mothers' skirts, hungry for food and affection, but the women were too tired, too down-trodden, too sad, to notice them. I looked for Nonna, who stood at the back, behind the women, holding the child by its hand. She said something to her and patted her head and there was such a look of tenderness on my old friend's face that it took my breath away. Surely all children had the right to experience such love?

The women's eyes were still on me, willing me to continue, wanting more. and I saw their rapt expressions and felt a shiver of excitement. I knew I had them in the palm of my hand. It was that same power I felt when I danced. I was drunk with it and, without thinking, I pulled up a crate and jumped up onto it, so that everyone could see me. This was what I had been waiting for, a chance to share my thoughts and dreams with these poor wretched women. I didn't just want to feed, clothe, educate or heal them, I wanted them to wake up and think for themselves. I wanted them to be free.

'My dear sisters,' I began. 'You all know me. I am Veronica Bertrame −daughter of a courtesan and wife to a wealthy man. I am more fortunate than you. I have money and food and rich clothes but I am still a slave.' I saw some of them whisper to their friends at this, but I shook my head. 'You think I am very different to you? I'm not. I may wear fine clothes but I am a woman, just like you. Men rule our Most Serene Republic and even the most stupid of them is still our master. I long for freedom, just like you.' I had a fleeting glimpse of Pazienza's raised eyebrows but I didn't care, I had the bit between my teeth. 'But our day will come, I promise you.' I raised my voice a little. 'I tell the truth in front of you all. I will be the first to act, setting an example for

120

you to follow. Will you follow me?' A murmur of approval rose amongst the women clustered about me. 'Would you fight with me, side by side?' I was shouting too loudly and I knew at once that I'd gone too far. The women glanced at their friends in alarm and muttered to one another. One or two ducked back inside their building closing the doors firmly behind them, shutting me out. I saw Nonna's startled expression. I should have stopped then, I wanted to, but I couldn't. 'Is this a life worth living?' I asked, sweeping my arms about me. 'Is this what you want for your children and their children?' No one answered. They stood with their heads bowed. Women like them were never asked for their opinions, they had been taught to keep quiet. Words were weapons used by men. 'When we too are armed and trained,' I continued. 'We will convince men that we have hands. feet and hearts like them, and although we may be delicate and soft , some men who are delicate, are also strong, and others who are course and harsh , are cowards.'

That was when I glimpsed Pazienza pushing her way through the women towards me. There were two feverish spots of rouge on her face, disguising a livid bruise under her eyes. A beating from one of her men, she had told me, almost with pride. 'But you should see him.'

'Move over, Veronica,' she hissed, and climbed up onto the box to stand beside me. She stared at me for a moment then shook her head, as if in despair. 'Veronica, Veronica? Where in God's name did that come from? '

'I've ruined everything haven't I? Why do I always go too far?' I turned to climb down from the box but she grasped my arm and we

121

stood arm in arm staring out at the women, who were watching us intently. When Pazienza spoke her voice was strong, compelling. 'Veronica is right, sisters. Men are cowards – all of 'em.' And the women cheered and clapped.

I was stunned. She agreed with me. 'There are one or two good ones. ' I whispered, thinking of my Carlo.

'Yeah, well maybe for the likes of you,' she said, ' but not for me, not for them. Men are all bastards.'

Her fearlessness gave me courage and I spoke again. 'But we have not yet realised our power. For if we should decide to do so,. then we will be able to fight men until death.'

'Trouble is they're the ones with cudgels and fists. Not much of a fair fight, eh? They're always gonna be stronger than us, whatever weapon we use. '

'But there is a stronger weapon,' Pazienza, we use words, Pazienza. They are the most powerful weapons in the world.'

'Oh yeah, but how d'you speak when the bastard's knocked all your teeth out?' There was laughter at this and I looked at her and then at this gang of wretched women, most of them younger than me, with bad teeth and crooked bodies. The bitter wind on the canal scythed through their tattered clothing as they huddled together for warmth. The sailors who frequented the Carampane would take any woman, young or old, diseased or maimed and these women's pathetic attempts to be alluring made me want to weep. Every woman there was a hero.

122

Telling Carlo

My triumphant day with the women of the Carampane spurred me on to the next important step. It was time to tell Carlo of my plans. He was a business man and would be able to help me with my campaign. I had discovered, early on, that my husband had a methodical brain and I needed to be absolutely sure of the practicalities of any idea before I discussed it with him. However there never seemed the time to discuss such matters. Carlo worked long hours at the apothecary and when he wasn't working we were practicing my new creations or attending balls, or meeting with his many friends.

I had never talked to him about my life before we married. Oh, he knew Mamma was a courtesan and Nonna had brought me up but we had other more important things to consider than my unexciting life story.

I was waiting for the right moment to tell Carlo what I wanted to do but it never seemed the right moment. My husband was a very liberal man, so why was I so worried about telling him? I would have staked my life on his support. All I had to do was tell him Ginevra's story. So, why hadn't I before? I rehearsed my speech to him in my head, word for word, I even wrote it down in my book and learnt it by heart but, in the end, it all tumbled out of my mouth one Sunday morning as we lazed in bed.

The cathedral bells were ringing, calling the faithful to the Mass and reminded me of my childhood in the campiello. As we lay in each other's arms I told Carlo about Sundays when I was little. How Nonna would round all us children up, very early, wash our faces and march us off to church for matins. I had never talked about my childhood to him or anyone before this, and he hung onto every word. He kept interrupting, asking questions. So I told him about Ginevra and my dances and about Pazienza, and how they had all disappeared from my life. One thing led to another and then I was describing what had happened to my friend and how she had had a baby. I couldn't stop talking, even if I had wanted to. It was like the cork had sprung out of the bottle. I missed nothing out. I told him about my terrifying experiences on the Rialto and how Nonna and I visited the women in the Carampane, taking clothes and blankets and food. I described the terrible circumstances in which the women lived − the filth and cruelty − and how I had vowed to make a difference in their lives.

When I was finally done I lay back on my pillows, exhausted. I had been so engrossed in what I was saying I hadn't noticed how quiet Carlo had become. He was out of bed now, getting dressed, his back to me. He had a very expressive back. I was puzzled because Sundays were his rest days, away from the business, and we often lay in bed all day.

'You would love Little Ginevra, Carlo.' I said, propping myself up on my elbows. 'Carlo? She is so beautiful. Just like her mother. She has plum red hair and green eyes. Would you like to meet her? Carlo? Did you hear me?'

124

Carlo was at his desk studying some ledgers, as if I wasn't there.

'Carlo?'

Still no answer. He was running his finger down the lines of figures. I don't know who he thought he was fooling but it was obvious he was just pretending to be busy. I jumped out of bed and ran to him, flinging my arms about his neck and kissing him on the back of his head. 'Stop teasing me.'

Shrugging me off he stood there, his hands pressing down so hard on the desk, that his knuckles were white.

Panic clutched at me. 'What is it? Are you ill? Carlo, please tell me.' Taking his arm I pulled him around to face me.

He pushed me firmly away. 'No, Veronica, I can't allow it.'

'What do you mean? Can't allow, what?'

He took my hands in his and stared earnestly into my eyes. 'I forbid you to be involved with these...women.'

I was too surprised to speak. This was my lovely husband, my understanding, kind, husband? Maybe I had misheard.

'You are my wife, Veronica, and you have my good name to uphold. My clients are from the patriciate and nobili of our Most Serene Republic and this foolishness would have a very bad effect on my livelihood and yours, and all the people who work for me. I forbid you from visiting these whores and their brats, as if I have given you permission.'

'But Carlo...'

125

He held his hand, palm outwards, flat in my face. '...You must do as I tell you. I am your husband, you must obey me.' Then he left the room and I heard our front door bang shut behind him.

I flopped back onto the bed. It was such a shock. I had never dreamt that Carlo might object to my plans, that he might not realise how important this was for me, and for the women and children. It was my stupid fault. I had handled the whole thing badly. I had been too impetuous, too unrestrained. I should have been more delicate and broached the subject bit by bit with care and understanding. But no, as usual, I had ruined everything.

Somehow I had to make him understand that I could never turn my back on the women. He loved me, I knew that he would always love me, so there had to be a way to make him see reason. In the arrogance of first love I was positive I would succeed, but, however much I tried, I couldn't persuade him, not even when I wept as I told him why I couldn't abandon Little Ginevra and the others. He was adamant and became furious each time I broached the subject. I couldn't bear to have so much anger and pain between us, so I capitulated and promised I would never visit my friends there again. What else could I do? Carlo was so relieved and hugged me so hard I thought he might have damaged my ribs.

Of course I was glad that he was happy but I had no intention of abandoning my friends. I kept my promise and stayed away from my friends but it didn't stop me sending Nonna in my stead, who took money and food and saw Little Ginevra. Occasionally Pazienza secretly brought the child to see me. We would meet in some crowded

126

thoroughfare, where we were able to vanish amongst the throng of people. I treasured those moments.

I didn't like going behind my Carlo's back, but I made myself believe that one day he would relent.

The time to dance

You might think I was unhappy disobeying my lovely Carlo but there was so much going on in my life that I didn't have time to feel guilty.

Little Ginevra was growing up fast and the money and goods I sent with Nonna were being put to good use. I would have wished to see more of the child but it wasn't possible. Sometimes I caught her expression as she peered suspiciously at me, over her Nonna's shoulder. It made me sad that I was a stranger to her, an exotic stranger in my fine dresses. It reminded me of another little girl, another beautiful Mamma. But I wasn't her Mamma. The child had no idea who I was.

When she was five I employed an old man, for a couple of hours a week, to teach her and the others to read and they tell me she is progressing well. I wished I might teach her to dance but I had to content myself by sending simple dance creations, via Nonna, so that Pazienza could show Little Ginevra the steps Alfonso was willing to play for them but I didn't want to involve him in my deceitfulness, so I hired a musician. Alfonso knew what I was doing, because one of his gondolas was hired to take Nonna regularly to Pazienza and the child. It would have been foolish and dangerous for Nonna to walk the calli of the Carampane with her pockets full of money. Nonna would often visit the market on her way home so, that if Carlo asked where she was, I could say, truthfully, that she was shopping. We both knew how my old friend loved getting a good bargain. Her three most favourite things in the world were Holy Mother Church, then Little Ginevra and then shopping.

Nonna made sure that Little Ginevra attended Mass in San Giocomo di Rialto every Sunday, and was delighted when the priest invited Ginevra and the others to take part in a devotional procession for the festival of the adoration of the Madonna. Nonna made costumes for the children, who were all from the Carampane. The priest was a truly good man.

On the day of the procession Nonna and I found a good vantage point amongst the onlookers on the San Marco side of the bridge and waited for the children to pass by. Little Ginevra came in the front, holding hands with an older child. She was in a group of six identically dressed little girls, carrying bunches of flowers, which they strew in front of the Madonna's stretcher, as it processed slowly along the via. The little girls were well rehearsed. They knelt as one, raised their hands heavenwards together and genuflected in perfect unison, but there was no joy in their bearing and I longed to take each child and show them the magic of dance. Nonna watched Little Ginevra with a look of dazed delight. The child was as graceful as the proscribed steps allowed, but her smile was guarded and her demeanour solemn. What else could I expect? She was growing up on the Rialto and had seen the horror.

When they were finished, the crowd dispersed and Nonna and I parted, so that she could take the child back to Pazienza, who had been unable to come. Little Ginevra was very excited and clutched the

129

bag of sweetmeats, that I had brought her. Nonna waved to me and whispered in the child's ear, but the child wouldn't look at me. She went off, hopping and skipping beside Nonna, without a backward glance and I turned for home.

But these small regrets were nothing compared to my new life as Signora Bertrame. I, who had only known the narrow life of the campiello and the poor and destitute of the Republic, was suddenly caught up in the rich and noble world of wealth and influence. My life blossomed overnight. Carlo had friends from all levels of Venetian society. I was introduced to patricians and nobles, artists, poets and musicians, and welcomed everywhere, as if I belonged. My husband was a famed apothecary but he also had a huge reputation as an exponent of the Dance. He, Alfonso and their band of musicians were much sort after at all Guild and patriciate balls and banquets.

I am told that before marrying me, many beautiful women vied with each other to be Carlo's dance partner, and my new 'friends' were only too happy to tell me about his numerous liaisons. He was thirty so I knew he must have had women in the past and I'm not jealous − well, not much, but I sometimes had to remind myself that Carlo had chosen me and when I danced with my husband and saw those strumpets still watching him, like cats with bowls of cream, I nailed them to the floor with my angry eyes.

In the evenings, when Carlo is rested, we practice the intricate steps of new creations, which Carlo buys from foreign Dance Masters. Alfonso plays for us. I'm relieved to say that by this time I had persuaded the boy not to wear that ridiculous turban.

130

There was no dance too difficult for us to master and wealthy Venetians competed with one another to secure our attendance at their musical soirees. The hostesses at these events adored our modern and sometimes daring interpretation of the music, where the passion was expressed in the dance. Not so long ago. each dance had been proscribed and every step written down and followed slavishly, whatever the accompaniment.

Now I was married I was free and the old excitement for the Dance returned. Nonna still whispered 'modestia' but there was a definite twinkle in her eye now. She knew that I danced for Carlo alone and she loved him too, so she forgave him for leading me astray.

As our fame grew, so the demand for new work increased. The renowned Dance Masters didn't work fast enough to satiate the Republic's insatiable desire for new innovative work, so there were decisions to be made. The boy was already an accomplished composer, so what could be more natural than he and Carlo working together on their own creations? Carlo Bertrame became the new Venetian Dance Master, at least that's what we allowed people to think. It would have been unwise to disclose that I, Veronica Bertrame, was the creator. Dance Masters were always men. I was a respectable married woman but I would never be totally accepted into the higher echelons of Venetian society. The Princes of the Church and the most Serene Republic of Venice still feared women who wouldn't or couldn't conform. Superstitious stories about ghouls and vampires, that caused the pestilencia, still stalked the dark recesses of men's minds. Women were sent to the fires of the Inquisition on the slightest pretext. The old

131

and bent, the troublesome courtesans, the ugly, different, outspoken, scholarly, creative women, were all treading a very dangerous path between what was acceptable and what was the work of the devil.

No one knew our secret, not even Nonna. She would have worried. The modern Republic still needed scapegoats for God-sent or man-made calamities and women were easy targets, so, for Carlo's sake, I kept silent. I didn't mind him being lauded for my work because I knew the truth and no one could take that away from me.

My generation of women had more freedom than our mothers and grandmothers − especially the well-educated and well-placed in society − but it was still unwise for us to step outside the conventional code of behaviour. Carlo was a modern thinking man but since our wedding he had forbidden me from roaming the streets alone at night, unless he was with me. I had given in to him about not visiting the women but this was different. Carlo was interfering in my freedom, I had had my fill of Mamma's rules when I lived with her.

But why,' I argued.

'Because,' he said, floundering,'…because it isn't seemly for the wife of a…' he stopped because he saw my face. 'It isn't funny, wife.' He tried to look stern, but he failed, so he turned his back on me. 'If you disobey me I will have to beat you.'

'What? You beat me and I'll run away. And don't call me wife.'

'What shall I call you then? Strumpet? Wanton whore?'

That's when I jumped on him and bit the back of his neck, to show him that I truly was a vampire. Then he wrestled me to the

132

ground and pinned my arms down and kissed me. All our arguments tended to end like that and I was repentant about the bite marks on his neck. He had to wear buttoned up shirts for some time. My temper was something I needed to control. However he never called me wife again and I stopped my lone night walking, but it was my decision and I made him go with me instead. It was still wonderful to be out in night-time Venice, and I think Carlo enjoyed the frisson of danger lurking down every dark alleyway, as much as I.

So, I obeyed the rules, after my own fashion. My life was full and stimulating. I would have a baby, but not yet, not while I was creating dances. I had also begun my book − *Amore per la danza*, which would include all of my creations. I will publish this book one day and then everyone will know who Veronica Bertrame is, but until then it is enough to see my work performed and hear that the most illustrious Antonio Negri applauds Carlo Bertrame's creations.

Mamma a didn't interfere in my married life. It was as if now she'd done her job she could relax and for that I was grateful. The only times I was sure to see her were at balls or patriciate gatherings where Carlo and I were invited to perform. She was invariably part of a group of nobili, including the Duke and his wife. In those days I was still surprised by such hypocrisy.

The Duke had always been on the periphery of my life but I had never been formally introduced. I was still naive about the formalities surrounding a nobili's contract with his mistress, so maybe bastard children weren't part of the deal. He had always been in Mamma's life but I didn't know him, nor did I want to.

So, I was less than pleased when Carlo informed me that we had been invited to perform at the celebration of the betrothal of the Duke's daughter, Caterina del Vassolo. She was a tall, ungainly girl with the heavy jaw line of her class. The gossips said her intended was an insignificant creature from Sicily, with the look of a bow-legged goat and that he smelt a little goat-like too. I felt almost sorry for the girl.

I had no wish to 'perform' for the Duke, but Carlo had been looking for an excuse to try out the Sobria—an exciting new dance sweeping the ballrooms of Europe. If I'm honest, the reason I didn't want to do it was because it wasn't one of my creations. I had begun to despise the Dance Master's work, but Carlo assured me that this Sobria was unlike anything we had done before. He was taking a chance, because it was rumoured to be extremely daring, but Carlo was the darling of the patriciate and an optimist.

I tried to persuade him from accepting the commission but he looked at me as if I'd lost my reason. 'The duke is One of the Ten, my sweet. It would not be politic to annoy him. People that say' no' to the Duke have a nasty habit of coming to a very bad end.' He smiled as he spoke but I knew he wasn't joking.

When Nonna heard what was entailed in this new dance she was very concerned. 'You must be careful, piccolo', she whispered, so that Carlo couldn't hear. 'You must guard your reputation.'

But I laughed her concern away. 'I am with my husband, Nonna. He would always protect me.'

So began an intensive period of rehearsals with Alfonso, the dancers, and musicians. As the rehearsals progressed I realised the Sobria was indeed as exciting and daring as Carlo had promised.

On the night of the ball the lanterns burnt brightly about the glittering ballroom of the Del Vasallo Palazzo. We had dined on the finest food and at last the feast was over. Word had got round that we were to dance the Sobria and there was a buzz of excitement in the hall. While Alfonso and his musicians tuned their instruments I glanced at Caterina, seated between her mother and father. Someone should have told her that white was not a becoming shade for someone with her complexion − a cross between sour milk and plain dough. I smiled at her sweetly and curtsied to her mother, who raised an elegant eyebrow at me. Mamma sat behind the wedding party and I smiled in her direction. As my glance slid over the assembled nobili I was aware that the Duke was looking at me. Feeling his eyes on me I saw Anna del Vasallo's eyes narrow, and as I turned away from them she leant across her daughter and said something to her husband. He shrugged and turned to talk to the Sicilian. Was she so stupid to think I might want her vile husband when I have my Carlo? As my husband took my hand and led me onto the ballo I kept my eyes trained on a spot somewhere above the heads of the illustrious gathering. I could feel the men's eyes on me. I am aware of my power. I know I am beautiful. I hate it and relish it in equal measure.

But now I must concentrate. Now, there is only the dance. There are six dancers in the Sobria – five men and one woman. We have chosen the four male dancers with care. They are all young and handsome, dressed in black tunics with black and scarlet striped hose and short, flared capes, attached at their shoulders. Carlo and my costumes are scarlet too He wears a velvet doublet, hose and tunic, with a red and black cap perched on the back of his thick black, lustrous hair. My dress is of rich Moroccan silk with a plunging décolletage. The dress is full skirted so that it whispers about me as I turn and twist. My raven hair is dressed in ringlets framing my face.

We six dancers assemble at the edge of the dance floor and the chatter quietens in anticipation. Carlo gives the boy a signal and Alfonso strikes the beginning chords. The music has all the exotic rhythms of the Orient and the seated guests sway in time. Even Anna del Vasallo is intrigued. She pretends indifference but I note the way her thickly drawn eyebrows come together in concentration.

As the music swells Carlo takes my hand and we walk slowly out onto the floor followed by the men, two by two. When I am in the centre of the floor Carlo withdraws to the edge. He is the watcher. All the men desire me but I will only respond to the fifth man, the one who first leads me into the ballo – my Carlo.

The four men surround me, two in front and two behind. The dance begins. The men circle me slowly and I feel their lustful eyes on me. They offer me their hands but I turn away disdainfully. They encourage each other to approach but I am aloof, unobtainable, however much they entice me. One holds out his hand beseechingly

136

and I go as if to take it but at the last moment I flick my fan in his face. The tempo increases and my suitors sweep about me, twisting and turning, getting closer and closer until they are brushing against me. I am trapped amongst them. And then my Carlo is there, his hand reaching for me, his other arm curling about my waist, bringing me out of the men and into his embrace. The others fall back and Carlo and I are alone. I have eyes only for him and we begin our dance of love. I see Alfonso's shining puppy eyes on me, as I spin, and I mouth a kiss to him.

'Naughty, Veronica,' Carlo brushes my ear with his finger as we pass. 'You must not tease the boy. It is unkind.'

'Who says I'm teasing, husband dear.' I whisper from behind my fan. 'Maybe I grow tired of my dull apothecary husband – always the stink of herbs and potions. The boy smells of youth.'

As we dance our moves become more provocative and sensual. I follow Carlo's lead effortlessly. And then at last, when he offers me his hand, I rest my hand on his, feeling the warmth of his flesh. Now I am in my Carlo's arms. I am his.

As the last notes of the music die away we leave the ballo to rapturous applause. The assembled guests rise as one and give us a standing ovation. Carlo bows low and I curtsy deeply. The clapping increases, so Carlo takes my hand and we promenade around the floor, acknowledging the applauding nobili. When we reach the Duke's party they too rise to applaud us, and they nod and smile at us. The little Sicilian jumps up and kisses my hand enthusiastically. 'Bellisima.

Bellisima ', he exclaimed. Up close he wasn't so bad and he had very nice deep brown eyes. I smiled at him.

The only person who didn't acknowledge us was the Duke. He lounged in his chair, one hand resting on the arm, the other propping his chin, as if to see me better. His hand on the chair-arm rose and fell in a parody of slow clapping. He was bored. I can't explain the look on his face but all I know is it made me shudder. I must have clenched Carlo's hand tighter and he glanced at me. 'What's the matter, my love?'

'Nothing,' I lie. 'I'm excited, that's all.'

Carnevale

In the daytime between performing with Carlo and creating new dances I continued with my work on the Rialto. There was a full time teacher in the Carampane now, and some of the women, including Pazienza, were learning to read and write. I had hired a large dry storeroom, which doubled as a schoolroom during the day and provided warmth and shelter for the women on stormy, cold nights when they waited for the men.

It pleased me to buy Little Ginevra books, pretty dresses, trinkets and, quite recently, strolling on the Lido, I had found the perfect gift for her. It was soon to be the Republic's famous Carnevale and there was a vendor selling fine ostrich feathers, meant for trimming ladies' hats and costumes for the festival. The feather I chose was the exact shade of the child's hair. The shopkeeper said the colour was Titian, after the great man himself. Maybe Little Ginevra would learn to follow the feather's commands better than her mother had.

Nonna visited the child two or three times a week now, in fact I think she would have liked to live with her if I had let her go. But I couldn't part with her. Was that selfish of me? I suppose so, but Nonna had always been with me and I couldn't imagine life without her. She absolutely adored the child and talked of nothing else and it was obvious the child felt the same about her, because she cried each time Nonna left her. It was lovely to see my old friend so happy and my determination grew, that one day, I would persuade Carlo to accept the child into our household.

It felt so good to be making a difference to the lives of the poor women and children and everything would have been perfect had it not been for one thing. Since Carlo had forbidden my visiting the Rialto, the child and Pazienza had to meet us on the busy calli of San Marco or Castello. Pazienza and I would talk and laugh together like old friends, while Nonna took care of the child. However, over time, Pazienza stopped bringing Ginevra and sent Giada, a young woman, in her stead. Even on the rare occasions when Pazienza came, she barely spoke to me. I missed the easy rapport we had once shared. I thought maybe she had misunderstood why I could no longer visit the Rialto. Perhaps she resented this? Once I asked her if there was anything wrong, if I had done something to offend her? She had given me a long look as if she might say something, but changed her mind, shrugged her shoulders and walked quickly away, dragging the protesting child after her. When I asked Nonna where Pazienza was she would say Pazienza was with a man, then turn away, pretending to busy herself with the child. I knew there was something Nonna wasn't telling me but I couldn't waste my precious time with Little Ginevra worrying about Pazienza.

It was soon to be the Carnevale and Pazienza had promised Nonna faithfully that she would bring the child to meet us at the children's carnival – which took place on the last day of the festival before Lent. This was only Little Ginevra's third Carnivale, and she was very excited. Normally she was a quiet, withdrawn child but being in disguise seemed to give her courage. She could be whoever she chose. She was a little mouse the first year, then a wild gypsy last year and this year she was to be Gnaga, the cat. I had bought her a beautiful black satin costume and, something very special, a half-mask with golden ears and jewelled eyes. I had seen the mask weeks before in a tiny shop off San Marco's square. It was expensive but perfect and I couldn't wait to see her reaction to it.

On the morning of the children's festival, held in San Marco's piazza, Nonna was to take the costume to Little Ginevra and then she and Pazienza would bring the dressed child to meet me in the afternoon. That's when I'd give the child her mask. Afterwards, I would have to hurry home to await Carlo's return before our evening commitments.

I had always loved the carnival. It didn't matter if you were rich or poor, ugly or beautiful, everyone was the same in Carnevale. When I was a child Nonna had taken me, Ginevra, Pazienza and the others to the Big Canal, to watch the parade of decorated gondolas drift by. I'll never forget it. There was music and dancing and huge flaring torches placed along the darkened waterways, where crowded boats passed by, carrying beautiful masked and costumed nobili, their gold and silver costumes glittering like jewels in the flickering torchlight. Nonna took us home before the revellers became too boisterous and drunken, but even safe in our campiello we could still hear the music and singing. I remember being scared and thrilled by the leering faces with their hideous animal and skull masks, the stink of sweat and wine and the excitement, as people pushed past us, wishing us Buono Carnivale.

Nonna disapproved of Carnevale. 'It is ungodly, and a disgrace...' she said every year without fail, '...and, His Most Serene Prince, the Doge, should put a stop to it.' But she always took us and sometimes I think I caught a wistful look in her eyes as some fine Harlequin floated by in jewel encrusted mask, dressed, in saffron, emerald and crimson robes, like a queen of the Orient.

Carlo and I loved to dress up too. This year we had chosen costumes that complimented one another. He was to be the terrifying Bauta, with full face white cloth mask, eye holes and no mouth. A black veil covered his hair and he wore a black mantle around the shoulders, topped off with a black tricorn hat. He would look truly terrifying. I was to be Colombina, female servant to The Bauta, dressed in ragged, yet colourful clothes and wearing a most dazzling heavily decorated half mask, adorned with feathers and jewels.

It was to be a busy day for me. I would go to the children's Carnivale first and then, in the evening, Carlo and I would join the Grand Parade of boats in Alfonso's finest gondola, covered in exquisitely fret-worked decorations in gold and silver.

Daylight hours are short in February so the plan was that after the children's carnival the child would go home with Pazienza before it got really dark. I didn't want Nonna to be on the streets alone on Carnevale night.

142

Nonna had a carnival mask this year. She had bought it with her own money. It was black velvet and several sizes too large for her. I thought it best not to tell her that masks like hers were usually worn by men to disguise them in gambling dens and whorehouses. I managed to keep my face straight while she talked. 'It's just to amuse the child,' she said sternly, poking it back up her nose with a finger, daring me to smile at her. 'You know I don't approve of Carnevale.'

I was still laughing when a ragged little urchin banged very loudly on the street door. Nonna went down to screech at him – campiello children often knocked on doors for mischief. I should know, I'd done it myself often enough. But when Nonna puffed back up the stairs she was carrying a scrap of paper. Pazienza's rough scrawl was difficult to read but clear enough for me to know she wasn't coming to the children's carnival. No explanation, no apology. I was surprised by how disappointed I felt. It would have been such a good opportunity to talk openly with her, surrounded by all those people in disguises but after my regret came anger. I gave Pazienza enough money to live on, so why wasn't she coming? Wasn't I doing my best for her, for them all? Did she not realise what I was risking by continuing to help her? I didn't want thanks but she might, at least, have been a little grateful and done as I bid her.

'Oh dear, oh dear.' Nonna said, 'I was worried that something like this might happen.'

'What d'you mean?'

'We can't leave the child to find her own way home to that terrible place, in the dark. She'll be murdered or....some bad man will carry her off, or the Jewes might take her, or...'

'...Stop this now.' I snapped, 'You're working yourself up in a state. I'll think of something. I'll get one of the servants to take her.'

'But they've all gone to the Carnivale.' she wailed.

'Please stop, Nonna.'

'But your evening will be spoilt.'

'I said, I'll find someone. Now wipe those tears away. It's not going to help.'

'...I could take her.'

'No, you couldn't.'

'I'll run all the way home.'

Normally I would have laughed at the idea of my little round Nonna running anywhere but I was too annoyed. 'I could murder, Pazienza.' I said. 'She's doing it on purpose. She hates me.'

Nonna was busy packing the costume for Little Ginevra into her basket with a pile of old clothes for the children. 'She doesn't hate you, Veronica.'

'She could have come today if she wanted. '

Nonna shook her head. 'She has...problems...'

'...What problems? Don't I give her enough money? '

'It's not about that.'

'Then what?'

'Do you never look at her? I mean, really look at her?'

'Of course I look at her.'

144

But I didn't, not really, and now there was no more time to talk because Nonna had to hurry away and I had to prepare myself for the Carnevale. I had been so happy but now Pazienza had spoiled everything.

I admit I have a bad temper but the one good thing about Veronica Bertrame is that her bad moods disperse quickly, like wispy clouds across the sun. At least that's what my Carlo says.

So, within a very short time, I had decided that Pazienza was not worth worrying about and I refused to allow her to ruin my day. I wanted to mingle with the crowds of festival-goers, to see their costumes and for them to see me, so, after dressing in my fine costume and donning Colombino's exquisite mask I dismissed the gondolier, who awaited me at our slipway, telling him to meet me on the Lagoon side of San Marco at sunset. I was going to walk to the children's carnival. It was a good decision because I attracted many admiring glances and received smiling compliments. I was in a much better mood by the time I arrived in the crowded San Marco Piazza and looked about me.

I spotted the child immediately. She was in a large group of assorted animals, who were barking, neighing or meowing, all at the same time. There were several cats but none as fine as Little Ginevra. She is tall for her age and very slender and I stood for a moment watching as she played with the others. The children screamed and ran in circles, hysterical with excitement.

Catching sight of Nonna I waved and she saw me and pointed towards Little Ginevra. I nodded. Nonna called to the child but she

145

didn't hear her and Nonna had to shout before the child tore herself away from her playmates. I had never seen her so animated. She was always shy and serious around me. When she reached Nonna she took her hands and jumped up and down excitedly. Nonna's mask slipped right down around her neck. The child thought this was the funniest thing she'd ever seen and they were laughing and hugging each other as I made my way to them through the frenzy of children. The child pushed Nonna's mask back where it belonged, then Nonna whispered something in her ear and they both turned to look at me. The child stood for a moment gazing at me, at my beautiful mask, then she clapped her hands in delight and rushed at me. She crashed into me so hard I was nearly knocked off my feet, then she clasped me tightly around my middle. I had never felt her arms about me before and I froze. I wanted to hug her, to kiss and cuddle her, but my arms refused to work. I stood ramrod straight and after what seemed like an age, the child's arms dropped away from me. Where there had once been excitement and joy now there was nothing. She stood quietly beside Nonna grasping the hem of the old woman's cape and looking up at her for reassurance.

'My, what a wonderful puss you are. Little Ginevra.' I said, too late, much too late. 'You are the finest cat in all Venice, ' I added lamely. 'Don't you agree, Nonna.'

'The finest,' Nonna said, 'In the world.'

'I'm sorry, Little Ginevra.' I took a step towards her but she disappeared further behind Nonna. 'You startled me. I wasn't expecting such a bear hug.' I gave her what passed as a smile but she wouldn't

146

look at me. And we stood like three strangers, awkward and ill at ease. Finally I got control of my brain and I remembered the cat mask wrapped in red silk, tied with golden ribbon in my satchel. 'This is for you.' I said, offering the gift to the child, but she wouldn't take it. Nonna took the child's hand gently and tried to give her the parcel but the child clenched her fist tight. Nonna looked at me despairingly over the girl's head. 'Signora Bertrame has brought you a wonderful present, piccolo. Shall I open it for you?'

The child didn't move so Nonna unwound the ribbon and held the mask out to the child, who peered at it suspiciously as if it might bite.

'Oh my', Nonna said, 'such a beautiful cat. What a lucky girl you are. Shall I help you put it on?' And Nonna placed it on the child's face, just as the setting sun gave one last defiant flare of light. The golden mask became a glittering, dazzling ball of imbedded sequins. The girl stood motionless, like a statue. I had to shield my eyes from the brightness and when I looked into the eye slits of the mask, all I saw was blackness.

'She's shy.' Nonna pleaded. Then turning to look at the child again. 'You must say 'thank you' to Signora Bertrame, Ginevra. Remember your manners. Where's that tongue gone? You must thank the Signora for the beautiful present.'

But the child said nothing and suddenly I'd had enough − of her, of Nonna and Pazienza, of them all. 'Maybe we should find some other little girl with manners who would like to be a cat,' I said vindictively, holding out my hand. I saw Nonna's shocked expression

147

but I kept my hand outstretched to the child, and when she didn't give the mask to me I plucked it off her face and turned on my heel.

I heard the child sobbing as I marched away from them into the throng but I wouldn't look back, I wouldn't say I was sorry and I would never speak to that child again. And for all I cared, Nonna could go to hell too. All I wanted was to get home and draw my drapes and cry myself to sleep. I was glad of my mask because no one could see my tears and I walked blindly through the crowd, not caring who I knocked out of my way. Too late, I caught a glimpse of an old woman with a stick hobbling towards me. I was walking too fast to side step her and I crashed heavily into her, sending her sprawling. She lay on the cobbles at my feet and I saw a line of blood. The crowd was like a wave, dividing and surging past us, intent on enjoying itself, oblivious to everything else. I took off my mask and knelt down beside the woman. She was lying awkwardly with one leg twisted beneath her.

'Perdonami, Signora.' I said, 'I didn't see you. Please, let me help you. I will call for a gondola and take you to a physician.'

'No, no,' she muttered struggling to right herself.

I put my arms around her waist and helped her into a sitting position. She was wearing a long black dress and cloak and, as I lifted her, I saw a row of livid bruises covering her legs where the material had risen up as she fell. I pulled the material down to cover her, trying not to stare at her thin, emaciated limbs. The blood was oozing from a cut on her shins and she dabbed at it with her cloak, then she touched her leg gingerly and attempted to stretch it out. 'Not broken, thank

God.' she said. Her voice was strong. Not like an old woman's voice at all. 'It's just a scratch. I've had worse.'

'I'm so sorry, Signora, I wasn't looking where I was going. Please allow me to give you money for a doctor.'

She waved my words away dismissively. 'No doctor. I will live to fight another day.' And then she pushed the hair out of her eyes and looked up at me. 'So, Veronica? Where were you off to in such a hurry?'

I sat back on my heels, too shocked to speak.

'Cat got your tongue, Veronica?'

'Pazienza? You came'. I said, lamely, wondering how Pazienza's strong voice could come out of this frail, old woman's body.

'Looks like it,' she said, painfully turning onto her knees and holding out for my hand, so that I could help her to her feet. Once up I kept my arm about her until she was steady enough to stand on her own, then I handed her the stick. 'So where's our girl? ' she asked. 'I couldn't miss seeing her in her mask, could I? Nonna tells me it is very pretty. The child loves pretty things. Did she cry when you gave it her? She always cries when she's happy. Just like her Mamma used to.'

'She doesn't have it yet,' I lied, pulling the mask from my satchel and showing it to Pazienza. She turned it over and over in her hands, a smile lighting up her face. 'It is the most beautiful thing I have ever seen. So? Heaven be praised', she said, 'I'm here in time to see the child's face when she first sees this? So beautiful, Veronica. She will be so happy. Come, we will find her and Nonna. That cat needs her whiskers.'

149

She held her hand out to me and hand in hand we walked slowly back to the piazza, to find a little girl in a cat costume, in need of a mask.

Little Ginevra saw Pazienza first and ran to her. I could see the child had been crying and Nonna too, by the look of her. Nonna managed a watery smile and came to me, putting her arms around me, 'Are you all right now?' She patted my cheek, as if I were five again.

'I'm so bad, aren't I?'

'No, just full of passion.'

'Will she forgive me?'

'Of course,' Nonna said, and we watched as the child clung onto Pazienza's hand, asking her questions, and investigating the blood on her leg. My friend caught me staring at her and smiled at me over the child's head. I saw the bruises on her face clearly now and how one of her eyes was swollen and puffy. What was happening to her? She was only four years older than me and she was already an old woman. I remembered what Nonna had asked me that day. Had I looked at my friend, really looked at her?

The child's eyes were on me now and Pazienza took her hand and led her back to where we stood. She came reluctantly but I smiled brightly and opened my satchel, taking out the cat mask and offering it to Pazienza.

She shook her head. 'No, you must give it, Veronica, it is your gift.'

But I pushed it into her hands. 'No, you. You're her Mamma.'

150

She gave me such a look of love it took my breath away, then she bent down to Ginevra and gently attached the mask on the child's face. 'This is from all your mamma's, sweet Ginevra,' she said, and we all clapped.

She looked as wonderful as I had imagined and jumped about us, shouting meow, and clawing the air like some ferocious beast. I rested my hand briefly on her shoulder and she turned to me and whispered. 'Thank you for my cat, Signora Bertrame.'

'Not Signora Bertrame, Little Ginevra. Please, call me Veronica.'

And quick as a flash she replied, 'And I'm not Little Ginevra any more, I'm big.'

I laughed outright at that and then Ginevra giggled, then Nonna, then Pazienza. We laughed as if it was the funniest thing anyone had ever said. Afterwards she took Nonna's hand and led her to the group of children, who waited for her, wanting to touch her mask. Then they danced in a circle and Nonna stood in the middle of them, doing the steps to an old peasant dance and clapping. Pazienza and I stood side by side watching until Nonna sent Ginevra for me and I joined them in the dance. It was one of the happiest days of my life.

When I returned to where Pazienza stood, Ginevra was teaching her friends a new cat dance while Nonna sat on the steps leading up to San Marco, fanning herself and getting her breath back.

'You have taught her well,' I said, after a while. 'She has the natural grace of her mother.'

151

Pazienza nodded. 'She is a quick learner, our Ginevra, she sucks up the dances like a sea sponge.'

'And since your...accident, you don't dance?' She knew I was asking a different question but she shrugged and turned her attention back to Ginevra.

'Only, you never used a stick before... '

She rounded on me. '... Veronica. If you have something to say, spit it out.'

'I'm sorry I don't want to ...'

'...You don't want to what?'

'It's not my business.'

'Ask me the question now or I'm going.' She saw my hesitation. 'I mean it,' and she turned to walk away.

I grasped her arm. 'Did someone do this to you, Pazienza? The bruises, your eyes, your leg? Did some man do this to you?'

She stood there, amongst the wild abandon of Carnivale, alone in the midst of all that reckless merriment and when she turned her face to mine she was crying silently, tears running unchecked down her poor ruined face.

I took her arm and led her to a darkened doorway, away from the crowds and waited till she had control again. 'What happened, Pazienza?'

'He happened. Broke my leg in two places. Made sure my dancing days are over. '

I was stunned. 'Who is he?'

'My protector....' she spat on the ground. '... my protector.'

152

'But why ?'

'Because he could. Because he didn't like the way men looked at me when I danced. So he makes me ugly.'

'Leave him.'

'You think I have an option? He's a powerful man – one of the patriciate. He will never let me go.' She saw my look of disbelief. 'Oh, I know what you're thinking. Why would a rich man want a broken whore like me?' She studied my face for a moment. 'We live in different worlds, you and I, Veronica, but sometimes you are such a child. I belong to him, forever. He likes strong women, he enjoys beating them into shape. I was a strong woman once.'

'You could go away, Pazienza, somewhere, anywhere. To terra ferma? I could give you money.'

She shook her head sadly. 'He would hunt me down, wherever I went, and besides, I can't leave.' Her eyes drifted back to the piazza, to where the child pranced with her friends.

'You think he would harm the child? '

She nodded.

'I could find a safe place for her and send her to you when you were safe.'

'You don't understand. She would never be safe, not as long as he lives. '

And then I understood her. 'He ...wants her?'

'Oh yes. Not yet, but soon, very soon. I've seen the way he looks at her. ' She drew her cloak around her and straightened her skirt, swiping at her tears with the back of her hand. 'We must go, Veronica. He will be waiting for me.'

'He didn't know you were coming?'

She shook her head defiantly, her old, strong self back again. 'But I don't care what he does to me because seeing the child like this makes my life worthwhile. Just one thing, Veronica,' and her voice was soft again, pleading, She clasped both my hands in hers, 'If ...something happens to me, you must take the child. D'you understand'

'Of course.'

'You promise? You have to promise.'

'I promise, Pazienza.'

Nonna and I stood together watching the pair of them as they walked away from us into the shadows. The slender bent woman, limping along with a stick, the child beside her, spinning to wave at us and blow kisses. And her laughter. I can hear her laughter still.

The Commission

My gondolier was waiting for us on the slipway and Nonna and I sat close together on the way home, lost in our own thoughts. I didn't tell Nonna what Pazienza had told me about her 'protector' but she knew already, I was sure of it. Nonna understood, better than most, the cruelties of our Serene Republic. I had seen her anguish each time she returned from the Rialto and made myself believe it was being parted from Little Ginevra that caused her distress but deep down I had always known there was something else worrying her. I had ignored her as I had ignored Pazienza. Was I so selfish that my desires were more important than anyone or anything else? Was I like my mother?

As we journeyed home Nonna took off her mask, looked at it one last time then dropped it in the rio. Mine lay in my lap, discarded, irrelevant. I prayed that Carlo would believe me when I pleaded a headache and wished not to go out again that night.

As we floated along the crowded rii, dodging in and out of larger crafts full of revellers, the noise grew louder and wilder. Music pounded in my ears. It was ugly and discordant and everything felt tawdry and stale. The freakish masks were funny no longer and the 'beautiful' costumes and masks were beginning to wilt, dropping cheap decorations in their wake.

155

My one thought now was how to save the child and Pazienza. If I could offer the child safe haven, then, with my help Pazienza could start a new life somewhere. I would talk to Carlo tonight, as soon as the opportunity arose. He would understand. I would make him understand. He was a kind man, a loving husband, a gentle person. As soon as he got home from the shop and we had eaten and we had danced and we had talked and laughed and maybe loved...then I would make him listen to me.

But all these plans flew out of my head because Carlo was waiting for us as the gondolier pulled into our mooring. My husband was shouting and waving a piece of paper over his head. His hair was wild. He looked deranged and as soon as we were near enough, he leapt into the boat, scooped me up and carried me into our house. He was laughing and crying and trying to speak all at once. Finally, putting me down, he kissed me, then he grabbed Nonna as she came slowly up the stairs behind us. He ran up the stairs with her over his shoulder shouting, 'I can't believe it, I can't believe it.'

When he finally calmed down enough to make sense, he sat Nonna and me down and told us what had happened. He said that just as they were shutting the farmacia for the night, a liveried man had delivered a message. Carlo passed the card to me and I saw Nonna's eyes widen with horror when she recognised the seal. It was addressed to Signor Carlo Gaudio Ranieri Bertrame and wife. It was an invitation for us to appear before the Senate at the Doge's palace.

Nonna shrieked and jumped up. 'You're going to the Chamber of Torment. You must run.'

156

Carlo laughed, pointing out that it was unlikely we would have been formally invited to appear before the Senate if we were going to be arrested and thrown into the deepest, darkest dungeon, looking out on the Bridge of Sighs. He meant it as a joke but she didn't laugh. This was something else for her to worry about. I kissed her little creased face before she hurried away to her room, to worry in private. 'It will be fine, my Nonna,' I soothed, to her departing back. 'Perhaps they wish to make my Carlo a Duke?'

After she'd gone Carlo strutted around the chamber with his nose in the air, bowing to me most prettily, pretending to be a noble. His eyes shone with excitement and I was caught up in his excitement.

It was only much later as I lay beside him, his arms close about me and his sleep-breath sweet on my cheek, that I had time to think. What was one more day in the scale of things? Tomorrow I would talk about the child.

157

Paradiso

But when I woke early the next morning, ready to do battle, Carlo had already left for the farmacia, leaving a note saying he was busy with several important clients and entrusted me to see to the many things that needed doing before our meeting with the Senate. I couldn't let him down and as my busy day progressed, so my resolve weakened. When this was over, nothing would stop me from talking to him about Ginevra, but for now there were more pressing matters to consider. I wrote a note to Marietta begging her to visit me as soon as she was able. My friend had mixed with the nobili all her life and would be able to answer all my queries. She would school me in how I should conduct myself in the presence of the Senate. I didn't even know how to address such eminent noblemen. After I'd finished the note I called for Nonna, so that she could visit Marietta for me on her way to the Rialto. But Nonna was nowhere to be found. None of the servants had seen her and when, at last, I heard her coming into our entrance hall I ran down the stairs and grasped her arm.

'Nonna? Where have you, been? '

She turned a tear-stained face to mine. 'I have been in the church all night, Veronica, praying to the Madonna for you and the Signore.'

I shook my head in frustration. 'For goodness sake, Nonna, will you stop this nonsense.' I tried not to raise my voice, while I explained, yet again, that she had nothing to worry about and we were not going to be arrested. Finally, when she was calm and managed a watery smile, I sent her off to my friend.

And the child and Pazienza? At the bottom of my list yet again. But after all this time what would a few more days matter? In fact it would help me, in affording me the space, to think out a proper plan to get them to safety. You see? I'm very good at excuses.

I was more than a little apprehensive as Carlo and I disembarked from the gondola on the day of our appointment with the Senate. As we entered the magnificent Ducal Palace I clutched Carlo's hand tightly and he turned and smiled at me. 'Take a deep breath, my darling. You have nothing to fear. They will love you.'

Two guards ushered us through the huge ornate doors and left us to walk side by side down the long Senate chamber, to where a group of stony-faced old men sat, at a huge table, facing us. They sat erect and expressionless apart from one man, lounging in his chair at the far end of the table, a supercilious look on his face. Marietta had advised me to keep my eyes lowered modestly but before I could look away I felt his eyes on me, boring into me, and I recognised him. It was His Magnificence, the Duke del Vasallo.

I refused to let the man's presence affect me and focussed on the other men. I smiled modestly at them but they weren't looking at me. When we reached the table Carlo took a step forward and bowed deeply before the men. I was struggling to stay calm but Carlo's confidence transmitted itself to me and I curtsied as gracefully as I could manage with legs made from jelly. I wasn't often scared but the power of these men was legendary. These were The Ten, the most powerful men next to The Doge, and even he had to be careful not to offend them.

We stood patiently as they appraised us until eventually a thin man with the face of a tortoise and the voice of a small dog addressed himself to Carlo. 'I am informed that you dance well − by those who enjoy such...diversions. '

He sounded doubtful that any such 'diversion' could possibly be of interest to him.

'You are too kind, your Excellency,' Carlo responded, inclining his head. 'We do our utmost to please.'

But tortoise face wasn't interested in us, he picked up a document and read from it. 'You are requested by the Senate to create a special dance-performance, to accompany the unveiling of Jacopo Tintoretto's masterpiece, 'Paradiso', commissioned by Our Most Excellent Doge and Prince, Girolamo Priuli, to replace the 14th Century fresco by Guariento, which was destroyed in a fire.' He took a sip from his glass. 'There is some urgency. Veronese was chosen to paint the replacement but he has died and Signor Tintoretto has undertaken the task and is most insistent that you perform at the unveiling.'

The Doge? Had he said The Doge? Carlo and I stared at each other in utter disbelief. Jacopo's Paradiso, was the talk of Venice. Could it be true? That Carlo and I were to create a dance for the Doge? If I had been the sort of woman to faint this would have been the

160

moment to do so, but the senator was speaking again and I wanted to hear every word from an upright position.

'Your performance should mirror a work so stupendous in scale, so colossal in the sweep of its power, so reckless of ordinary steps of conception...' He spoke ponderously as if doubting our intellect and I tried to concentrate, as he droned on and on, but there was a bubble of mirth growing inside me. '... or methods, so pure an inspiration of a soul burning with passionate and visual imaging...' he plodded on. I don't know who had written his speech, but whoever it was, wasn't worth his hire....'and a hand magical to work in shape and colour. And lastly a work to be viewed with awe.'

I mustn't laugh, I mustn't laugh. When I know I'm going to disgrace myself I often grab the first thought that enters my head, to avoid a catastrophe, so I looked straight at the senator and said, 'You do us much honour, Your Lord, but we will need to see the painting before we can accept the commission...' Too late I saw the shock at my impertinence rippling through the assembled men. I looked down, wishing the floor would open at my feet so that I might disappear. What was I doing? Carlo rested a hand on my elbow.

'You must excuse my wife's ...impetuosity, my Lords, but she is ...excitable.' He allowed a moment to pass then added, 'It is ..that time?' The men's grey beards waggled up and down in unison, the anger clearing from their faces. The loathsome Duke was smirking. Oh yes, they all had first-hand experience of such aberrations in their own households. Carlo pinched his fingers into my flesh and gave a slight shake of his head at me. 'Would you wait outside, my Lady? While these worthy gentlemen and myself discuss this great honour'. I curtsied deeply and stumbled out of the room.

As I waited for Carlo, my mind was already racing with the possibilities of the dance I would create. I could see the colours and movements and passion I would include in the piece, to portray the unrestrained glory of the painting. Because of course, I didn't need to see 'Paradiso' to decide if we would accept the commission. Not many people know this but Carlo and I are in Jacopo's wonderful painting. If you look very closely, Carlo is in a blue robe − one of the multitude of saved souls − and I am in white, standing beside him, staring out at the glory. I thought it the most beautiful painting I had ever seen. And joy of joy Jacopo is our very dear friend. To be commissioned to create a dance for such a wonderful work of art, painted by Carlo's best friend, was truly a God given gift.

When Carlo and I were first married Jacopo had welcomed me into their household like another daughter. Jacopo's father was Giovanni Robusti, a master dyer with a love of vivid luxurious colours in the dyes and tints he used. Jacopo was named 'Tintoretto' after his father's occupation and had inherited his father's love of vibrant colours. We had some of Giovanni's glorious wall hangings in our house. People said they were as fine as any you might see in Alexandria. The tints were supplied by the foreign traders, who also supplied pharmacological products to the Bertrames. Jacopo and Carlo had grown up together.

Jacopo was nicknamed Il Furioso because he worked so quickly on his huge canvasses. Marietta had told me once that her

162

father was apprenticed to Titian, as a boy, to learn the fundamentals of painting. However, Jacopo had been sent home after a very short time because the gifted young artist had already acquired his own style and would not benefit from Titian's tuition. This was the official story but gossip had it that Titian was jealous of this young upstart's prodigious talent.

The Republic's opinion on the painting was divided. Many, like us, thought it Tintoretto's finest work, while others despised it. There are always people who whisper in corners at the success of others and it was rumoured that Master Titian thought Tintoretto's Paradiso a ludicrous failure. He accused the younger artist of losing his wits, but whatever the gossips said, His Most Serene Prince, the Doge, had commissioned it and that was all that mattered. Tintoretto's masterpiece would always be remembered in our dance, long after the paint faded and cracked on the canvas and we lay cold in our tombs. This dance would be my and Carlo's masterpiece and my epitaph.

As I waited for Carlo I remembered the very first time he had taken me to meet the great man. The artist had gone out of his way to put me at my ease. Back then I had no social graces and was awkward and very nervous, but I needn't have worried because he welcomed me like a member of his family and he became like an older brother to me. We were often invited to eat with him and his family. It was a lively place with noise and children running everywhere. It was only when Jacopo's wife, Faustina appeared, that order was restored. 'Mamma is coming' was like a clarion call and by the time she appeared in the doorway the children would be seated, demure and well-mannered. Faustina and my Mamma had a lot in common.

Marietta was rumoured to be Jacopo's love child and treated with cool disdain by Faustina. She was a talented artist in her own right. I loved her work and we spent a lot of time together. I had commissioned her to paint me a series of pictures of dancers performing. I planned to include them in my book, although I didn't tell her this, even though I trusted her. I was learning caution.

Jacopo and Marietta were also accomplished musicians and often played with Alfonso. He designed gowns and tunics for myself and Carlo and had a passion for all things theatrical. There was something of the actor about Jacopo but his wife discouraged this flamboyant side to his character. However, when she was absent, we sometimes taught him our latest dances. He especially liked the naughty ones. When we were rehearsing he and Marietta would come and sketch us.

In the weeks leading up to our performance I barely slept. If I wasn't working on the Dance I was dreaming about it. My creation was like a sinuous line of ivy, wrenched from the stubborn undergrowth of false starts and tedious passages. My Paradiso; had to be perfect in every way. Sometimes the work went well but at other times it felt as if I was going backwards. There was so much to do. There were fittings for costumes and auditions for extra musicians, plus interminable rehearsals for the musicians and dancers. But it was worth all the hard work. I had never felt so fulfilled and fortunate, and would have been the happiest woman alive except for one thing. The truth is I sacrificed Pazienza and the child for a dance – and that's what is was, just another dance, however much I tried to justify its importance. There was no room in my life for anything or anyone else, so, I pushed money at Nonna, begging her to watch over Pazienza and the child. She did my bidding willingly but I saw the strain on her. She was a worn out old woman, what could she do? May God forgive me.

Our Most Excellent Prince, The Doge, hosted a lavish banquet in his palace on the night Jacopo's 'Paradiso' was unveiled. The cream of Venetian society attended. The patriciate, including the Council of Ten, sat amongst illustrious foreign dignitaries. Jacopo and Faustina were placed beside The Doge, in front of the huge shrouded canvas. Faustina was smiling so widely I thought her plump cheeks might pop, while Jacopo looked about him, a stunned expression on his face, as if he couldn't quite believe where he was. On the Doge's other side sat his Magnificence, the Duke de Vasallo and his wife..I watched him as he laughed at something The Doge was saying but then he glanced in my direction and looked straight at me, as if he had sensed my eyes on him. He nodded in acknowledgement but I ducked behind the huge floral display on our table pretending I hadn't seen him.

Before my marriage I had only ever glimpsed the duke in profile, seated in his carriage, waiting for Mamma outside her palazzo. I wasn't allowed outside if he was there but I used to peep from behind my drapes until Nonna caught me and shooed me away. Now it seemed as if he was shadowing me. He hadn't spoken to me, or

165

touched me but I felt...what did I feel? I felt...violated by him. I know that sounds ridiculous , that I'm over reacting , being dramatic, but I came to dread his presence. He never took his eyes off me while I danced and there was always the same look on his face, as if I were some succulent morsel of meat on his plate. I could feel his eyes searching me out now. My aversion to him was visceral. He literally made my flesh crawl, as if a hundred biting flies were feasting on my flesh. I couldn't tell my Carlo any of this because he would have reacted badly and I didn't want him to get into trouble because of me. The duke was a very powerful man.

Taking a deep breath I made myself think of something else. I searched the room for Mamma. She was sure to have been invited. Eventually I spotted her at the end of a long side table of lesser nobles. She was, as usual, beautifully dressed in a gown of crimson, her black hair coiled on her head and studded with pink pearls. She looked pale and suddenly older, or maybe it was the bright light in the room, leaching the colour from her cheeks. I tried to catch her eye but she was too busy putting on a great show, of not caring that she had been excluded from the first ranks of society. Venice was awash with rumours that the duke had taken a new lover but the Most Serene Republic was always full of stories , mostly untrue, so I ignored it.

Soup was being served and I turned my attention to my own table. I was determined not to have my evening spoilt by Mamma or her duke. Carlo and I were seated amongst the Republic's most famous poets and artists. It was certainly the most interesting table. As a rule Carlo and I would be the most flamboyantly dressed at any function

166

but tonight we were demure in our 'Paradiso' costumes. My dress was ice blue velvet and close fitting. It had a high neckline and long sleeves, with no bombast. The overall effect was simple and chaste. Carlo was dressed in a velvet, tight fitting tunic with black and grey striped silk breeches. The guests at our table, women and men alike, were dressed in the most outlandish clothes, in bright colours, made from sumptuous materials. There was much lively debate and people were arguing and laughing at the top of their voices. It was like being in a giant cage, full of Moorish parakeets. However, there was one subdued corner at our table, where a group of artists huddled around Titian and his protégées. They sat morosely, toying with their food and I felt their jealousy rising from them like the warm, fly-studded, stench of a dung-heap. The maestro caught my eye and managed a thin-lipped smile. He had painted me, twice, so I smiled sweetly at him, but beneath the table I squeezed Carlo's thigh in delight. I loved intrigue. Carlo said it was the peasant in me.

I never ate much before I danced but that night I didn't dare eat a thing. I had dispensed with those terrible creaky corsets long ago, but I was wearing a tight stomacher and my breasts were subdued beneath boning. Fortunately I had at last come to terms with my breasts. Maybe Carlo's love of them had transmitted itself to me. I had always been voluptuous but I had put on extra weight around my middle. Too much polenta and rich food. But I was very happy and when I am happy I eat, so, tonight there wasn't room for food.

I dipped my spoon in the soup, just to appear sociable. It was almond cream with the succulent flesh from three pigeons. It was meant to be shared between two people and was usually a great favourite of mine but on that night, even the smell made my stomach heave. Fortunately Carlo has a large appetite and ate it all on his own.

I sat through course after course of elaborate food, trying to control the excitement building inside me. Nonna marvelled that I never got nervous when I was going to perform. But why would I? I was doing what I loved more than anything in the whole wide world with the man I adored. I watched him as he ate his split- roasted skylarks with lemon sauce, and talked animatedly to the woman on his other side. I shot her an evil look but she was too engrossed with my Carlo to notice. Hussy.

When the banquet was over, servants removed the dishes and the guests reclined on chairs and sofas surrounding the ballo. Alfonso and his musicians appeared from where they had been patiently waiting for hours. They took their places on a raised dais beside the painting and played softly in the background.

Then came several tedious speeches and Jacopo's response to the great honour that The Doge had paid him by commissioning 'Paradiso' and finally the painting was revealed. There was a stunned silence, which went on for such a long time that people began to glance at each other nervously and raise their eyebrows. I saw Jacopo, he had his head down, and Faustina was muttering in his ear. Carlo reached under the table and squeezed my hand. Then, someone shouted 'bravo;', and another and another until the room was a bubbling cauldron full of clapping and cheering people. I saw Titian's

168

expression and was pleased to see that he was nodding his head in approval.

The painting was a triumph. I had seen it before, but not here in this magnificent setting. It was indeed a truly remarkable work of inspiration and religious passion and Jacopo deserved every accolade. He was obviously delighted and not a little relieved and even Faustini was smiling. She was quite an attractive woman when she looked happy.

It was very late when we were finally announced. There was a ripple of polite applause but everyone was tired and ready for their rest and their strained, white faces stared out at us. Lost faces, lost souls. The candles were extinguished in the main hall, while the dance floor was brightly lit by hundreds of towering candelabra. I felt the tiniest twinge of self-doubt as Carlo led me to the centre of the floor. What if my creation wasn't equal to the sheer majesty of Paradiso? Would it be a disaster? What if I let Jacopo down, and Carlo and Alfonso and...

'...Veronica?' Carlo's voice came from somewhere far away. 'Come to me.' Then I looked into my sweetheart's eyes and saw his love and all my doubts disappeared. I walked into his embrace, sure in the knowledge that everything would be perfect. Alfonso and the musicians began the hauntingly beautiful introduction. It was a simple, devout, yet triumphal piece of music. Alfonso had excelled himself.

And then our 'Paradiso' began. There was nothing lewd or provocative in our dance, there was only adoration and humility. It passed like a dream and my feet whispered over the floor. There were tears running down my cheeks when the music came to an end and we

169

all knelt as one and prayed to God. It was a triumph and the company rose and bowed their heads as we left the floor. No one spoke but every face was bright with joy and wonder. I walked behind Carlo, smiling, basking in the glory as people congratulated him. This night was the pinnacle of my life.

A surprise

Hard on the heels of our success came Carlo's busiest period of the year. It was the designated time for the making of the new batch of theriac – Bertrame's famous, cure-all. Carlo's treasure.

My husband worked from dawn till dusk, checking deliveries of the rare, priceless ingredients, visiting clients, dealing with officials. I hardly saw him. I woke to an empty bed and fell asleep alone. I missed him but I was busy too. I had many notes of congratulation to respond to after our 'Paradiso' triumph. These were followed by invitations to perform our dance at glittering events. Our future fame was secure.

It would have been perfect if only I wasn't so exhausted. On some mornings I could barely drag myself out of bed. And then there were the belly cramps. Sometimes they were so painful, they caught me unawares and I would cry out with the pain. I rested in bed for most of the day and only rose, just before Carlo came home, when I pretended all was well. I didn't want him to worry about me.

I saw very little of Nonna at this time. She spent most of the days going backwards and forwards to the Rialto. I could see she was exhausted and worried but she never complained, however, I couldn't rid myself of the nagging fear for Pazienza and Little Ginevra. When I asked Nonna how they fared she would say they were fine and then busy herself with some household task, so that she didn't need to look me in the eye. Nonna was not a good liar and wore her fears like a carnival mask, but I deliberately ignored her increasing anxiety, telling myself that her obvious unease was centred on me.

I comforted myself with the half-formed plan I had dreamt up for my friend and Ginevra's child, to escape from that brute of a man. And when everything was back to normal and I was better, nothing would stop me from getting them away from Venice to safety.

But the pains increased until the morning came when I couldn't stand. Carlo had already left for the Guidecca, but he must have forgotten something because, just then, he came back into our rooms and found me doubled up on the bed, moaning with pain. He was frantic and urged me to see his physician. He made me promise and I agreed just to make him leave. I knew he had an important meeting with the Magistrati alla sanita −State Health Authority − that morning and he didn't need the extra worry of an ill wife.

When I was recovered enough, I found Nonna and told her about Carlo's doctor. She made a face. She didn't trust these *foreign devils and their magic potions*. She thought their *modern* methods dangerous and un-Christian. She had always relied on natural herbal remedies for any ailment and she put my malaise down to being over-excited by all the fuss − her words not mine − and prescribed a good purging. I dutifully drank her *medicine* and was immediately and violently sick.

172

The next morning I couldn't even get out of bed and Carlo's face was rigid with worry as he left the house. 'I will send Alfonso for my man, Veronica. He trained in Arabia in the great University of Alexandria. He has experience of the finest modern medical knowledge in the world. Please, my darling, say you will do as I bid?'

I knew that some crucial ingredient for the theriach hadn't arrived and I didn't want to add to Carlo's concerns, so I gave in, ignoring Nonna's tight-

In fact the doctor wasn't an Arab at all but a Roman. But that was still foreign in Nonna's eyes and she reverted to speaking in her thick Venetian dialect, so the poor man had no idea what she was muttering. I thought it unwise to translate for him. She stood between him and me, and carefully peeled back my underskirts so that he might examine my belly but nothing more. He had to reach around her to examine me and her eyes narrowed as he touched my skin and pressed down. While he pummelled me he asked me questions, about my general health and how long I had had the pains, and was I putting on weight and how often did I bleed? I answered him truthfully, determined not to blush as he touched very private parts of me and asked me intimate questions.

When he was finished he sat down opposite me and wrote something in a notebook while Nonna fussed about me, replacing my skirts and helping me up into a more dignified position. She made the physician wait until she was satisfied that my modesty had been restored, then she pointed at him, motioning him to speak. He rested his chin on one long slender hand and smiled. I found this quite

173

offensive, because I was in pain and we were paying him a great deal of money.

'Signora Bertrame? I am happy to tell you that there is nothing wrong with you. In fact,' he said, 'you are in remarkably good health for a Lady halfway through her term. There is no need for treatment, but your woman here must make sure you have a good diet, not too many sweet things, fresh air and gentle exercise, no more tight stomachers and,' he added, looking straight at Nonna, 'no more purging.'

But Nonna wasn't listening, she was screeching like a hen laying a very large egg and clutching at her chest, as if she was going to have a fit. 'A baby. My Veronica is going to have a baby.' All pretence at not understanding the doctor had melted away. She was shaking his hand now and then she was hugging me and helping me up from the couch, her arms about me, so I wouldn't fall.

I couldn't think or speak as the doctor packed his bag, said his farewells and a servant showed him out. I was truly dumbfounded. Me? Having a baby? We had been married for five years but not getting pregnant had never concerned me. I was far too busy enjoying my life why would I want a baby? Finally I found my voice. 'A baby?' I stuttered. 'I'm going to have a baby?'

Nonna laughed. 'Why so surprised? You are married, my Veronica, and when you are married you have babies.'

I was very quiet while she prattled away, making plans. I didn't know what to feel. I knew that Carlo would be happy but what about me? Carlo was mine and I didn't care to share him with some bawling

174

infant. And what if he stopped loving me when I was fat and ugly? My childhood experiences with babies in the campiello were of screaming, smelly little bundles, attached to their mother's breasts like leeches. And what if my Carlo loved this baby more than me? What then?

Nonna had one hand resting on my belly, stroking it as though the baby was already alive. I pushed her hand away. 'It's all right for you, Nonna,' I snapped. 'You won't have to bear the brat and wipe its disgusting bottom and feed it and..'.

'...But a baby. Veronica. Yours and Carlo's baby. You are so lucky.'

'You like them so much why didn't you have one?'

If I'd been looking at her I would have seen the tears springing in her eyes but I was too busy feeling sorry for myself. I wanted to hurt her. Why? God knows. I'm not a nice person. I happened to glance at her then, and saw her staring at me, her old eyes red-rimmed and clouded with tears. 'I had a baby once, Veronica,' she whispered. 'A little girl. So small, so beautiful. But I couldn't keep her. She didn't belong to me.'

'What d'you mean? You had a baby? It belonged to you.'

She shook her head. 'He took her.'

'You're making no sense, Nonna. Who took her?'

'It doesn't matter. It was a long time ago. '

'No, please, tell me. What happened ?'

She took a deep breath. 'My father sold me to the Inn keeper when I was very young. I was a slave in that place. Do this, do that. Sleeping on rags in the corner of the kitchen. Then...when I was old

175

enough...' She raised he eyes and looked at me. She didn't need to say any more.

'Oh, Nonna, I am so sorry.'

'You wonder why I let your mother speak to me the way she does, but she was the only one who ever showed me any kindness. Her mother bought me as a maid for her, but I was always too clumsy so I became a scullery maid, then, when you came along she gave you to me to look after and said I would be your Nonna. It was the happiest day of my life.

'And your baby? What happened to your baby?'

She shook her head sadly. 'Every child I see I think maybe she's mine. But she's gone, Veronica. Only God knows where. I pray for her every day, that she has been treated kindly.'

'But why didn't I know this before? Why didn't you tell me?'

She shrugged. 'You never asked me. And why should you? I'm your Nonna and that's enough for me.'

I pulled her little body into my arms and rocked her gently. How could I have lived with her all my life and yet know so little about her? I had just accepted her love and loyalty as if it were my due. We stayed like that for a long time, until I felt her exhausted body surrender to sleep, then I laid her gently down on my bed. Taking off her shoes I pulled the covers over her and kissed her. 'Sleep well, my Nonna.'

Soon afterwards I heard the outside door crash open and Carlo's footsteps as he took the stairs, two at a time. I put a warning

176

finger to my lips as he burst into the room and, taking his hand, we tiptoed outside. I shut the door quietly behind me. 'Nonna is unwell.'

But Carlo wasn't listening. He held me at arm's length and stared into my eyes, his face grey with worry. 'What is it? Veronica? Are you ill? Tell me, please, I've been frantic. If you died I'd...'

'...I'm not going to die.' I gently smoothed the deep furrow away from his forehead with the back of my thumb. 'Everything is wonderful, Carlo, 'And suddenly it was. Our child would be loved and that is really all that matters, isn't it? I took Carlo's face in my hands and kissed him on the lips. 'We are having a baby.'

I needn't have worried about Carlo's reaction. He was so delighted his joy was infectious. I had no doubt he would be a good father The little ones loved him. I had seen him in action with Alfonso's little sister, Sofia, and Jacopo's youngest, Frederico.

I wanted a boy but Carlo shook his head and kissed my belly. 'No, it is a little girl. Feel, Veronica, she is dancing already,' and he laid my palm against my small bump and I felt the butterfly-wings of tiny feet and fingers. 'We will have a beautiful daughter, just like her Mamma,' he said, picking me up in his arms and dancing me around the room. 'We will devise a new baby dance, not too energetic, not too wicked, something befitting the arrival of our little Veronica.'

So life went on, except that now I had two fussy carers. Nonna wouldn't let me do anything strenuous and fed me like a prize pig, while Carlo was the opposite, urging me to eat things that were good for me and the baby. He lectured me day and night about resting and not getting overly excited. He was still very busy in the farmacia but he kept popping in during the day to make sure I was alright and wasn't over-taxing myself.

Once again I allowed my worries to drift away while Nonna continued to reassure me that Pazienza was managing. She said that the child was flourishing. I'm not blaming her, it was all my fault. I should have known.

As the day of the Making approached, Carlo spent less and less time at home. Dancing was out of the question now and my night ramblings had ceased. My sickness had passed, I was feeling a lot better but I was very bored and desperate for stimulation. Marietta came when she could but she was very busy. She was married now and had just had a baby. Little Francesca was like a beautiful little doll.

There was nothing left for me but to take an interest in the making of the theriac. My husband loved his work and was an exceedingly good apothecary, so when I asked him to tell me about the making of the theriac he was thrilled, and his enthusiasm transmitted itself to me. Science was thought to be beyond the mentality of feeble women so Carlo went very slowly to begin with. This was to enable my puny female brain to comprehend the big words. He plodded on like this until I could stand no more and screeched at him to hurry up. However, I was suitably impressed by his knowledge, even when he repeated it ad nauseam. His was fascinating work and I had watched in awe as he and his assistants processed the unguents, salves and potions

178

of the day. *'To heal and to make beautiful,'* he used to say, with his wicked grin, *' but poisons can kill as well as cure.'*

The exact recipe for the theriac was a spezieri secret and I had to swear on the bible that I would never disclose it to anyone. We were in bed when he first told me, and he pulled the covers over our heads, like we were little children in a cave and whispered the list of ingredients in my ear. It was hard not to giggle when his breath tickled my ears. There was viper 'dust' from live snakes, opium, powdered stag testicles, unicorn horn or narwhal, exotic spices from Arabia.... The list went on and on. Apparently, theriac could cure everything including the plague, infectious diseases, scorpion bites, viper stings, rabid dog bites, putrid fever, stomach ailments, tuberculosis, sight defects. I was most impressed but then Carlo spoilt it all by saying it was also used by wealthy women as an anti-wrinkle cream and I couldn't resist saying how sad it was it hadn't worked on Anna de Vasallo. Carlo punished me for that remark but...I always liked his *punishments.*

When he was done explaining the making he unlocked a drawer in the dressing table and brought out a wonderfully ornate little phial made from lapis lazuli and studded with flecks of gold. He uncorked the bottle and wafted it under my nose. I took a deep breath, then wished I hadn't. It was the most disgusting thing I had ever smelt. 'And that is the famous, theriac?' I managed, between gulps of fresh air. 'People pay a king's ransom for that?'

He nodded. 'You have to understand your market, Veronica. If I made it smell sweetly, and I could by adding a little of this and a

179

little of that, then the nobles would think it was for children. No, it must be powerful medicine to smell like the pit of Hades.'

'So it's quackery?' I meant it as a joke but I saw the hurt in his eyes. I tried to hug him but he held me at arm's length.

'No, Veronica, I would stake my life on the theriac. It is indeed a magical elixir.'

I wagged a finger at him in mock horror. 'Magical? Be careful, Carlo Bertrame, someone might hear this heretical talk.'

My husband was not amused and I should have kept quiet but I could never resist having the last word. I told you I was bad. I had to make one last jibe at my husband's life's work. 'Well, I sincerely hope that we never have reason to take the theriac. I'd rather die than drink that.'

'Then, we just have to pray you never have need of it, Veronica.' Carlo's voice was stiff with disappointment. 'We Venetians are proud of our skill in medicines and pharmacologia. Learned professors from all over the world would pay a king's ransom to obtain the recipe for theriac. They are not fools.' He didn't speak to me for a whole day after that and I learnt not to mock Carlo's precious elixir. It was his passion just as dancing was mine.

Each year's new batch was stored in a locked chest at the back of Carlo's workplace, with each phial carefully labelled and dated. The key to unlock the chest was the one he always kept on the gold chain around his neck. There was also, another much smaller chest containing the potion. He showed me where it was hidden beneath the cellar floor. This, he told me, was for emergencies only, or if the other

180

chest had been stolen. No one knew about this except him, and now me. He gave the key for this chest into my keeping and we found a hiding place.

He explained that the new theriac takes many months of fermentation and then years for it to mature, hence its exorbitant price. Each year's new batch was stored carefully in labelled phials until it was ready for sale. The Magistrati alla Sanita oversaw the entire process so as to avoid malpractice. Apparently it could be administered as a potion or salve, a plaster or just eaten in chunks by adults. The ingredients could also be pulverised and reduced to a sweet tasting gum mixed with honey for children–Venetian treacle. If I ever had need of the elixir I knew which version I'd favour.

As the day of the making drew closer, Carlo and Alfonso slept at the farmacia. Food was prepared for them in our kitchen and ferried over to the island.

I spent the long lonely days working on new creations for the Dance to include in my book. Sometimes Carlo allowed Alfonso to visit me for an hour or so and while he played the lute I tried out my latest ideas in my head.

I saw little of Nonna at this time because, now I was over the early months of pregnancy and feeling better, she could visit the child regularly, as before. Sometimes, in the evening, I caught sight of Alfonso helping her from his gondola. She didn't know I was watching and I saw the weariness in her as she hobbled into our house, shoulders hunched, head bent. Once or twice I saw Alfonso half carry her to our door.

Later, when she came to my room with my meal she would be the old Nonna again, smiling and chatting, as if she hadn't a care in the world. I had stopped asking her how things were with Pazienza, and she had stopped telling me about the child. We were playing a game of cat and mouse and it had come close to souring our relationship. The simple truth was I was jealous. Jealous of Nonna's close relationship with the child, and jealous that Nonna might love the child more than she loved me. Often I would excuse myself when she came to sit with me in the evenings, saying I was tired and needed to lie down and she would kiss my forehead and leave the room without saying a word. Sometimes, at night, I heard her restless pacings in the room above me, where she slept.

Marietta still visited me occasionally. Little Francesca was beautiful and rarely cried. So I would sit nursing the baby while Marietta and I chatted. She told me about her confinement, skilfully avoiding my questions about how much the birth hurt. I loved to hold the child and smell her sweet baby smell. She would stare up at me through big dark eyes, as if I were some imponderable puzzle.

Marietta needed stimulation too and one day, as I nursed the child, she got out a pad and pen and sketched me. The finished drawing was very good and she asked if she might do a portrait of me. I agreed, as long as she painted me from the bust up. I didn't want to look fat. Marietta called the painting, 'Portrait of a Lady' and I loved it. She caught me gazing away to the left, wearing my favourite rose coloured bodice with embroidery and beading over a white ruffled undershirt. I wound a dark velvet wrap about my shoulders.

182

Carlo insisted that we hang Marietta's work in pride of place in our reception room. My friend signed it with the Tintoretto 'T' and everyone who saw it swore that the Master had excelled himself in this work. Marietta and I enjoyed the joke, as did Jacopo. Nonna was the only one who didn't like Marietta's painting. She refused to say why but I knew she didn't approve of my friend. Maybe she was jealous or maybe it was because Marietta wasn't religious and poked fun at the priests and the Church.

It was a perfect early spring day when we gathered outside the shop for the making of the theriac. Carlo promised I should have pride of place to watch the proceedings. My belly felt as if it were about to burst and my back hurt abominably. It was unseasonably hot for the time of year. The blue Venetian sky framed the terracotta buildings and huge pots of heavenly lavender, placed outside our shop, were alive with bees. The scent hung like a gauze curtain over the piazza.

Carlo had been on edge all morning, shouting at the workers, complaining about everything. It was only when he caught my worried glance and bent to kiss me full on the lips and the men and boys cheered, that he relaxed.

The precious ingredients had been displayed in silver caskets, outside our establishment for the specified three days. A rota of guards protected them from thieves. At noon Carlo's assistants brought out the heavy bronze cauldron, in which the theriac would be made, and set it on the paving stones. Silk covered chairs were arranged in a semicircle around the cauldron for the patricians and state officials. Nonna and I sat near the front, in the shade of a lemon tree.

Lastly a large barrel containing the vipers was rolled out and placed beside the cauldron. I was glad to be at a distance from them but I still heard their evil hisses. I hated snakes. The serpents had emerged from hibernation three days earlier and would normally have been sleepy and easy to handle but the warm weather had enlivened them and they were a coiling, boiling mass of hungry, thirsty and very angry snakes. The children from nearby streets ran shrieking around the barrel, screaming with excitement, poking sticks at the maddened creatures. One hysterical child dropped his stick in the barrel and before anyone could do anything about it a snake slivered up and over the lip of the barrel. Carlo grabbed the snake by its tail before it could escape and waved it about his head. He was smiling at the children. 'Who is the bravest amongst you? See, I hold him tight he cannot hurt you. Come, touch his skin, feel how soft and dry he is.'

Everyone was laughing now, even the stony-faced officials. The children stood a safe distance away, not sure whether to laugh or cry, and Carlo was capering about making them giggle. But he didn't see the snake suddenly coil itself around his arm and sink its fangs into his flesh. I screamed and he leapt backwards and collided with the barrel, overturning it. He fell in the midst of the maddened serpents. I watched in horror as those small evil heads struck, again and again. 'Carlo,' I shrieked, and ran to him, all terror for snakes forgotten. Someone grabbed my arm and pushed me aside, before I could touch him. It wasn't happening. I wouldn't let it happen.

184

The men beat the snakes off and someone ran for the theriac, but it was too late, Carlo had too much venom in his blood. I cradled him in my arms as he died and I cried out to God and all the saints to save him, I swore I would attend Mass every day and never wander the streets at night again, or Dance, or be proud and immodest, but as I clutched him to me I saw his dear face turning livid and swollen from the snake's venom. His eyes fluttered open once and he tried to smile at me but then he was gone.

Staggering to my feet I ran at the barrel of snakes but Alfonso caught my arm and swung me off my feet. I kicked and screamed and clawed at him but he held me fast against his strong young body. It wasn't my beautiful Carlo's body but it was someone with blood coursing through his veins, someone who had loved my Carlo with all his heart. I stopped struggling and buried my head in the boy's neck, tasting his tears.

'Please, please.' I whispered. ' Let me die, Alfonso. I beg you.'

But he shook his head. 'No, my Lady. You must live and have your baby – Signor Bertrame's baby.'

He carried me to where Nonna waited, her arms outstretched and pain pinned to her face. 'Oh my, child. Oh my poor, poor, child.'

They sat me down and knelt beside me, holding my hands, while the shocked company drifted away. The guards cleared the street and eventually the coffin bearers came. When they tried to take Carlo I screamed at them to leave him but Nonna whispered, 'Come, my Veronica, we will take the master inside and pray for him. Come.' Then, with one on each side of me they led me into the house. I would

185

have fallen but the boy's arms were strong about me. It wasn't happening. It wasn't happening. 'Is it true?' I kept asking. 'Is it really true?'

I have no real memory of the long days and nights that followed Carlo's death. I was like a sleepwalker. People came and went. Even those I had once loved like Marietta and Jacopo were strangers to me. There were words and tears and people touched me, saying. 'It's God's will,' and 'He's in a better place.' But I didn't want their words or their touches or their tears, all I wanted was my beloved.

My lovely boy was interred in a cold dank crypt beneath San Pietro Castello. My Carlo, so vibrant and full of love and passion, laid to rest in a cold dark space. How he would have hated it. When I dream of him he is always in that crypt and I wake shivering. If I had had my way I would have placed him in the most beautiful gondola in all of Venice and set him adrift in the Lagoon, to sail the high seas.

All I really remember from that terrible time was Nonna's pleading voice. 'Please, Veronica, you must eat, for your baby. Just a spoonful, please, my little one.'

But how could I eat, when he was dead?

I was near my time when I fell down the stone steps of the house. I'm not sure if I threw myself, or whether it was an accident. I will never know, but I will always feel guilty.

The pains began immediately and a doctor attended me for three days and nights before I gave birth. Nonna and the doctor whispered in corners, shaking their heads. 'Too small,' they murmured, voices full of pity. Nonna tried to take her away from me but I fought and screamed at her to leave me alone. I wrapped my baby in the shawl I had made for her, and held her gently in my arms to keep her warm. I felt her little heart pulsing against mine, like a baby rabbit's, and I kept her close until her eyes turned milky and she lay still and cold in my arms. I think I was mad after she died. I wanted nothing but to close my eyes and never wake.

On and On

But life grinds on doesn't it? On and on.

I am told that Mamma came often as I lay on my bed too shocked to move or speak. She brought me delicacies to tempt my jaded appetite and little trinkets that might amuse me but I have no memory of these small kindnesses. All I remember is that Nonna was never far away from me, sleeping on a pallet just inside my door. And sometimes I caught sight of Alfonso's stricken face, as he hesitated in the doorway.

I inhabited two worlds. There was the real, terrible one, where I suffered a life without hope, and then the blessed, imaginary one, where Carlo and I danced through the calli and along the rii, holding the hands of our laughing little girl as she twisted and turned between us.

I experienced the same day over and over again – the same dark, terrible day. I don't know how long this went on, it could have been weeks or months, but then, one morning, I remember waking and watching as sunlight flooded into my chamber and my drapes trembled in a gentle breeze. I felt fresh cool air on my clammy skin and heard strong male voices, drifting up to me from the canal below. A boatman was singing. Covering my ears with my hands I turned my face to the wall. The world was going on without my Carlo, without my child, and I wept, as if I would never stop. Nonna ran to me. She had been praying and her rosary beads hung from her hands. I grabbed them and hurled them as hard as I could across the room.

'Get out.' I screeched. 'Get out and take your God with you. I hate your God.'

'No, no,' Nonna pleaded, trying to touch my arm. 'Have faith, my Veronica. Your loved ones are in your heart forever and the good Lord has them in His embrace.'

'Good?' I screeched, 'What compassionate God would take my Carlo and our beautiful baby? They were innocent, blameless. If He wanted a sinner, why didn't He take me?'

'Shh, shh,' she whispered, reaching out for me. 'You don't know what you're saying.'

I slapped her hand away. 'I swear to you, Nonna, I will never set foot in your church again, or hear any words of religion spoken in my house'. Nonna was speechless, her eyes full of tears, but I was adamant. 'If you disobey me you will pack your bags and leave. Do you understand me?'

She raised her hands to her face in shock and I could see her little body shaking as she turned and hobbled out of the room.

I sat on the edge of my bed, shaken by the vehemence of my outburst. I was so sad to have upset Nonna but I had meant every word. I loved her and would make it up to her but, if I were to survive, I had to be strong and not rely on anything or anyone but myself.

189

The sounds from beneath my casement were increasing so I swung my legs over the edge of my bed and got unsteadily to my feet. I was still very weak and had to thread my way slowly across the room, from chair to chair, until I reached the window. A barge was moored below and several men were unloading heavy chests onto the towpath. Mamma was with them, shouting instructions and overseeing that the boxes were carried safely into my house. I heard the men's heavy tread on the stairs, as they passed my door and continued on up to the next level, where there were unoccupied rooms. Pulling on my wrap and going to the door I found Nonna standing behind it watching the men. She flinched when she saw me and I took her hand and squeezed it. She turned her dear face to mine and breathed out slowly, as if she'd been holding it for a very long time, and I kissed her cheek. Two men puffed past us, battling with a very large and heavy box.

My mother's voice pursued them up the stairwell. 'If anything is broken or damaged in any way. I shall hold you responsible.'

I looked at Nonna. 'What's happening?'

Nonna held my hand tightly. 'I think your Mamma is moving in with us.'

I had never been interested in my mother's affairs, but I was aware – the whole of Venice was aware – that her duke had finally taken a new mistress. It had happened some time after Carlo's death but I hadn't the emotional energy for anything outside of my own misery. If I had been able I might have felt sorry for her, because she must be suffering. Mamma had always been 'in charge' but now she had to cope with losing her lavish life style and, even more importantly, her status.

Later, when the men had clumped down the stairs for the last time, someone knocked softly on my door. 'Veronica, may I come in?' I was sitting beside the window while Nonna gently brushed my hair. I raised my eyebrows at Nonna. Mamma had never knocked on my door before. 'Of course, Mamma. Please, enter.'

She slipped inside the room and stood there avoiding my eyes. We waited for her to speak. It was an awkward silence and eventually I took pity on her. 'How can I help you, Mamma?'

She looked up, surprised, as if, for a moment, she'd forgotten where she was. 'Ah, Veronica. Yes... I've decided to find a more suitable apartment. The palazzo is far too large for me and the cost of all those servants is ridiculous. After all, how many personal maids does one need?...'

Was she asking me?

'I thought I had found the perfect house , close to the Grand Canal, but it was taken before I could make my offer. The property market is exploding. So many foreigners buying up everything they can lay their hands on.... So in the meantime I find myself homeless.'

'Your palazzo is sold?'

She nodded and then looked away quickly. I thought she might be crying but she took a deep breath and squared her shoulders. 'I promise I won't need to stay with you for long....' She trailed off, absent-mindedly picking at the stitching on the hem of her shawl. 'It

191

will only be until I find something…more appropriate. I won't intrude in your life. You will hardly know I am here.'

What could I say? It must have cost her dear to beg, especially as my humble dwelling wasn't what she was used to. I lived in a backwater of San Marco. Neither Carlo nor I had cared what people thought about us or where we lived. This was our home and we had been so happy here, and now he was gone it was even more precious to me. He was never far away from me while I was there.

At first Mamma's presence had no impact on me. I still lived in that dark place, barely aware of anything beyond the walls of my wretchedness. However, gossip in Venice is like the tenacious lichen that scrambles between the cobbles and gallops across the stone walls of our city, finally forcing its way into your consciousness. A market vendor told Mamma's woman, who told my servants, who told Nonna, who told me, that my mother was receiving a pension from His Magnificence, the duke de Vasallo, one of the Ten, and one of all men like him − the pious, powerful hypocrites of our Most Serene Republic. These were the same men who judged the poor and crippled, the same who kept whores but tortured poor women for their immorality. Nonna told me once of a poor, young serving girl who had been violated by the son of a rich nobleman and, when she became pregnant, had been publicly flogged for her licentiousness. Her beating had been so savage that she lost her baby and then she drowned herself. The rapist was sent to France on important state business.

But Mamma's duke was kind and generous, she insisted. He had allowed her to keep her jewels, her gowns and the furniture. How

192

gracious of him. But then he'd thrown her out of her home, like some old used toy. She wouldn't have a word said against the man but, however she justified it, her life had been drastically affected. She had been diminished by that vile man and sadly she had no one to turn to but me, her ungrateful daughter.

She didn't have friends and had always lived a solitary life. In fact Anna de Vasallo seemed to be her closest confidante. I don't think she liked women very much. Maybe she saw them all as competition? However, she was a consummate actress and declared, very convincingly on many occasions, that all she wanted now was to live out what remained of her life in a simple and dignified manner. She was probably in her early forties at that time, although I never knew her exact age.

Little by little, as the days ground wearily on, I started to feel emotionally stronger, although still weak from lack of sleep. The only way I could get any rest was to take the powerful sleeping draught, that Carlo's physician prescribed for me. I was glad of it but it left me dazed and confused the following morning. Nonna ran the house for me and Alfonso saw to my business.

At first Mamma was an insubstantial shadow, drifting listlessly from chamber to chamber. She would sit for hours in my room gazing out at the rio, a kerchief clutched to her nose. It was summer now, and as the water levels shrank, so the stink increased. I was used to it but she wasn't. She didn't complain, she just had that way of sighing and shaking her head as if she couldn't quite believe what was happening to her. Her unhappiness made me uncomfortable but I should have made the most of it because, all too soon, everything changed.

The first indication I had that something was amiss, was one morning when I woke to the sound of raised voices outside my door.

'But I must talk to Veronica, my Lady. I have an important message for her.' Nonna's voice had an edge of panic to it that alarmed me. Nonna was always the calm one.

'Must? Must?' Mamma screamed at her. 'How dare you. I decide who talks to my daughter, not some common, serving woman. D'you hear me?'

'Yes, my Lady,' Nonna was crying now, 'I meant no offence but I need to talk to Veronica. She...'

'Veronica? Your mistress is Signora Bertrame to you, and don't you forget it.'

There came a light tap on my door. 'Mi scusi, Signora Bertrame. May I enter...? '

'No you can't, you stupid fool.' Mamma screamed. ' Signora Bertrame is resting.'

'But...'

I heard a scuffle and a noise like a slap and Nonna's cry of pain.

'Get back to the scullery, where you belong. And from now on you never enter Signora Bertrame's room without my permission. Now, get out of my sight.'

And I heard my friend stumble away. I was attempting to get out of bed when Mamma burst in. 'That woman is impossible,' she

194

snarled, 'and what do you think you're doing? Get back into bed at once. '

I wanted to tell Mamma she couldn't treat Nonna so cruelly, but I couldn't countenance an argument with her – not yet.

So began Mamma's new regime and, even in my stupefied state, I understood what was happening. It was simple. Because Mamma had lost control of her own luxurious, ordered life, she had decided to take control of mine. What else was there for her? However, even though I understood her motivation, it didn't lessen the impact her vindictive behaviour had on me.

I needed Nonna beside me and mourned her absence. She had loved my Carlo too and we had shared our suffering. Losing her comforting presence and compassion was like another bereavement to me. I never saw her unless Mamma permitted her to carry a tray to me or make up the fire. She only had to smile at me or touch my hand and my mother berated her. She was always there, bullying, hectoring, as if Nonna were a dog.

She hired a new serving woman who saw to my personal needs. I was careful not to say anything in front of this woman, because she went straight back to Mamma with everything I did or said.

Mamma had total control of me and my household, except for one thing. At night I heard my old friend moving about in her small room above mine and sometimes the creaking, as she toiled up the rickety outside stairs, that led to her room directly off the street. Her

195

chamber was no larger than a broom cupboard but Nonna loved it. If it had been larger, no doubt Mamma would have taken it from her. It was such a comfort to know she was still there, close to me and when, suddenly, I didn't hear her for two nights in a row I was terrified that Mamma had thrown her out. Where could she go? She would be destitute. I was frantic with worry, but then, the next night, I heard Nonna's footsteps once again.

I could read my old friend's mood from the way she walked. When she was tired, she dragged her left foot, but when she was happy she walked like a much younger person. Hearing her was such a small thing but I was learning that it was invariably the inconsequential things in life that see us through terrible times.

Day by day I was building up my resolve to confront Mamma but that time hadn't quite arrived and I was forced to acquiesce as my servants were dismissed one by one, some of whom had worked for the Bertrame's all their lives. Alfonso was only allowed to see me about farmacia business, and then Mamma was always present. He barely looked me in the eyes as he showed me bits of paper to do with the business. I couldn't concentrate on anything but would nod at anything he said, or sign any order.

Marietta never came now. She was very ill and I heard one of the servants saying that Jacopo had taken his daughter to Terra Ferma, to seek a cure. I longed for news of her.

My mother had begun to sit with me at night, while I drank my bedtime drug-infused milk. I think she wanted to make sure I took it. As distressed as I was, I had to put a stop to her ranting, so, unbeknown to her, I had been attempting to sleep without the drug for several nights. I had tipped away the draught and filled the bottle with water.

Eventually the morning came when I awoke refreshed after a natural night's rest, the first in a very long time. I was in my robe by the window eating breakfast when Mamma burst in. She was already in full voice as she entered, as if she and I were continuing some previous altercation. '...And why didn't you put a stop to his ridiculous behaviour? All that showing off, and for what?' she sneered, 'to make you love him more? Look where that got him? She needed a scapegoat to blame for her fall from grace, and who better to vilify than her dead son-in-law? Whenever she wanted something, or someone slighted her, or just because she could, she poured vitriol on my poor Carlo's head.

Her venom took my breath away. How could she be so cruel? She must have seen the pain she was causing me but she ignored it. All she saw and felt was her own humiliation.

'...And why didn't you make sure he made proper provision for you?'

I looked her straight in the eyes. 'You know the law as well as I, Mamma. The widow has no monetary claim on her husband's inheritance. And my dowry is long gone.'

'There are always ways around such obstacles.'

'But we have enough money, Mamma, and this house and the farmacia are mine. Carlo was a kind, generous husband, and we all profit from his open-handedness.'

197

But she wasn't listening, she never did. 'I had such plans for you, Veronica, and now look at us, ruined, because you couldn't keep Bertrame alive long enough to make proper provision for you and your family, and now this odious little distant cousin from Milan, inherits everything.'

She tossed a letter at my feet. I picked it up and glanced at the heading. 'But this is addressed to me, Mamma.'

She waved a dismissive hand in my direction. 'We will fight this, Veronica.'

I was busy reading the letter. 'If money is all that interests you, Mamma, we are rich. See?' I waved the letter at her. 'It says here, I keep the farmacia.'

'But he inherits all the money.'

'I have the theriac.'

She curled her lip. 'That filth? Who will buy that quackery when the whole of Venice knows it couldn't even save Bertrame's life? And remember, girl, the shop is nothing without the Master.'

She was right, of course, and even in my distress I knew that Carlo's business was collapsing. I had seen the anguish on Alfonso's face. My heart was beating wildly but I made myself smile at my mother. 'Alfonso and the men work very hard. You'll see. We'll build the farmacia up and be rich once more.'

'Rich, rich,' she sneered.

I sighed, recognising the look in her eyes. She was going to give me the lecture again.

'Any whore can be rich. I wanted a name. I wanted them to look up to me.'

I was tempted to join in. I knew it all by heart. I'd heard it enough times. We could do a duet.

'We wear the same clothes, have our hair dressed like theirs, mix with them but they know who we are. You don't know how fortunate you've been. My mother was a procuress and sold me when I was ten...'

Strange, I thought, she was nine the last time I'd heard this diatribe. If I could have laughed I would have.

'...I could never choose who I serviced. You didn't have to please some, stinking, fumbling old man. I wanted something better for my daughter. My ungrateful daughter. I lavished everything on you, you were educated and cultured. You had dancing and singing lessons. I kept you out of harm's way. I could have pocketed a fortune by selling you to one of my patrons with a taste for young girls. The Doge himself wanted you but I refused him. Instead I arranged your marriage to Carlo Bertrame, the owner of the most illustrious spezierie in Our Most Serene Republic...'

And suddenly I could take no more, '....Enough.' I screeched, jumping to me feet and jamming my hands over my ears. 'Not one more word, Mamma.'

She narrowed her eyes at me. 'What?'

'I forbid you to speak of this matter ever again.'

She was quiet for a moment, a puzzled look on her face, but then she carried on, as if I'd been some minor annoyance that could be

199

ignored. '...I found you the most influential apothecary in Venice and you let the stupid man slip through your fingers.'

I went to the door and flung it wide. 'This is Carlo's house, Mamma, and he was the best, the kindest man I have ever known. You will never speak ill of him again..'

She stared at me open-mouthed.

'I think it's time you found alternative accommodation, Mamma, don't you? It would be best for both of us.'

She hesitated for a moment, her eyes wide with surprise, then she swept past me, wanting to bang the door but I stood with my back to it, depriving her of the satisfaction. I could hear her screaming at some poor servant as she stormed down the stairs.

My heart was beating wildly and I was shaking. I could hardly believe what had just happened but it felt so good, so very, very good.

Recovery

After several nights of blessed sleep I woke with enough strength and courage to take charge of my life once more. Mamma was still living with me but I never saw her, nor did I want to. She spent her days scouring San Marco, looking for suitable accommodation. I wouldn't throw her out until she found something but she knew her days in my house were numbered.

That morning I waited until I saw her and her maid leave my house, then I summoned Mamma's new serving woman and told her to find Nonna and bring her to me.

The woman was surprised. 'But she is busy at her work, Signora. The mistress says she has been neglecting her duties and sent her to work in the kitchens today...'

'... Did you not hear me?'.

'But may I not serve you, Signora? The mistress....'

'...Who is this mistress you talk of? There is only one mistress in this house and that is me.'

'But Signora Bracci ordered that I alone see to your needs. The old woman is not to be admitted to your chamber. She is not fit...'

I took a step forward and the woman must have seen the look in my eyes, because she stood meekly aside to let me pass.

I discovered Nonna in the kitchen on her hands and knees, scrubbing the floor. Two young scullions stood by watching and giggling. When they saw me they hurried back to their tasks.

Nonna had her back to the door so hadn't seen me. I knelt down beside her and put my arms about her. She went stiff for a moment, as if expecting some rebuke, then she turned and saw me.

'Veronica,' she sighed, and closed her eyes. 'May God be praised.'

I got the servants to help me and we half carried Nonna to my rooms. I instructed them to bring food and drink then I sat beside Nonna on my bed and held her against my heart. 'Oh, Nonna, I've missed you so much.'

She took my hands in hers and raised them to her lips. 'I have been so worried about you, Veronica. Are you well?'

I nodded and we sat close together for some time, hand in hand, allowing the peace to settle about us and for Nonna's breathing to become more regular. 'Everything will be alright now, Nonna,' I promised. 'We will never be parted again.'

She smiled but there was something hiding in the corner of her eye. I knew that look. It was fear. Stroking her arm I tried to calm her. 'There's nothing to worry about now, I promise. It's all over. I am well again and soon Mamma will leave my house for ever. Everything will be as it was. '

But my words didn't calm Nonna, they seemed to have the opposite effect. She wouldn't look at me and her hands were trembling. She was muttering something, over and over again, under her breath.

202

'What are you saying, Nonna? I can't hear. '

'You'll never forgive me, Veronica. You'll hate me.'

'I could never hate you, never. Now tell me. What is this nonsense?'

But she wasn't listening. 'I didn't know what to do when the message came. Your Mamma forbade me from giving it to you. She turned me away from your door. I knew it was important but what could I do?' She clutched at my arm. 'Please, please say you'll forgive me.'

'Nonna,' I said. 'You are being silly. It is I who should beg your forgiveness for not standing up to Mamma, when she was so cruel to you. I am so sorry.'

She shook her head frantically. 'No, no, no. You don't understand. it's...it's not about your Mamma, or me, it's something else.' Her words ended in a wail.' I couldn't help it, Veronica. I didn't know what to do.'

At that moment there was a slight noise from somewhere in the house and my old friend jumped, as if she'd been struck. Maybe she thought that Mamma was about to burst into my room and order her away again. I touched her hand. 'It's all right. Nothing is going to hurt you. I'm here.'

She struggled to her feet and hobbled towards the door. 'You must come with me, Veronica.'

'Where? Where must I go?'

'You will know what to do.'

'Please, come back, sit down, tell me what this is all about. You're not making any sense, Nonna. '

But she stood at the doorway, waiting patiently, her eyes pleading. I had no option but to humour her. I was frightened that my old friend might be deranged. So, I took her hand and allowed her to lead me out into the hall, then up the crooked little staircase that led to her room above mine. At her door she stood aside for me to enter before her. The room was as it always was, bare except for Nonna's small cot, a bedside chair, a chest and crucifix. In the corner there was an alcove with curtains drawn across, where Nonna hung her clothes. I was puzzled. 'Well?'

Nonna stepped into the room beside me, then she whispered. 'It's me. You can come out now.'

After a moment the curtains twitched and a child's face appeared between the drapes. The eyes focused on me and widened, then the curtains closed quickly. Nonna went to the alcove. 'It's safe, piccolo. Take Nonna's hand', and she reached in and gently pulled a child into the room. It was a little girl and she was clutching Nonna's doll.

'Ginevra?' I was stunned.

The child hid her face in the old woman's dress.

Nonna stared at me over the child's head. 'Forgive me, Veronica.' she pleaded. 'There was nowhere else for her to go. I had to help her didn't I? Veronica? Please say something.'

'Forgive you?' I went to my friend and put my arms around both of them. 'Forgive you, Nonna? I bless you. I thought there'd never

204

be joy in this house again. Thank you.' And I kissed both of their heads.

The child ducked from my embrace and hid behind Nonna, her fist clutching at Nonna's dress. Everything had happened so quickly it was hard to keep track of my emotions. Of course I was happy to have my Nonna back and delighted that the child was safe in my house at last, but if the child was here, then where was Pazienza?

Ginevra moved and I saw the child's expression. I had never seen such terror in a child's eyes before. I was frightened. 'Is she hurt, Nonna? Shall I send for my physician?'

Nonna shook her head. 'I fear there is no cure for Ginevra's malady, Veronica. Every night in her sleep she cries out in terror and I hold her close, until she is quiet again. I was so frightened someone would hear and her presence would be reported to your Mamma. Did you not hear her?'

'Until the last few days, Nonna, I have been taking a sleeping draught,' I explained. 'Nothing would have woken me. Can she tell you what she dreams?'

She shook her head. ' She has spoken little since the night we came here .'

'We?'

'Alfonso. We travelled here in his gondola from La Guidecca, the day after he brought her to the farmacia from the Rialto. '

'And what of..?'

Nonna put a finger to her lips and glanced worriedly at the child. I understood and lowered my voice. 'Did...she not come too?'

205

Nonna shifted uneasily. 'You must ask Alfonso. I am too muddled, and besides...'

We both looked at Ginevra. She was sucking her thumb and clinging to Nonna as if her very life depended on it. The child was obviously in shock. Whatever had happened that night was best not discussed in front of her.

'And no one knows she's here?' I asked. ' Not even the servants?'

'Alfonso carried her up the street stairs to my room and she has been here ever since.'

'And you kept her here in secret, all that time? You were very brave. '

'Not brave. I was away for two days, Veronica, and no one missed me or bothered to climb the stairs to visit me. Why would they? I have been invisible in your Mamma's household.'

'I missed your footsteps, Nonna. I was so worried that Mamma had thrown you onto the streets. And there was something else too. A messenger came with a note for me and you tried to deliver it. Mamma chased you away didn't she? Was it from Pazienza?'

Too late I saw the child's stricken face. 'Mamma, Mamma,' she whimpered, over and over again.

Nonna held the child close, calming her, while she talked. 'The boy said it was from her and it was urgent. I was so frightened something bad had happened...but I didn't know what to do.'

I could see that Nonna was very close to breaking down, so I turned my attention to the child. 'So, Ginevra?' I said, making myself smile. ' How would you like to come and play in my big bedroom?'

The child kept her eyes down and shook her head, vehemently. Then she whispered in Nonna's ear.

Nonna looked at me over the child's head. 'She says she doesn't want to leave this room.'

I knelt down beside Ginevra, not attempting to touch her. 'I know you love it in Nonna's room, but you don't have to hide anymore, Ginevra . Every room in this house belongs to me and you can go wherever you choose. But if you want, you can come back here whenever you wish. Please come with us, it is time to eat and I am hungry, aren't you? I think there may be cake today. Shall we see?'

She looked at me and then at Nonna, who nodded encouragingly, then she slid her hand into Nonna's and they went to the door. At the door she hesitated and looked up at Nonna, her eyes bright and trusting. 'Will my Mamma come for tea? She likes cake. Sometimes she gives me a cake if I rub her legs for her when they hurt. '

I dug my nails into my hand determined not to cry. 'When we've had our tea, Ginevra, I will show you all my dresses and pretty jewels. Would you like that?' No answer. 'And you can laugh and shout as much as you like. You don't have to be as quiet as a baby mouse, when the cat is on the prowl.' No answer, but I could see she was listening. 'You can go where you like in my house, Ginevra, and roar like a lion if you so wish. I say what happens here. '

207

Ginevra looked solemnly from Nonna to me and then she let go of Nonna's hand. 'I'm not frightened of lions. I am ...Daniel in the Lion's Den and if we meet any lions I can make them purr like kittens. I saw the lion in the theatre play in San Marco. Do you remember, Nonna? You were frightened but the funny man was Daniel and he tamed the lions. They all lay on their backs and had their tummy's tickled.'

Nonna and I laughed too loudly at the child's joke, then we went down the stairs to my room. I didn't look at Nonna, nor she me. Ginevra rushed into my room, almost colliding with the serving girls, who were bringing trays of food and drink. I saw their startled expressions and nodded to them. 'Ah, good. We are all hungry. Put the food over there.' They couldn't take their eyes of the child. 'Oh, and this is...

'...Daniel,' Ginevra shouted. 'I am Daniel in the lion's den.'

The girls giggled as Ginevra roared and showed her claws. I could hear their brains ticking.

'This is Signor Bertrame's niece.' I said, plucking the lie out of the air. She will be staying with me for the time being, while her .parents are away. Get the boy to move the cot in here from the other room...' My baby's room. 'You will find bedding in the chest. That will be all for now.' The girls' eyes were wide with surprise but they managed to curtsey as they backed out of the room. I heard their excited chatter as they clattered down the stairs.

The child jumped on my bed, cramming cake into her mouth as if her very life depended on it and I placed two caskets full of my

208

jewels beside her. When Ginevra looked inside them I swear her eyes nearly popped out of her head. We watched as she searched delightedly through the treasure, stringing the necklaces about her neck like garlands of flowers. I was smiling and when I looked at Nonna, so was she. I tried to focus all my attention on Ginevra but my mind was elsewhere and, eventually, I could stand it no longer. I touched Nonna's arm. 'Please,' I whispered. 'We must talk.'

I led the way outside, leaving the door ajar, so that the child could see us. 'What's happened, Nonna?' I asked softly. 'Where is Pazienza?'

'I don't know...'

'... Is she ill? Has she had an accident?'

Nonna looked at me despairingly. 'I know nothing, Veronica.'

'But Alfonso must have told you what the message said?'

'He didn't, Veronica. I only knew he was going to Pazienza and he said it would be too dangerous for me to go with him. I was to wait in the shop. The hours crept by, night had fallen, and still he hadn't returned. I have never been so frightened. I didn't know what to do...'

'... Why did he say it was dangerous?'

She hesitated. 'I can't remember. Forgive me, but it's all so confusing.'

I could see I was making my old friend flustered so I gave her a moment to collect her thoughts. 'When you can,' I said more gently, 'start from the beginning, Nonna. I need to know everything that happened, however trivial.'

209

She hesitated for a long time. I wanted to shake the words out of her but, somehow, I managed to hold onto myself. Then, at last, she took a deep breath and began. 'It all started on the day when the boy brought the message.'

'Yes, I know about that.' I snapped, unable to stop myself.

'But you said start at the beginning, and that is the beginning.'

'The message, Nonna. Was it from Pazienza?'

'Yes, and the boy said it was urgent, that he needed a reply straight away. But I couldn't give him a reply. Your Mamma stopped me from giving it to you. Do you remember?'

'Yes, yes, yes. What did you do next?'

'What could I do? I can't read and I didn't trust anyone here to read it for me, so I thought about Alfonso and I took the gondola to La Guidecca..'

'And?...'

She looked at me blankly.

'Did he read it?'

'Yes, then he got his coat and ran out of the shop. He said I must wait for him and to keep the fire alight, and that he would be bringing the child with him.'

'That's all?'

'Yes.'

'And when he returned?'

'He didn't speak, I don't think he could. I have never seen him so weary. He could barely walk. Once he had settled the sleeping child in front of the fire, he pulled a cloak about himself and lay down beside her. I watched over them that night. The child twisted and turned all night, calling out in her sleep. Once, she sat bolt upright and I thought she looked to me. I went to her but when I touched her shoulder she struck out at me, shouting, 'No. no.' I lay beside her cradling her against me until she fell asleep.' Nonna was silent for a moment, gathering her thoughts. 'I must have dozed off then because when I woke the child was still sleeping but Alfonso was gone. I could hear him talking to someone in the shop. I wasn't sure what to do. Not long after that he came in, putting a finger to his lips. He gave us food, then whispered that we should stay there and not make a sound. It wasn't a problem keeping the child quiet because she didn't say a word. At first I thought it was because she was exhausted but as the day drew on I realised that it was something else. She clung to me and sat on my lap, sucking her thumb − something she hadn't done since she was a baby − she seemed so unlike herself. I don't know what happened to her that night, Veronica, but it must have been something very bad.'

'And you were in the farmacia all that day?'

'Yes but as soon as the shop closed that night and the workers left for home, Alfonso took us to his gondola and brought us here. It was very dark, the calli were deserted and there was little water traffic. When he tied up, he picked up the child and we climbed the street stairs to my room. He warned me over and over again that no one should find out that the child was in your house, or who she was, and I must never tell anyone, but you.'

'And, he said nothing of Pazienza? '

211

She shrugged helplessly. 'He said it was best I didn't know anything, in case I was questioned.'

'Questioned? I don't understand. Who would question you?'

'The Signori della notte,' she whispered, as if, by merely mentioning their names, they might materialise. She didn't need to say more. Everyone in the Republic had heard about these men of the night, who kept our Most Serene Republic free from sin.

I was sure that Nonna had told me everything she knew about that night but it wasn't enough. There were still more questions than answers. I had to talk to Alfonso. Nonna sat with the child while I scribbled a note to him. When I was finished I rang for Mamma's serving woman. She arrived a few moments later, red-faced and out of breath from her hurry to climb the stairs to do my bidding. I gave her the note and told her to hire a messenger and have the note delivered into Signor Ortha's hands at the farmacia on La Guidecca. I knew she would read the message so I was careful not to say anything incriminating. I simply requested that he attend me concerning important business matters. I saw her eyes on Ginevra, as she hurried out. Mamma would be informed of our new lodger before the day was out, but I had far more important things to worry about than her.

The truth

Later that day I was resting on a chair beside the bed, where Nonna and the child slept, when I heard raised voices on the stairs. I hurried out to stop the noise before it woke the child and saw Alfonso leaping up the steps towards me. I caught a glimpse of the serving woman's frightened face below and motioned for her to go away.

As Alfonso reached my landing I put a finger to my lips but he gave me no acknowledgement and pushed past me into the room. The child was still asleep and Nonna lay close beside her, snoring, eyes closed, 'resting them', or so she said. Alfonso went straight to the child. 'Thank God she's safe,' he muttered.

I barely recognised my boy. He had always been very particular about his appearance but today his immaculate jerkin was undone, his shirt untucked and stained and his feet and calves bare and dirty. I attempted to touch his arm but he shrugged me off and glared. 'Alfonso?' I said, 'What ails you?'

He didn't answer. All his concentration was focussed on the child: and; leaning over her, he brushed her cheek with the back of his fingers very gently, as if he couldn't quite believe she was real. She stirred in her sleep, but didn't wake.

'Come, Alfonso,' I whispered. 'We must talk. ' And I led the way to the door.

He glanced at me and then back at the sleeping child.

'She'll be safe here.' I said.

He still hesitated.

'I swear that she will come to no harm in my house, Alfonso.' I led the way down the stairs, trusting that he would follow me, and after a moment I heard his step behind me. Once inside my dayroom I closed the door and offered him a seat, but he prowled restlessly about the place. His eyes were bloodshot and his hands shook.

He went to the door and opened it, staring up the stairs. 'And no one knows she's here?'

'Nonna hid her in her room until today. I have only just met her.'

'But your Mamma?' he asked, anxiously.

'Not yet but the servants saw her and they are Mamma's women, so... I told them she was Carlo's niece and I was looking after her while her parents were away. There's nothing to worry about, Alfonso, the child is in my care. Please, my friend,' I begged, 'be seated.'

At last he did my bidding and sat down opposite me. I filled a cup with wine and pushed it towards him. He didn't drink.

'So how are you, my friend?' I asked gently. 'And your family? Little Sofia must be growing up so fast, and your dear papa? How are his legs?'

'His legs?' he repeated, staring at me as if he didn't understand the words.

'Yes,' I smiled at him. 'It's such a long time since you and I talked about such things. I've missed you, Alfonso.'

He shook his head as if waking himself up from a deep sleep, then he scrambled to his feet. 'My Lady,' he mumbled, 'Forgive me...I am not myself,' and he pulled off his cap and stuffed it in his pocket. His hair sprang up, just like it always did and his hand went automatically to smooth it down. He was my boy again.

'Come, Alfonso,' I said, pushing a plate towards him. 'Take some refreshment.'

He sank back into his chair. 'I am so sorry, my Lady. I fear I have forgot myself'.

'Have you been ill?'

He shook his head, 'No, no. I am well but... And you? Are you recovered?'

'Recovered? No, Alfonso, I shall mourn my Carlo forever and...my child.'

'You have suffered much, my Lady.'

'But now you have brought me little Ginevra to light my life. I owe you a debt of gratitude, my friend.'

We sat in comfortable silence as he reached for his wine and ate a little. I waited until he was finished before I spoke again. 'Can you tell me what happened that night, Alfonso? When you brought the child to my house? My poor Nonna is ...very muddled and I was indisposed at that time.'

215

'Of course,' he said. 'I will do my best. How much do you know?'

'Very little, except that a note arrived from Pazienza, but Mamma wouldn't let Nonna deliver it to me. I kept to my chamber at that time.'

He looked worried again. 'Your Mamma saw the note?'

'No, Nonna took it away. Mamma has no say in my house anymore, Alfonso. As soon as she finds somewhere she is moving out. It may take her some time, you know how particular she is but I am mistress in my house once more. It is the beginning of a new life for me, Alfonso, and I trust you will be part of it. I know I have neglected the farmacia of late but we shall meet very soon to discuss the future. In the meantime be assured that you will always find a welcome in my home.'

He smiled at me.

'But for now,' I continued, 'my sole concern must be for Pazienza and the child. What news of my friend? Do you know where she is hiding, so I can send her aid? I pray she has found a safe haven, far away from that brute.'

Alfonso shifted uneasily in his chair and I saw his discomfort. 'I'm sorry, Alfonso. I'm going too fast aren't I? Can you bear to start at the beginning? Tell me what the note said and then what happened afterwards? I will be patient.'

He nodded, cleared his throat and began. 'After Nonna brought me the note I went straight to the Rialto.'

'What did she write?'

216

'Just a few scrawled words, my Lady, hard to read, as if she were in a hurry, or... She wrote that she entrusted the child to you, and... that you must forget her.'

'Forget her? '

He nodded.

'And what else?'

'She said goodbye.'

'Goodbye?'

'And that was all?'

'That was all.'

'I know Pazienza, Alfonso.' I spoke more sharply than I intended. 'And she would never have just said goodbye, without an explanation.'

He shrugged.

'And when you saw her later? What did she say when you saw her? Alfonso? She must have said more.'

'She didn't ...she...she was ...' He shook his head despairingly.

'What is it? Why didn't she speak?' I was fighting to keep control of myself. I had to stay calm. 'Let's go back a bit. When you got to The Rialto, who did you see? Was the girl there, Giada? The one who kept an eye on Ginevra when her mamma was ...busy?'

Alfonso shook his head, 'Later, I saw her later, but, when I first got to the Carampane it was deserted.'

'Deserted?' I couldn't keep the incredulity out of my voice. 'That place is always full of people at night. I've been there, I know what it's like. Why are you lying?'

217

He shook his head.

'You were frightened weren't you? Afraid that something bad would happen to you if you asked too many questions. I know what an evil place it is.'

He shook his head. 'It's the truth, my Lady. As I said there was no one about and it was so quiet, eerily quiet. The calli were deserted and there were no lights shining out from the tenements. Even the street torches were dim. There were no women with their men outside the inns or crowding the street corners, no noise or drunken singing, no shouting or screaming...nothing, just silence...cold silence, and the feeling that someone was there in the shadows, watching me. I am used to danger, my Lady, especially there on the Carampane. A blackamoor is treated with disrespect and often violence, even in these enlightened times. I am always armed at night in such places and I know how to protect myself. I am not easily frightened but that night I wanted to flee, to hide. There was evil there, my Lady. I could feel it.'

He was quiet for a moment, then he reached for his cup and drank slowly, as if dreading the moment when he would have to speak again. 'I ran as fast as I could through the streets to Pazienza's room. Thank the Lord I was barefoot and made no sound. My plan was to find the child quickly, but when I reached her door it was hanging off its hinges. The room had been ransacked. All the furniture was upturned much of it broken, pots and pans, crockery, food, rubbish, bedding and clothing spilled all over the floor and... and then I saw it, a pool of blood on the ground and you were right, my Lady. I was frightened... I still am.'

218

'Oh, God,' I could feel the room spinning. 'Pazienza?'

'All I saw was the blood... and the smell of it, the stink of it.' He was gasping for air. 'I thought there was no one there and I turned to flee but then...I saw him...her man. He was sprawled on the floor eyes wide, staring. I thought he was unharmed but then I saw the small gaping wound in his thigh and a ribbon of blood still pumping from it...' He groped for his cup.

Thank the Lord. It wasn't Pazienza. She wasn't dead. It was that beast, that bastard. A mighty wave of relief washed through me, but I had to make sure. 'Was it him?' I asked, at last. ' The one who beat her?'

He nodded.

'And he was dead?'

'No one could lose all that blood and live.'

'I'm glad,' I said. 'He deserved to die. He was a monster. I wish I'd stuck a knife in him too. But what of Pazienza? Did she escape? I pray she is safe. Alfonso? Tell me she's safe.'

He couldn't look at me. 'She was there in the room, my Lady, crouching in a corner, her cloak wrapped tightly about her. I stood in front of her and said her name and she lifted her head. She was holding a small square-ended knife in her hand, like the sort fisherwomen use to fillet fish. Such a little blade, my Lady, yet so much blood. And as I stood there I heard the tramping of many feet and men shouting orders. I tried to pull Pazienza to her feet, so that we could run, but she couldn't stand, she was broken, my Lady. Her face... her poor, poor face. I tried to pull the knife out of her hand but she clung on. "Go', she

219

pleaded. 'Save her.' The men were almost upon us and I sprang away from her and ran, may God forgive me, I left her to those fiends.'

He hung his head and I saw his misery.

'Poor Pazienza.' I said, taking Alfonso's hand. 'But you did the right thing. She wanted you to save Ginevra. You had to leave her.'

He rested his head in his hands and wept.

'Do you know where they've taken her, Alfonso? We can help her. It wasn't her fault. He was torturing her. The Magistrati will be lenient when they see what he did to her.' Kneeling beside Alfonso, I put my arms about his shoulders. 'Listen to me. Pazienza was brutalised by that man. He is the criminal, not her. There must be something we can do to help? Someone to bribe or coerce. I have some money still, we must find a good lawyer to speak for her, to explain what happened. Anyone who saw Pazienza would see how he mistreated her. She will be pardoned. Ginevra will have her mamma back once more.'

He raised his head and looked at me. 'She doesn't want to be pardoned,' he muttered.

'What? But that's nonsense, you said she didn't speak, except to tell you to save Ginevra.'

'It wasn't Pazienza who told me, it was Giada, and , but for her, I would be dead or imprisoned by now. When I fled Pazienza's room I didn't know which way to run. The tenements are a warren of ill-lit streets, all tumbling in and out of each other and I was confused. The sound of the advancing guards was getting closer but I couldn't tell which direction they were coming from. The sounds echoed up and down the alley ways and I stood there paralysed with fear, waiting until I saw the flickering shadows of men and torch light leaping around the corner of a nearby calle. I turned on my heels and ran from them, but they must have seen me because there were shouts and I heard them crashing after me. I expected a blade in my back at any moment but suddenly a doorway opened up beside me and someone pulled me inside. We stood side by side with our backs to the door. I was gasping for air but the person clamped a hand over my mouth. The shouting increased, heavy footsteps clattered on the cobbles. They came to a halt quite close to where we cowered, but then, finally, an order was given and they moved off.

We waited until we were sure they had gone and then my rescuer removed their hand and I heard a flint being struck. In the flickering light I saw a girl's face. It was Giada. 'Thank God you've come.' she whispered, 'We have the child safe but you must leave now, before they return.' She pushed me in front of her into a tiny storeroom, hidden behind a pallet, stacked with blankets. This was in darkness too and at first I thought the place was deserted but then, as my eyes adjusted, I saw another young girl watching over several sleeping, smaller children. Ginevra was there too, squatting on the floor with her doll, eyes blank, rocking, rocking.... I scooped her up in my arms. She felt like a doll, my Lady, rigid, unmoving. I carried her to where Giada waited by a low door that opened out into a small back alley-way.

She hurried me along the winding, secret paths of San Polo, until we reached the rio and found my gondola. When we were safely

221

there she told me what had happened. Pazienza had been on edge for days. She knew her man was coming to take the child and there wasn't much time left to get the child to safety. She repeated over and over again that Veronica would come for Ginevra. Veronica had promised. She was feverish and Giada thought she had lost her wits, after the last vicious beating at that man's hands. All the women told Pazienza she had to accept losing her child. It was life, it was their life. They had seen it all before, it had happened to their children. But Pazienza said she would rather die than let him have her child.

'Oh poor, Pazienza,' I moaned. 'I'm sorry, I'm so sorry.'

Alfonso was still talking. 'Pazienza planned to bring Ginevra to you that morning, my Lady, but, she didn't get the chance, because her man came early. Pazienza had seen to it that Ginevra was safe with Giada, while she packed a few things to take with them. Her door was locked and when the man demanded entry, she told him the child was out playing and would be back later. He didn't believe her and told her to open the door, and when she refused he broke it down and proceeded to destroy everything he could lay his hands on. He was already drunk and Pazienza kept refilling his cup, hoping that he would fall into a stupor but the drink just made him crazy. He kept ordering her to bring the child and each time she refused he beat her. All the women heard her screams but there was nothing they could do. They knew they would suffer too if they interfered. They had children of their own to care for. But the hysterical child tore herself away from Giada and ran to her mamma's room. Giada tried to stop her but it was too late. The child watched as her mamma was being beaten to death.'

'Oh, poor, poor Pazienza. And the child? No wonder she is as she is. The horrors she has seen.' A sudden thought struck me. 'She was there when her mamma knifed the man, wasn't she? Alfonso? Heaven forbid. Did she see it happen?'

He looked away from me.

'She did didn't she?' I couldn't speak for a moment. 'Oh, that poor little girl. But Pazienza had to do it. That brute had to die. No court will condemn her. It was self defence. I will find good people to speak for her. She will be pardoned. And as for Ginevra, we will love her so fiercely we will make her forget what happened. I will spend the rest of my days making Ginevra and her mamma happy.' And assuaging my guilt, my inner voice comforted.

Alfonso shook his head in despair. 'No, no,' he moaned, and I saw that little seven year old blackamoor once more, gazing up at me through big tear-filled eyes. 'Pazienza has already confessed and is held in The Doge's dungeons.'

'No.' What was he saying? 'You're wrong. She saved Ginevra, Alfonso. She saved her from that vile man.' I was babbling now. 'No one will blame Pazienza for killing that monster, no one. She was defending herself and the child. If there's any justice in this precious Republic she will not be judged harshly. I will do everything I can to see her go free.'

'She doesn't want to be free,' his voice was so soft I thought I'd misheard.

223

'What? Of course she wants to be free.'

Alfonso leant in towards me, breathing hard. The look in his eyes frightened me. 'Don't you understand?' he said. 'It wasn't Pazienza who killed her man.'

'What? You're talking in riddles. You say she's confessed.'

'She has, but it wasn't her...'

'...Then who? Some other woman he had mistreated? Who? Tell me, Alfonso. It doesn't make sense.'

Alfonso continued the story. As he spoke it was as if he were seeing the scene unfolding before him. 'Giada tried to hold onto the frantic child but Ginevra fought and scratched until she was free and could run to her mamma. She picked up the knife from the floor and screamed at the man to leave her mamma alone. He saw the child waving the little blade in her hand and laughed at her, opening his arms to her. His hands were already on her as she shrieked and stuck the knife into his leg. Just one little stab, that's all it took...and he fell, spread-eagled on the floor, still bellowing and cursing and trying to get to his feet screaming at them, telling them what he would do to them when he caught them. They watched as he crawled about the floor bleeding to death.'

I staggered away from Alfonso. No. I hadn't heard that. He hadn't said that. I was dreaming. It wasn't true. 'No. No. Not the child. It's not true. It's a terrible mistake. Giada was lying. Maybe it was she who knifed the man. Maybe...'

He shook his head. '...No, it was Ginevra.'

'No. Please. It can't be true.'

'How many times do I have to tell you?'

'Liar,' I yelled, jumping at him and punching him as hard as I could in the chest. He staggered backwards, a look of indescribable shock on his face, but I followed him relentlessly, fists flailing. He didn't retaliate, he let me hurt him. 'Stupid, stupid boy' I shrieked.' Of course it wasn't her, she's a child, a little child.' And when I was finished, totally drained, we stood face to face breathing heavily.

'Yes, your Alfonso is stupid.' he said. 'But you needn't worry because if they find out I have protected a murderess my life will be forfeit, and yours too, and Nonna, and Giada and all the other women. Our only hope is that the child doesn't talk, doesn't remember, because if she does we are damned.'

'Forgive me.' I was so ashamed. I touched his hand. 'It was such a shock. I am so sorry I hurt you. '

'I have had worse beatings for less reason.'

'Pazienza is giving her life for Ginevra?'

'Yes.'

'But it's not fair, Alfonso. Pazienza never hurt anyone.' The whine in my voice sickened me. This was the real world and I was reacting like the spoilt child. Always promising things I couldn't deliver, always failing. 'I know we have to honour her wishes, Alfonso. But we must make them understand. That man deserved to die.'

He nodded. 'Yes, he did, but he was a nobili, and he has been murdered by a whore. You think they will spare, Pazienza? Never. The judges are nobili, The Doge is a nobili, the Church is nobili. '

225

'But what can we do? There must be something we can do.'

'There's nothing, unless we give them the child, and I doubt even that would save Pazienza. The Ten know how the people would relish the spectacle of the double execution of a whore and her brat. Such entertainment.'

'Is that what we are, we Venetians? Nothing but drooling savages?'

He touched my hand. 'Your friend had come to the end of her life, my Lady. That man had been killing her, little by little, since the first day he used her – when she was not much older than Ginevra is now.'

'Can we see her, Alfonso? Take her some comfort?'

'I don't know, but they say she is to be executed within days. She has confessed and the courts have found her guilty. The sooner the better for the Magistrati, to show the people how efficient they are at punishing wrongs done to the nobili. A warning for us commoners to keep in our place.'

I didn't want to ask but I had to. 'How will she be...?'

He knew what I was asking. '...The man was a patriciate, my Lady, so she will be publicly executed.'

'Oh God'. I knew about such horrors. The condemned were flogged around the city and finally executed in San Marco's piazza surrounded by the jeering rabble. 'So we must stand by and watch her die, so cruelly?'

'It's what she wants, my lady. She wants the child to be free.'

226

Secrets

We told Nonna that Pazienza had killed her man in self defence, had confessed, and was to be executed. Nonna, like us, was truly shocked and saddened for our poor, wretched Pazienza, but she believed that our friend was in God's hands and He would be merciful to her. She spoke with such conviction I wished that I could share her faith. I envied her.

Nonna managed her grief for Pazienza by dedicating herself to the child. She saw this as God's will. It was her duty to safeguard, love and cherish Ginevra for the rest of her life.

We kept the child indoors and close to us at all times, not risking that she suddenly talk about what had happened. She was still traumatised and hardly spoke but we couldn't relax our vigilance. We also wanted to shield her from news of her mamma's fate. There were posters displayed on every street corner concerning the forthcoming execution of the sinful whore condemned to death for slaying an innocent, God-fearing nobili − an honourable man who had spent his life supporting the poor and needy. There were renewed calls, especially amongst nobili and patriciate matrons such as Anna del Vasallo, that the Magistrati alla Sanita should have the evil, disease-

227

ridden Carampane, razed to the ground, along with its depraved whores and their bastard spawn.

The worst was yet to come. I had heard rumours from my serving women and refused to believe them until Alfonso swore it was true. Pazienza was to have her hand severed – the one used to kill the man – and hung about her neck, as she was flogged about San Marco.

'But this is the sixteenth century.' I shrieked, angry with Alfonso for bringing such horrors into my house. 'We're not barbarians.' Anger is what keeps me going. After my outbursts Alfonso and Nonna shrug and stare down at the floor. They know better than me, what our Glorious Republic is capable of.

I am driven to praying again. Each morning I go down on my knees, on the most uncomfortable, rough bit of the floor, as if this makes my supplication more sincere. I call on all the angels and saints, to hear my prayers for Pazienza and that her end be quick and merciful. Nonna doesn't question my new found devotion but kneels beside me contentedly saying her rosary over and over again, her soft monotone like the hum of pollen-laden bees. Sometimes the child kneels beside us, bringing her doll's hands together in prayer. I wonder what she prays for.

At night Ginevra sleeps in Nonna's room or mine. Sometimes, when she wakes crying out for her mamma, we all sleep together. With Ginevra it is like living on the top of Mount Etna, where they say it is tranquil for days, weeks, months in a row, and then one day it spews out seams of red hot coals into the blue Sicilian sky and its fires blast across the firmament. Ginevra's night terrors are lessening but when

228

she has a very bad dream I wake at once and run to her, holding her close, her face buried against my chest, comforting her, but also muffling any words she might scream out. At these times I am grateful for Nonna's increasing deafness.

I attempt to fill Ginevra's every waking moment with distractions, to take her mind off the horrors. At first she didn't want to do her lessons or dance, so I would read her stories and perform little dances for her. I even did the sun and moon dance once. The child sometimes stood beside me, mirroring my steps. She has her mother's grace. Alfonso plays for us when he can, although he works long hours at the farmacia. The child loves Alfonso. She likes to sit at his feet and watch his long, slender fingers plucking the strings. At these times she almost smiles and we hold our breath.

One of her favourite diversions is helping Nonna in the kitchen. She loves having her hands in a bowl of flour, breaking eggs, mixing in milk, licking the spoon. The young scullions play games with her but even at those times she would sometimes stop in the middle of some nonsense and burst into tears. Nonna used to tell me that sadness waits patiently for its moment, like a hawk in the bushes watching for the fledgling.

While the child slept and Nonna was on guard I sent message after message to my one time patriciate friends, begging that they speak for Pazienza to the authorities. I needn't have bothered because I soon learnt another of life's lessons. I discovered that a wealthy widow – even an ugly one – has power and an assured place in society, but a poor widow is worthless – even one with admirers and beauty and

229

education. It soon became apparent that people knew more about my perilous financial situation than I did and I knew that very soon I would have to address these problems. These 'friends' had been Carlo's people, never mine. They were either 'sorry', that they couldn't interfere in our Glorious Republic's justice system, or, didn't even have the grace to acknowledge my missives. Even my good friends were unable to help. Jacopo was still on Terra Ferma with Marietta.

Tragedy and comedy come and go in these days like clouds on a sunny day. One day I found Ginevra in my reception room staring up at Marietta's 'Portrait of a Lady', and copying it into a book. That same day I have news that Marietta is dead. I mourn her passing and wish I could have seen her one last time. They say her death has affected Jacopo very deeply. I never saw him again. I miss him. Ginevra asked me if I would teach her a new dance this morning, so I have given one of my old gowns to Nonna to make dresses for the child. I have no need for these fine gowns now. I will wear black until the day I die.

A Prayer answered

The day of Pazienza's execution draws ever nearer and I have given up begging for her life to be spared, now I only plead for clemency. That she might not suffer the public execution and the horror that entails, but be executed out of sight, on the axe-man's block. Surely this is not too much to ask? But who is left to ask?

Ginevra remains withdrawn and weeps for her mamma almost every day but she has never mentioned what happened on that terrible night, or the man. Mercifully, her recollection of that dreadful time seems blocked. Alfonso and I pray it will remain so. Pazienza still lingers in prison and I so wish I could see her before she dies. They say she is frail and crippled and that she may not live long enough to be executed. I pray they are right. I send my friend warm clothes and food but I don't know whether it reaches her, they will not let me visit her. The gaolers promise my messengers they deliver the goods to the condemned woman but I don't trust them.

Mamma has the instincts of a ship bound rat and doesn't want to be aboard my sinking ship when Bertrame's farmacia is ruined. And if the procession of trades people, carrying fabric swatches and rug samples to her rooms, is anything to go by, she won't be with me for much longer. She said she was sorry for my problems and I almost believed her. She could afford to be magnanimous now that her dignity and social standing had been restored and my wealth and reputation had been ruined. I think this pleased her more than anything.

I didn't care what she thought. I was just glad she was going. I had my reasons. Since the Duke del Vasallo's new found generosity towards my mother, he had begun to call regularly at my house. When I object, Mamma said he was only there to finalise and legalise his settlement on her. On more than one occasion she had invited me to join them in her rooms for refreshments. I always made some excuse. Of course Mamma didn't believe me. Why should she? She knew I despised the man.

'What have you got against him?' She kept asking me. 'He never treated me badly. He's a noble man.'

'And I'm the Queen of Sheba.'

The duke's visits were innocent, she insisted, but I knew better and so did she. 'It wouldn't hurt you to be nice to him, Veronica,' she complained. 'You owe him much and you never know when you might need a friend with his influence.'

I refused to be drawn into any discussion about him, so she would sigh, take a deep breath, then straighten her shoulders as if preparing for battle. 'A little gratitude wouldn't go amiss. Play your cards right, and…'

But I never let her finish that particular sentence. It didn't take an old crone with second sight to work out why the duke was suddenly so interested in my welfare. He sent me good wishes and small

232

comforts, via Mamma. He said he was concerned for my future now that I was alone but I knew what he really wanted. Stupid, stupid man. Did he not know that I would rather bed a one legged beggar with leprosy, than him?

But he wasn't going to give up so easily and sent a formal invitation, delivered by Mamma, inviting me to perform a dance at a ball, held in honour of the birth of the duke's first grandchild. So the Sicilian goat had done his bit? I tore the card into small pieces and tossed them in the air.

'But what harm would it do, Veronica?' Mamma pleaded. 'Your mourning period is over. His lordship has paid you a great honour. He could have secured an illustrious Dance Master but he chose you. It's just a small intimate affair, all he requires is you, your dancers, and the musician, what's his name? He has always been fond of you and I know he would be very generous.' '

I laughed out loud at this. But at least she had the good grace not to look me in the face as she said it.

'He's One of the Ten.' She insisted. 'The Republic's most excellent Councillor, next in rank only to Our most Magnificent, Serene Prince. I have never understood your aversion to him, Veronica. He is trying to be kind, for my sake, to help you.'

I stared at my mother. Did she really believe what she was saying? We both knew he had waited a long time for this opportunity. He was like a wolf closing in on its prey, watching and waiting, that mean smile on his face, as if there was some joke that only he was

233

privy too. There were many ugly, rich men in Venice but none of them appalled me as much as this duke.

Mamma found my aversion to him insulting. After all, she said, he had been her lover and my benefactor for a long time. I disputed this statement. He was her lover and her benefactor. He was nothing to do with me and never would be. At least that's what I thought then but what a difference a day makes.

No longer welcome in my rooms, most of our exchanges took place halfway up or down my stairs. This particular day Mamma was waiting for me, third step down from the top, while I was on my way to my bedroom. She liked to look down on me. It was fortunate because I wanted to talk to her too. 'Yes, Mamma,' I said, pleasantly enough. 'How may I help you?'

'Why is she still here, Veronica? The whole of San Marco can talk of nothing else.'

'Sorry?' I asked, innocently. 'Who are we talking about?'

Drawing in a deep breath she let it out slowly. I was impressed by her self-control but it didn't last long. 'You think I gave my life up for you to sneer at me, at your mother?' she stormed. 'Where would you be now if it weren't for my sacrifice?'

I smiled at her. 'Tell me Mamma. Where would I be?'

She raised an elegant eyebrow, sensing my mockery, but it didn't stop her. 'You would be with those disease-ridden whores, who you love so much, that's where you'd be...and I demand that you do something about the brat. It's not fitting to shelter that murdering whore's bastard in your house.'

234

Somehow I kept the smile on my face although it wobbled a bit. 'Whore's bastard, Mamma?' I asked sweetly. ' Like me, d'you mean?'

She would have liked to strike me then, but thought better of it.

'Just keep her out of my sight, is all I ask of you. And when his lordship attends me, take care she is in your rooms, out of sight. '

I wasn't surprised that she knew who Little Ginevra was. In fact I was surprised she hadn't mentioned it before. I was about to retort that I wouldn't let her odious duke anywhere near my beautiful Ginevra but I stopped myself in time. 'Are you expecting the Duke today?' I asked. 'If so I will make sure Ginevra is occupied. She likes to help Nonna in the kitchen. She makes those little pastries that you love so much. '

Surprised by my amiability she narrowed her eyes at me, but I smiled again. 'I'm so glad you've found somewhere more appropriate to live, ' I said, without a glimmer of irony and she seemed to accept it as such.

'The Duke will be here this afternoon.' She said, as she passed me on her way down, to where her woman waited patiently, holding her mistress's cloak.

'Oh, and Mamma,' I called, after her retreating back. 'I was thinking, it might be pleasant to join you in your rooms for refreshments this afternoon? It could be the last chance we have to say goodbye, before you move into your new apartment.'

She was so surprised she nearly lost her footing. 'Be careful, Mamma,' I warned, running down the stairs and putting my hand on

235

her arm, steadying her. 'Let me help you to the door.' She brushed me aside and hurried down the remaining steps unaided. 'This afternoon, ' she called over her shoulder. 'We'll expect you this afternoon. And don't wear black.'

That afternoon I waited until I saw the duke disembarking from his ostentatiously decorated gondola, and heard his tread, then his hesitation as he passed my door on the way to Mamma's rooms. I gave them a few moments alone before I climbed the stairs to join them. Their murmuring voices ceased as I tapped lightly on the door. 'Come in, my dear.' Mamma's voice was a little shrill, almost school girlish. 'Silly girl.' She trilled. 'No need to knock on your Mamma's door.'

They were seated on silk-backed chairs in her small withdrawing room, overlooking the rio. I hadn't realised what a lovely view there was from up here. Mamma had arranged herself artfully on a chair, where the reflection from the sunlight on the water, flickered onto her hair and spangled her dark dress with gold. I wanted to applaud her. She looked magnificent.

I curtsied and the duke stood and bowed, then came towards me, hand outstretched. 'Signora Bertrame,' he murmured, kissing my hand. Then he led me to the third chair, set between theirs. His skin felt dry, warm and a bit scaly like the little lizards that scampered over the campiello walls when I was a child.

My black dress was demure but close fitting and made from luxurious black velvet – so black it looked dark, dark, green. My hair was coiled and plaited around my head. I wore no jewellery but my

236

wedding ring and as I moved, my skirts swung about my hips and I felt their weight, tugging at me, wanting me to twirl and spin. The material had a dance in it. That thought made me smile and the duke noticed, thinking it was for him. I looked quickly away.

There was a tray of sweet Marsala wine and tiny apricot biscuits, laid out on a table, and the duke poured a tiny glass and offered it to me. I took it and he raised his glass to his lips. I did the same, and our eyes met. It was like one of those games I'd played as a child, where you stared at someone until you were either forced to blink or look away. The one who lasted the longest was the winner.

My eyes began to prickle and water but I forced them wide, determined to keep them from closing. I saw his wry smile —the smile of victory, but then Mamma suddenly said, 'Well, this is most pleasant isn't it?'

I could have kissed her. Finishing the wine I replaced the glass on the table and the duke lifted the bottle to refill my glass. I placed my hand over it. 'No more thank you, your lordship.'

He didn't speak and neither did I. Mother prattled away filling the uncomfortable silence but I wouldn't be intimidated by his tactics. This was how he unsettled people, made them uneasy, forced them to say silly things, to incriminate themselves. A thought flashed through my mind. Had this man questioned Pazienza? Had he ordered the Signori del Notte to torture her? Was it his judgement that she be publically executed and horribly maimed?'

'You are pale, Signora.' His voice made me jump.

237

'It's nothing.' I managed.' I feel a little light-headed, that is all. It is so warm in here. My rooms are cooler.'

He strode to the casement and drew back the shutters and I felt the cool breeze calming me.

'Thank you.'

'Your loss has been intense, Signora. It must have been a very difficult time for you but I am glad your mamma has been here to support you through your grief...'

'...I keep advising Veronica...' Mamma interrupted, '...that the time has come for her to enter society once more. She has fulfilled the period of mourning.'

I saw the duke stare at my mother and the message was very clear. Be quiet, his eyes said. Be quiet, until I give you permission to speak. And she obeyed him. Then he smiled at her and said, 'Could we have some more of these delicious pastries, my dear?'

Mamma nodded and went to the bell pull.

'No,' the duke shook his head. 'Don't let's drag that poor old serving woman up those stairs again. You go,' he said, looking pleasantly at my mother again, and she immediately got up and left the room, leaving the door ajar. He rose swiftly and closed the door firmly behind her.

Returning to his seat we sat in silence. He knew I had something to say, so he could afford to be patient. Why else would I be there? As we sat he idly twisted the stem of his wine glass, so that his jewelled rings reflected in the amber liquid, turning it to fire.

At last I found my voice. I had decided to be direct. 'I think you know that my friend Pazienza Bagnio has been arrested for the killing of a man on the Rialto, my lord?'

A frown appeared between his eyebrows. 'Arrested and convicted, Signora Bertrame. The whore is to be executed for the foul murder of the most gentle of noblemen.'

I bit my retort back.

'I must say, Veronica − I may call you by your given name, may I not? I must say, I am surprised that such a...sordid affair is a suitable topic for a young Lady, such as yourself. I had hoped we might find more pleasant conversation.'

I was not going to play his games. 'I have no one else to turn to, my Lord. You are my only hope.'

He waited.

'They say that my wretched friend is to be publicly executed and...' I stopped for a moment, gathering the courage, '...and to have her hand cut off.'

He shrugged. 'We Magistrati debate long and hard on such horrific crimes and we are careful that the punishment should fit the crime. This impresses on the most brutal, uneducated mind that a convicted criminal will always suffer the severest of punishments. As for your...friend, our Most Serene Prince, The Doge, has taken a personal interest in this despicable act. The murdered nobili was a friend and loyal supporter of our beloved Republic.' He took my hand and I steeled myself to let it stay in his. 'I am sorry, my Lady. There is nothing to be done. Any reduction of the sentence would be seen as a

239

weakness. And we cannot disappoint the worthy trades people of Venice can we? The business that attends such public executions is incalculable. '

Snatching my hand from his I stood up. 'So ...my friend will die in agony in front of the blood thirsty mob in order that the pie-sellers make a profit and the nobili take their revenge?' My loathing of him and all that he stood for was like a piece of rank, raw meat in my mouth but I managed to hold onto myself because I knew this man's secret. I knew his desire for me was eating him away. So I didn't throttle him or scream at him. I laughed. This startled him and he took a step away from me, as if he thought me mad, but the more surprised he looked the more I laughed. Then, I drew back my hand and made as if to strike him. He saw it coming and caught my wrist forcing me back down in the chair, and then he was on me, his hands all over me, his mouth on mine.

Finally I fought him off and we stood facing each other, wild eyed and gasping for breath. I was trembling so much I thought I might fall but I managed to reach the door.

'Veronica, wait. Please.' His voice was soft, almost pleading.

I hesitated.

'There may be something I can do. To help your friend.'

'What?' I asked, turning to face him.

'I can't be specific. All you have to do is agree that I will be rewarded for my trouble.'

I deliberately misunderstood him. 'Rewarded? I am sure you are well aware that my business is failing. I have little money, my Lord."

He took a step towards me, anger flaring in his eyes. 'Do not toy with me, girl. You know my price, and it is not in ducats. Now answer me.'

'And you will help her. You promise? You will help my friend?'

He nodded.

'I will require written confirmation.'

'What? Is the word of a nobili not enough for you?'

I wasn't prepared to back down. 'I would prefer a business relationship.'

'You amaze me, Veronica.' Was he smiling? 'Maybe that's your appeal. Always pushing the boundaries, always doing the unexpected. It's why you've kept me intrigued all these years, and why I've helped you.'

He saw my surprise.

'Did you never ask how your mother managed to buy Bertrame for you. Um? All the wealth she possessed was from me.'

"I think my Mamma earned that money, your Grace.'

He ignored the implied insult. 'And would his most Serene Lord, The Doge, have commissioned you to create a dance to celebrate Tintoretto's painting, without my word in his ear?' He let this sink in for a moment and then he smiled lazily like a cat with the cream. 'Alright. You shall have your written confirmation but in return you must do as I bid?'

Maybe his good humour gave me courage. 'I will, but I will not pay your price until you have kept your part of the bargain.'

'D'you take me for a fool?' He wasn't smiling any more. 'No, no, no. It doesn't work like that, Veronica. You pay the price and then you are rewarded.'

I started to argue but he held up his hand. 'You are lucky. I am feeling generous today, Veronica. My demands are modest. All I ask is that you promise to dance for me and my friends – a private function, you understand?'

I was stunned. 'You want me to perform a dance for you? For your new grandson?'

'No, that opportunity has come and gone, Veronica. This will be a...different occasion. A more intimate affair. Do you understand?'

I nodded.

'And further,' he continued. 'It will not be just any dance, Veronica, it must be the Sobria. You may bring the blackamoor and his usual musicians and dance troupe to accompany you. Inform them that they will be paid handsomely.'

I couldn't believe it. I was so relieved. Just one dance. 'Thank you, thank you, my lord. I promise you, this will be the best dance performance of my life.'

'Oh it will be, Veronica, be sure of that. You may go now.' he said, waiving me away with one hand.' I have business to discuss with your mamma.'

242

'As you wish.' I pushed open the door.

'Oh, and Veronica? '

I waited.

'Bring the child. Your mamma tells me she dances most prettily.'

I stood in the doorway my back to him, my blood turning to ice. 'That won't be possible, my lord. I don't allow her out at night. There are too many licentious men roaming the streets of our Glorious republic seeking innocent children to debauch.'

'As you please, Veronica,.' he replied, refusing to rise to my insinuations. I fled down the stairs but his words followed me.

'If you should change your mind, there will be ducats for the child.'

I was in my rooms before Mamma returned with the pastries. Nonna and Ginevra were still busy in the kitchen so I sat, staring out of the window, trying not to panic. Did the duke know something about Ginevra or was he just goading me? I prayed it was the latter. Surely if they had discovered what the child had done they would have taken her long ago? I would do whatever was necessary to help my friend but let him have the child? No...never.

The longer I sat there staring out at the peaceful rio and the gondolas drifting past, the better I felt. I was worrying unnecessarily. Mamma had told him about the child, that was all. Yes, that was it. I must concentrate on what I had to do to help Pazienza. It was surprising that he just wanted me to perform for him and his friends, it seemed too easy, much too easy, but sitting there in the peace and quiet, I allowed myself to hope. The duke was One of the Ten. His power in the Republic was legendary. He was the man who could save Pazienza.

Mamma left my house on the same day the duke and I made our deal. I kissed her cheek, wished her well and then she was gone. Nonna, the child and I watched from my room as three men in the duke's livery waded through ankle deep water on the towpath − the rio had flooded again in the night. They were loading Mamma's goods onto a barge. When they were finished they carried her and the serving woman into a gondola and then the crafts moved off.

'It is over, Nonna.' I said. 'No one will ever part us again. '

'If it be God's will, 'Nonna murmured and turned her shining face to mine. It was so wonderful to have my Nonna and my house back again.

La Guidecca

Early the next morning I woke with renewed energy. My house was free from Mamma's control and so was I. After a hurried breakfast I ordered my gondola. I was going to see Alfonso. Before I could make any plans for the future, I needed to see how bad things were. I must look to my failing business and visit the farmacia.

I hadn't been outside the house since my baby's death and Nonna threw up her hands in horror 'Out of the question, Veronica. You are not recovered.'

'I am as strong as I will ever be, Nonna, and I have neglected the business for far too long. Poor Alfonso has borne my troubles on his own, it's time I shared his burden.'

She saw my determination and offered to go with me, but we both knew she couldn't leave the child alone, so she entreated me to take a servant. I refused. This was something I had to do on my own.

I travelled to the farmacia, hidden behind the feize in my gondola. I was dressed in my habitual black, my face and hair covered by a veil. As the gondola slipped quietly between the waking houses, the rising sun sent quivers of gold into the water from between the buildings. I smelt orange blossom and heard birds singing. Life. It was spring.

While I journeyed I thought about the shop and what might be done to save it. Alfonso had tried to discuss the business with me before but I had refused to acknowledge there was anything wrong. There was one thing certain, if we were to survive we needed to be able to make new theriac. However, Alfonso could never become a member of the Apothecary Guild and only guild members could make the elixir. If only we could hire a guild member to join Bertrames, but I wasn't sure we had the money to entice someone with the qualifications to join us. I knew Alfonso could do the job but he was a foreigner, a Moor, and although the Republic was a liberal, cosmopolitan society and welcomed strangers to its shores, only Venetians could be Guild members. It was true that the elixir had fallen out of favour since my Carlo's death but there were still people with money, prepared to try anything in extremis. There was Carlo's old chest, full of phials of mature potion and also the secret cache that I held the key for, but if the pestilencia didn't come soon it would all be over for us. Who was it said? 'Be careful what you wish for.'

That morning I arrived before the start of trading, so that I could look at the books before Alfonso and the others arrived. I had Carlo's key to open the shop.

My gondolier walked me to the farmacia and waited outside as I entered. Once inside, I lifted my veil and stared about me. The shop's shelves were empty except for a few dirty, fly-blown phials and old pots of congealed unguents. When Carlo lived I had often visited the shop and been enchanted by the hustle and bustle of the place. Each

246

assistant scurrying around, pursuing his allotted task, everything orderly, customers seated on silk-backed chairs with Carlo or Alfonso seeing to their requests. Servants bringing lemon juice and small sweet cakes. There was a vitality and eagerness in those days but now it was quiet and gloomy. Where had the displays of exquisite skin products and beauty potions for the rich women of Venice gone?

I made my way to Carlo's small back office, where they kept all the files and ledgers. And there at the desk I found Alfonso asleep, a gutted candle placed beside him, surrounded by ledgers, his elbows resting on the open books, his head on his hands. When I put my hand gently on his shoulder he woke with a start and struggled to rise. I pressed him back down and he raised his weary face to mine. 'Signora Bertrame.'

'I should have come before this, Alfonso. Please, forgive me.'

'No need, my Lady.'

I hadn't looked at him properly for such a long time. He had lost weight and he was like some different version of himself. Suddenly, with a shock, I realised that he had a look of his father − his old, frail, father.

'Has something happened, my lady?' he asked, 'Is it Pazienza? Or the child? '

'No. Ginevra is well and there are plans afoot for our friend. Has Giada been allowed to deliver the food and clothes to Pazienza yet?'

He shook his head. 'No, the gaolers take the goods but no one is allowed to see her.'

247

'I have hopes for our friend, Alfonso. But it is too early to think about it yet. Today, I need to talk to.'

Jumping up he sat me in his chair, then he drew up a stool for himself. He fussed with his jacket, trying to make himself presentable, attempting to smooth down his hair. Reaching forward I took his hands in mine.

'Will I call the boy to run and bring fresh bread, my lady?'

I shook my head.

'Or I could make some ...'

'...I don't want anything, except the truth. Alfonso.'

He looked serious, took a deep breath, but then his face crumpled. 'I am so sorry, Signora. I have tried, we have all worked so hard, but....'

'...How much do we owe?'

I could see him trying to work out a kind way of giving me bad news but I shook my head at him. 'The truth, Alfonso. I need the truth.'

He squared his shoulders. 'The Jewes are clamouring for settlement or they will prosecute... The master gave them a bond.'

'A Bond? What bond?'

'He promised them a portion of the new theriac in payment of our loans. He always promises the same but...'

'...But no new elixir this year?'

'They will take you to court if the bond isn't honoured.'

'Can we delay payment?'

He shook his head. 'They say a bond must be paid by its due date or...'

248

'...Show me how much we owe.'

He flicked to the back of the ledger and passed a document to me. It was a large amount but there was enough 'treasure' in Carlo's chest to cover it.

'Come to my house in the morning and I will have the theriac ready for you.'

He gave me a worried glance. 'And your Mamma, is she...?'

'...No, Alfonso. Mamma has moved out. I am in charge of my life once again. '

He smiled. 'You look, forgive me Signora for my presumption, but you look like the young Signorina again.'

I patted my hair. I hadn't looked in a mirror for such a long time. 'You are too kind, Alfonso, but I think I am in need of Bertrame's beauty products, or is it too late to rescue my good looks.?'

He looked away. 'You will always be beautiful, Signora.'

I touched his hand. 'Veronica. Remember? Not Signora. Now is the time to call me by my name.'

'I couldn't. It would be disrespectful, my lady'

'How long have we been friends, Alfonso?'

He nodded shyly. 'I will try.'

'So, 'I said, wanting to put him at his ease again 'back to our beauty products, Alfonso. How do they fare?'

'We have sold the little we had but we need raw materials.' He looked at me, hope flaring in his eyes. 'Signora...Veronica? Can we buy new ingredients?'

I shook my head. 'Unfortunately not, a distant cousin inherits the money. but I still have the farmacia and the theriac and the warehouses. They are full of ingredients. I have seen them. Carlo showed me. He was so proud. We must make new products. You and your workers are skilled at making such potions? Alfonso? Look at me.'

But Alfonso kept his head down. ' The warehouses are empty. '

'What? No...you're mistaken. I've seen them. They are full.'

That was a long time ago.'

'How much is left?'

'As I said, the warehouses are empty.

I got to my feet and leant across the desk, staring down at him. 'But why didn't you tell me, Alfonso? You should have told me.'

'I tried, but you were... I couldn't. You had so much to bear and your Mamma wouldn't let me talk to you.'

'I know, I know, it wasn't your fault.'

'There is nothing left to sell and the men haven't been paid for months. They will be sad to leave your employ – they have worked here all their lives– but they must find work or their families will starve.'

I pulled the veil back over my face and stood up. 'Take me to the warehouses.' I wouldn't believe it until I saw it for myself.

He got to his feet, staggering a little.

I took his hand, steadying him, and we walked together side by side out into the shop.

Several workmen and assistants had gathered at the far end of the room, watching us with worried frowns on their faces. I smiled at them, thanking them for their loyal support and pledging to pay them what they were owed. Then I wished them good luck and a good day.

My waiting gondolier escorted us to the gondola and I bade him wait till I returned. Alfonso handed me down into the craft, slipped off his shoes, then took up the oar. I watched as he skilfully controlled the oarlock and steered us out into the main channel of the canal. He would always be a gondolier.

All along the rio, we passed ferrymen unloading goods onto the towpaths, while shop keepers haggled with early customers. The everyday clamour and energy of the place felt like a slap in the face. and I longed for the rain, the storms.

Alfonso took my arm as he guided me up the stone steps to the first of our huge warehouses. Once inside I stood in the huge echoing, store- room, where the smell of exotic spices and herbs still drifted, like cobwebbed dreams. There was nowhere to hide. Alfonso stood beside me, head bowed.

'Empty,' I whispered, 'empty, empty. Are they all like this?' He was quiet. 'Alfonso? Tell me. Are they all empty?'

When he looked at me his eyes were full of sorrow.

'Nothing left?'

He sighed. 'There's no shame, Signora. You have tried, but it's over.'

'What to do, Alfonso? We are ruined.'

'You must stop trading, my Lady. I'm so sorry. I'm so very sorry.'

Saying goodbye

Alfonso came for the theriac early the next morning and my bond debt to the Jewes was paid in full. At the same time I engaged one of their men to act as an intermediary for me, in the business of selling my assets. My valuable jewellery — except for the pearls, which would be Ginevra's dowry. My fine furniture and furnishings were sold, along with most of my ball gowns. I sold Marietta's portrait and Jacopo's father's priceless wall hangings and, with the accrued monies, I was able to settle my outstanding debts and pay the farmacia workers and servants. The only 'treasure' I kept was my home, the shop on La Guidecca, and my personal cache of theriac.

With the servants gone, Nonna, the child and myself retreated into the house like hermit crabs withdrawing into their shells. In some ways it was like the old campiello days, except there were no free food handouts here. But Ginevra blossomed. She was the happiest I had ever seen her. No longer confined to my and Nonna's rooms she roamed the empty house, dancing and singing from room to room, discovering treasures and secret hidey holes.

On the day I closed the doors of Bertrame's for the last time, Alfonso locked up and handed me the keys.

'Please, Alfonso.' I said. 'I have no money to pay what I owe you. You must take the shop in recompense. Do what you will with it. Sell it or live here and then, one day, perhaps you will open another

253

farmacia and people will come from all over the Republic for Alfonso Ortha's potions.'

At first he refused but I begged him and, at last, he put the keys in his pocket, touching them reverently, as if he were blessing them. 'I will bring my family here. My father and mother lived here once many years ago. You have blessed us.'

My sadness at parting with the farmacia was softened by the knowledge that Alfonso's family would live here. We stood in silence staring at the shop's dirty, spider-webbed windows and murky interiors. Carlo's pride and joy come to this. My gaze travelled upwards to the shuttered windows of the rooms above the shop, where we had lived when we were first married. It was never elegant nor fashionable and it had lacked a woman's touch, but it was where Carlo and I had first loved one another. I stood for a moment engulfed by the memories. Alfonso stood beside me and we both cried and didn't care who saw.

Alfonso swore he would never leave me. 'Please,' he sobbed. 'I have the gondolas still and my father's traghetto here on La Guidecca. We could all live in the farmacia and I will ply my trade as my father did. I could provide for us all. Please, you must let me protect you.'

I took his hand and held it against my lips. 'Ah, Alfonso, my friend. You have many mouths to feed and your father is too old to work. Never fear, I will survive. '

'But, how will you live?'

'I will manage.' I tried to smile. 'Don't forget I am my mother's daughter. But, there is something you can do for me.' I tried to keep my tone light.

'Anything, my Lady.'

'If, for any reason, our little Ginevra ever needed a safe haven, would you be prepared to give her a home?'

I saw his startled look. 'Is she in danger? Has she remembered?'

'No, no, nothing like that. In fact she seems to be more like her old self. There's nothing to worry about at the moment but just in case she should need help. My future plans are...uncertain and she needs a stable life.'

He frowned at me. 'Do you doubt me? Send a message and I will come.'

'Thank you, Alfonso. But this isn't goodbye. You will always be our dearest friend and I hope we will meet each other as before. Ginevra would be so sad not to see you, and I hope you will still play for me, sometimes. Who knows, maybe I could make a living from my dance creations?' This wasn't such a bad idea because Carlo had been paid for performing at functions and, always a generous master, the payment money was distributed between the musicians and dancers. 'In fact,' I said, before Alfonso could interrupt. I had been plucking up the courage to tell him about my promise to the duke. I knew how he would react. 'I have been commissioned by the Duke del Vasallo. He wants us to perform the Sobria, for a special private function he is planning.'

I spoke quickly as though it was of no consequence but Alfonso was no fool and he stared at me as if he couldn't quite believe what I had just said. 'It would not be proper for a widow to dance on her own.'

'He has promised that you will all be paid handsomely.'

'Do you think I care about his money?'

'No but...'

'...And you? Will he pay you?' He couldn't keep the revulsion out of his words.

'Alfonso, please, try to understand. He has promised to help Pazienza. That is all the payment I desire. She will be free. Imagine the child's joy.'

'And you trust this man? The Duke del Vasallo?' He shook his head at me sadly, as if he doubted my sanity.

I tried to take his hand but he pulled away. 'Please, my friend, try to understand why I have to do this. I must help her. Don't you see? I failed her. I always fail the people I love and this is Pazienza's only chance. Say you'll play for me. Please. It's just one little dance.'

He stood there quietly, staring out at the Lagoon, and then, at last, he sighed and nodded. We returned to La Guidecca in silence and Alfonso walked me to where my gondolier waited. As soon as I stepped down into the boat Alfonso turned and walked away. 'Come soon,' I shouted after his retreating back. 'We will need to rehearse.' And he raised his hand to show he had heard me.

If I'm honest the collapse of Bertrame's was no surprise and I determined not to cry on the way home. I had no more tears to waste on futile regrets. There was some small sense of liberation in the knowledge that things were as bad as they could get. When there's no further to fall, the possibilities of rising again are boundless.

After tying up on our slipway my gondolier and I talked for a few moments. He had agreed to take my gondola as payment for his owed wages and we parted on good terms. I was sad to see him go. He had been my boatman since I was sixteen and he had always worked for the Bertrames.

He doffed his cap and wished me well before he pushed off and glided out onto the glittering rio. I watched as the craft went under the bridge and disappeared into the heat haze that hung on the Big Canal. I felt chilled to the bone.

One little dance

Within a few days of my meeting with the duke, Mamma delivered my contract for the performance. There were also monies for the hire of musicians and dancers. Mamma couldn't look me in the eye as she handed the document over, so I knew she'd read it.

My stomach knotted as I read what was expected of me. I had known what he wanted and I was prepared for it, but to see it written down made it horribly real. But I had to make myself believe that his demands were worthwhile. Nothing mattered but that my friend's sufferings would cease. I didn't tell Nonna the truth. A far as she knew I was just performing at one of the nobili's functions.

By then Alfonso had moved his family into the farmacia and was very busy working the traghetto. I didn't tell him what the duke expected of me. I couldn't.. I was frightened he might do something terrible.

When the six young male dancers and Alfonso and his musicians began rehearsals in my house, Ginevra begged that she might come and watch us. I agreed although Nonna tut-tutted when she heard we were dancing the Sobria. She insisted on accompanying the child and sat on the most uncomfortable, straight-backed chair I possessed, hands folded in her lap, watching disapprovingly. My dancers made a huge fuss of her and it wasn't long before her little, lined face was flushed and wreathed in smiles. We tempered our Sobria when the child was present and sometimes she danced some of the steps with me. I see her mother so clearly when the child dances.

Before the night of my performance, the duke sent me a gown to wear. It was a shimmering red satin dress, tight-fitting with a décolletage that plunged to my navel. He knew I only wore black but he had made it clear I had to obey all his stipulations before he would help Pazienza. There was no lace modesty insert in the gown's neckline and Nonna took one scandalised look, then ran from the room her head in her hands. She returned with her sewing box and made an insert for me. I took it to pacify her but I knew I wouldn't wear it.

On the night of the performance the duke sent his most elaborate gondola to carry me to his palazzo. Nonna was dressed to accompany me but the gondolier's orders were to carry me alone. I watched her stricken face receding as the gondola moved swiftly away towards the Big Canal. There was no feize to hide behind and I was told to sit in the centre of the craft, in full view of any passerby.

On arrival I was led straight to a small intimate space, lit by candles and heady with the smell of incense. Alfonso and his musicians were already playing when I entered the room. I had not eaten and felt slightly sick and dizzy. My dancers waited for me and my partner came to me and took my hand. I was trembling so much he squeezed it and smiled kindly at me. I took a deep breath as we waited for our music to begin and I dared to look about the room.

259

There were six men seated on low silken chairs, surrounding the ballo. They lounged with their jackets off and shirts unbuttoned. Each man was attended by half-naked whores. Servants ran between the men refilling glasses. When my partner led me to the ballo, the men jeered and shouted obscenities at me. I had never experienced anything so ill-bred and coarse, outside of the Rialto. There was no etiquette here, no code of behaviour. It took more courage than I thought I possessed to remain standing there, when all I wanted to do was run. My legs were shaking so much I thought I might collapse.

And that's when I saw the duke. He was seated in the centre of the circle of chairs, lazily examining me from head to foot. When he was satisfied he raised his glass and saluted me. His companions were very drunk and the air was charged with danger. Even my dancers were apprehensive but I spoke to them, giving them the courage I didn't feel myself.

The musicians were seated behind the men and I saw Alfonso. I tried to catch his eye but, when he saw me, he turned his head away and struck the beginning chords of the Sobria. 'Just one dance,' I kept repeating to myself, 'Just one little dance. Then my Pazienza will be safe.'

'Now', I whisper to my dancers and I lead the way slowly and languorously through the assembled men to the centre of the floor. I murmur in one man's ear, and tap my fan on the fingers of another, who reaches out to touch me. I have promised that this will be the best dance of my life and I will fulfil my part of the bargain. My lips are parted invitingly but my nails drip blood. There is no fear left in me,

260

just shards of anger, like stilettos, sharp enough to pierce any flesh. My 'suitors' surround me, while the one I 'love' stands at the perimeter of the floor, waiting to claim me.

As my suitors approach me one by one and I rebuff them, the nobili shout encouragement. My dress's heavy train swings provocatively about my hips and I turn and twist. My hair coils around my face and the pearl necklace hangs about my throat. Women like us are allowed to wear pearls. Mamma has taught me well, and, at last, I have learnt my place.

The dance begins. This is the same Sobria I danced with my Carlo but this travesty of a performance bears no resemblance to the dance of pure love and desire that I and my love performed. This is bestial, obscene.

My movements are immodest but I perform them automatically. I have closed down my mind. This is not me or my body, this is the dance and I am merely the follower. 'Modestia'. Is that my Nonna's voice in my ear? But it is too late for that, far too late.

I keep my eyes on the boy. He plays, head bent, determined not to see me. His mouth is clenched in a tight line of concentration, selecting each new chord as if it pained him. He glances up and our eyes lock for a moment but there is nothing there. He is a stranger. Just one dance. Just one little dance.

But I delude myself. It was never going to be just one dance was it? And when it is over and the duke walks slowly towards me, to claim me, I know the pretence is over. He stops in front of me and smiles, then he puts a hand out and twitches the dress off my shoulders with one finger. I am naked.

He is the first, taking me there on the floor of the ballo, my face pressed into the hard wood floor, my screams muffled by his shout of triumph. Once I think I hear Alfonso's voice, calling my name, but then I push it all away, until there is nothing, apart from my fear and humiliation and the men's hands and bodies on me.

I will not speak of it. It is nailed in a box in the back of my head. I will never open it. So don't ask me. Never ask me. I wanted so much to believe it had been worth it. All of it. I had to believe that or I would go mad.

'Look for her near your dwelling, Veronica,' he said at last, tossing me the dress and a thick red shawl to cover my nakedness. 'That's where you'll find her, your friend, the wretched whore.'

'And you've kept your word?' I whisper, not looking at him. 'She's safe?'

'There will be no public execution. I am a nobili and we always keep our word. Now go. Oh, and next time, Veronica, be sure to bring the child.'

The same gondolier was waiting for me but I stumbled past him, ignoring his entreaties to carry me home. I ran through the dark streets, not caring that my chest burned with exhaustion and my bare feet were bruised and cut. No one tried to stop me, even the feral dogs fled from my bloody path, sensing my rage. On reaching my house I tore off the dress and hurled it into the rio.

262

Once in my room I shivered in a basin of water by my washstand, whilst I sponged myself with water, then I wrapped myself in a blanket and sat by the window to wait. It was a dark night, no stars or moon. As I waited there my arms and legs jerked spasmodically from the cold. It felt as if I had ice running through my veins. I would not sleep that night, I might never close my eyes again, because I dreaded the images that might rise. Would I ever be able to forget?

I had to believe that Pazienza would be free. *'Look for her near your dwelling.'* That's what he'd said and I had to believe she would come. That was the only thought in my head.

It was that dead first light, that heralds the dawn, when I heard voices below. Peering down I saw a group of figures, grey in the early light, huddled beside the rio. They were the sewage workers who patrolled the rii at night, mending stonework and unblocking outlets. One of them was pointing at something in the water. Two men stood further down the bank with grappling hooks.

I dressed quickly in my street clothes and pulled a black cloak around my shoulders and head to hide my face. Then I slipped out of the house and joined the people watching the men struggling to drag something out of the water. At first it looked like a mass of black twisted ropes and jetsam, maybe thrown overboard from some ship. The tides brought many such things into the rii. One man knelt and unravelled some of the ropes that were tied around the bundle, then they took a side each and attempted to heave the whole thing up onto the bank. They struggled with the weight of it and some of the

263

workmen went to help. At last they managed to pull it out of the water and a woman in front of me took one look and shrieked.

Pushing my way to the front of the crowd I saw what she had seen. It was a body– a woman's thin emaciated body – the arms and legs no thicker than a child's. They were shackled together and the chains attached to a huge slab of rock. The men turned the body over and I saw a face staring up at me. It was pale, lifeless, colourless, except for a vivid purple scar running across the sunken cheeks.

There was no time to weep. I ran into my house and up to Nonna's room, where I found her sleeping. The child lay curled close against her, thumb in her mouth, doll in her arms. I woke Nonna carefully, trying to keep the horror out of my voice and not to disturb the child, and I told her to get dressed, collect Ginevra's belongings, and take her down the metal stairs, directly into the back courtyard at the rear of my house. I placed money on her table. 'Catch the ferry to Guidecca and take the child to Alfonso, and hurry.' I urged, as Nonna struggled out of bed, still dazed with sleep. 'Stay with the child until you hear from me. Nonna? Do you understand? She mustn't come back here until I let you know.' She nodded, hearing the panic in my voice, and set about fulfilling my orders, her eyes wide with shock but she didn't ask any questions and kissed me softly. I closed the door as she gently roused the child.

I will kill the loathsome man. I could slice out his black heart but I want him to suffer like my poor friend has suffered and I will find a way. I promise you my friend, you will be avenged.

264

Delirium

I am set adrift in a moiling, boiling sea of violent colour and putrid richness. Upturned boxes and caskets, spew their obscene contents on the Persian carpets, like jewelled bird-shit. I am like some wrecked ship's waterlogged spar, rolling on the seabed, lurching in time to the vagaries of the current, whilst necklaces, earrings, golden combs, ornate ivory fans and lace mantillas, shoal past.

Books lie on the seabed, pages turning in the currents, for fish and drowned sailors to read. I had been searching for a book. Was it only yesterday? The book is bound in the finest red Moroccan leather and suddenly it is in my hand. I clutch it to me. My clammy fingers stick to the leather, like limpets to their mark. 'Amore per La Danza' by Veronica Bertrame. I trace the gold lettering with a trembling finger. This is my first, my only, published work. This slim volume contains everything that is Veronica Bertrame. I will take it with me to the Island —that and the pearl necklace —the pearls my mother gave me, for women like us. It is not for sentiment but for its value.

Who's there? Hiding in the shadows? Come out, show yourself. You can't frighten me. Silence. My eyes focus on the empty room. I have begun to see things that aren't there. It is delirium, I knew it would come. The dreadful stages of the pestilencia, each one written down, each new symptom worse than the last.

The room spirals about me. I try not to move my eyes. The violence of this attack has left me helpless but I must be patient and wait for it to pass. It always passes.

How many days have I lain here? The bells of San Marco have tolled three times for Sunday matins, but they say ten days is the limit for survival of the pestilencia. Why am I still breathing? Is God prolonging my agony to punish me for my apostasy? The nausea is passing but my head is pounding and my bones ache. The slightest movement sends the pain shooting through my body. Why is the sun so bright? It must be spring somewhere, only not here, not in this death chamber. I hate the sun and the new growth. Send the black night, winter's winds and rain and let the foul waters swallow Venice and all its vanities.

An honourable occupation

I managed to secure a plot for Pazienza in an ancient, overgrown churchyard on the outskirts of San Polo. Executed criminals were usually thrown in the pits but I bribed an official in order to claim the body. I paid two grave diggers and watched as they unshackled her hands and feet. My poor ruined friend. I covered her in a white shroud and then they laid her in a coffin.

Giada and some other women came for her funeral and Alfonso brought the child. He had not spoken to me since the night of the Sobria and even at the graveside, he stood apart, not looking at me. We watched in silence as the two men lifted the small coffin into the hole. There was an adult woman in that coffin but it was so small. Such a little death.

The disused graveyard was no longer consecrated ground so there was no priest but Nonna knew every prayer in the missal and spoke for our friend. I was glad the child would have somewhere to come and visit her mamma. Throughout the ceremony Ginevra knelt, staring down at the grave. She was white faced and silent, clutching her sprig of blossom. I hope she had a box to nail her grief in.

After Nonna's prayers for the dead, Ginevra stood and slowly circled the grave in a solemn dance. As she moved, she plucked the sweetly smelling petals from the blossom, and cast them high into the air, so that they fluttered down onto her Mamma's coffin. 'I love you,' she said. 'I love you, Mamma.' She didn't cry, but we did. We hadn't allowed the child to see her Mamma before the coffin was closed but I saw her, and I don't think I'll ever be able to forget it.

Afterwards I said some words to Giada and the others and then Alfonso and Nonna took the child back to his family on the Guidecca. He and I parted without a word. Ginevra clung to me and I told her I would see her soon.

'Veronica?' she asked, before leaving. 'Do you think Mamma saw my dance?'

I nodded, not trusting myself to speak and kissing her head.

The child smiled. 'Shall I call it Mamma's petal dance, Veronica? Would that be proper?'

I missed Ginevra so much but she seemed happy enough with Alfonso's family and I was just glad she was safe. Nonna went as often as she could but I knew I wasn't welcome and besides I had begun to think I was being followed. I still feared for the child's safety. I never told Nonna what had happened on the night of the Sobria and she never asked, but she seemed to understand why I didn't visit the island with her.

The little money I had left went on Pazienza's funeral, so now there was nothing to sell, except the house, my cache of theriac and myself.

268

I would not sell my house and the theriac was useless, so, I became a courtesan. It was a simple choice. What else was there to do? We had to live, I must keep helping my sisters and then there was Ginevra's future.

After my Carlo's death I vowed I would never bed another man, but my circumstances had changed, and you know what my vows are worth. When I was Veronica Bertrame, wife to Carlo Bertrame, famous apothecary, I could ignore the advances of princes and politicians and laugh at the foolish, ugly men behind their backs. However, now I had to reconsider.

I had survived the duke, I reasoned, so I could survive anything or anyone, however vile. I knew that men lusted after me. I was beautiful and famed for my wit and intellect. I wrote poetry and danced and I could be charming, when it pleased me.

When I told Nonna my decision she sighed and patted my hand, as if it were inevitable. Her eyes were bright with love for me. I think, in her mind, being a courtesan was an honourable occupation. I had problems seeing how this fitted into her religious views on morality, but she had grown up with my Mamma and had first-hand experience of much worse things than being a courtesan.

I surprised myself by asking Mamma if she would be my go-between – I hated the word procuress. She was surprised too but didn't gloat when I told her. In fact she seemed pleased that I had chosen her to act on my behalf, and listened patiently to all my conditions. I would pay her a fee, of course.

The only thing she wasn't pleased about was when I told her I would never take the Duke del Vasallo as a lover. I would rather sleep with a dog.

'But he's...he's an old friend. Veronica. He cares for me still, and for you.'

That made me laugh. 'Oh, mother, you may have been very beautiful and clever but you are a very bad liar.'

She pretended to be offended.

'I'm only going to say this once more, Mamma, I will never, ever, sleep with that odious creature. And if you don't like it you can leave now.'.'

'I know you had an...unpleasant experience, Veronica, but you brought it on yourself. The nobili don't like to be made fools of.'

'Maybe I could forget what he did to me, but he wanted me to bring an eight year old child for his pleasure.'

'Well? I wasn't that much older than the whore's brat, when I was first bedded.'

'And you think that makes it right?'

'This is the real world, Veronica. Not one of your stories in a book'.

'But it's wrong and I swear I'll protect that child with my life, like her mamma did, her brave beautiful Pazienza.'

Mamma huffed and puffed but she listened to the rest of my plans without interrupting. I would decide who I took as lovers but she could deal with the arrangements. After all, she had connections with all the nobili and patriciates. She would keep an appointment's book for me and act between myself and whatever man I favoured, fixing the price, the terms of entitlement, where and when we met, the social standing of my patron, and finally draw up a legal settlement for the end of a liaison. I insisted that I visit my patrons where they chose, but they would never enter my Carlo's house.

It wasn't long before Mamma had arranged my first meeting with a middle-aged nobili, whom I had met on several occasions. I knew he liked to dance, so at least I would have some entertainment while I earned a living. 'I felt surprisingly calm about everything except one thing, how would I tell Alfonso? Stupidly, I mentioned this to Mamma and she raised an elegant eyebrow at me. 'Why concern yourself with the boy, Veronica?'

'His name's Alfonso,' I replied, immediately annoyed.

'Whatever his name is, is immaterial. He is a blackamoor, a gondolier. Yes, he has shapely calves but he's a servant, a nobody.'

'He's my friend, Mamma. My very dear friend, and without him I would not have survived.'

'Everything is such a drama with you, Veronica. This boy is unimportant. Forget him. Your life is about to change into something magnificent and you don't need such people about you. Which reminds me, you need to employ a Lady's maid, more suited to your new position in society.'

'No, Mamma. I am not getting rid of Nonna, ever, neither am I going to turn my back on a dear friend. And,' I said, holding my hand up to stop her arguing with me. 'I will not discuss this again. Now, I must leave, I am late for my dressmaker.'

271

Soon after this, Nonna informed me that Alfonso was coming to collect some more of Ginevra's things. Nonna couldn't carry heavy bags any more.

I knew he didn't want to see me but I had to talk to him, so I waited until I heard him going up to Nonna's room. When I entered, a few minutes later, he was on the floor with his back to me, packing clothes into a pannier. Hearing me he turned smiling, expecting Nonna. When he saw me he jumped to his feet. I hadn't seen him properly at the funeral but now I did. There was a dark purple bruise down one side of his face that pooled inside his eye socket.

'You're hurt, Alfonso?' I stammered, holding my hand out, as if to touch him, but he took a step away from me. 'How did it happen? Were you brawling?' I meant it as a joke but he ignored me and got down on his knees again, hurriedly gathering up the rest of Ginevra's things and stuffing them into the bag.

I had carefully planned what I would say but now I was flustered and it came out all wrong. 'Do you need more money for Ginevra's lodging? Because if so, I shall soon be earning enough to pay you regularly. I don't want you to be out of pocket, Alfonso. I will have the means.'

That's when he looked me full in the face. 'The means?' He repeated. 'You will have the means? How so, my Lady?'

If I didn't speak now I never would have the courage, so, I drew a deep breath and I told him my plans. I held nothing back. He watched me as I spoke and I saw his grief.

272

When I was finished he dropped to his knees before me, swearing he could make enough money for us all, but I couldn't let him sacrifice his life for me. He had old parents, young brothers, a little sister and now Ginevra. He was already hollow-eyed and exhausted from his work, and if I am honest, a gondolier and lute player would never have enough money for me to live the life I wanted, as well as helping my sisters on the Rialto.

'You are so kind, Alfonso, but I cannot accept your offers. 'Please, I don't want to offend you.'

He got to his feet and stared at me. 'Offend me, my Lady? You don't want to offend me? You made me stand by and watch what they did to you and you don't want to offend me?' Each time he said 'offend', he smashed his fist against the door. His knuckles bled.

I took his hand and wiped the blood away. 'They beat you? That night? You tried to...save me?'

'But I couldn't. I couldn't. They threw me out like a beggar at the door.'

'I'm so sorry, Alfonso.'

'And it was all for nothing.'

'No, not for nothing.' I wouldn't believe that. 'She must have drowned quickly, and they didn't cut off her hand and...and we have her grave. Ginevra has her Mamma's grave.'

I knew he would never accept my decision but I didn't want to be diminished in his eyes. His good opinion of me was a treasure I hoarded and I couldn't bear to lose it, so what was left for me but to go on the attack?.

'You don't understand,' I accused. 'Women have to manage in any way they can or they will be ground under men's feet.' He was a man, I continued, so didn't know what it was like to be a woman, to be used and abused by men and then tossed aside like dirty trash.' I had worked myself up into a frenzy by then but he just stood there watching me, as if he were memorising every detail of my face. His passivity enraged me.

'How would you like to be treated like dog shit on some man's shoe?' I roared.

He stared at me long and hard and then he took my hands and pressed them against his face. I tried to pull away but he held me fast.

'Tell me. What do you feel, Signora?'

' Let me go, Alfonso.'

'Answer me.'

I didn't like the anger in his voice. I was the only one allowed to be angry. 'I feel...you, Alfonso, your skin. Now stop this or I shall call Nonna..'

'And does my skin feel like yours? Signora?'

'What is this nonsense?'

'Simple question, my Lady. Is my skin like yours.'

'Of course.'

He let my hand go and stood before me, shoulders slumped , eyes dead. He was saying something very softly and I had to lean closer to hear the words.

'There are worse things than being a woman, my lady. Being me is worse....'

'...What?'

I saw the tears wet on his cheeks.

'I am a worthless blackamoor, Signora, a worthless, lazy, dirty, blackamoor.'

'That's not so'.

'It must be so, my Lady, because I hear it a hundred times a day, and worse, much worse. But whatever they do to me, my Lady, I would never sell myself to them.'

I started to protest, to tell him he was wonderful, my best friend, my only friend and he wasn't worthless he was precious. I attempted to hold him but he opened the door and stood there for a moment, looking back at me. 'You must do as you see fit, my Lady. I will always be your... boy. If you need me, send a message. And as for the child, I will guard her with my life.' And then he walked away from me and out of my life.

Four years on

There is good news on the Rialto. Giada and some of the women have started a small business as dressmakers. Giada is a skilled seamstress. and their reputation grows. I am so pleased for them.

Ginevra will be almost thirteen now— a young woman. She is still living with Alfonso and his family. I pay for tutors for her and Alfonso's sister, Sofia. I would have her live with us but the life of a courtesan means I am rarely in my house in the evenings and get to bed very late, then sleep most of the day. It would be lonely for a young girl without the company of a family.

I have lost some of my fear for Ginevra's safety and I travel to La Guidecca when I am able. Nonna visits her daily. Alfonso avoids me on the days I see the child. 'He is working,' the family say to excuse his absence, ashamed to lie to me. But I smile and we talk pleasantly about the business and how Alfonso has built up the traghetto once more. His younger brother is learning the trade now.

As far as I know Ginevra has never talked about that terrible night when she killed Pazienza's man on the Rialto. Maybe she never will. I hope it's locked away somewhere and will never find its way out. Sometimes I ask her questions about past events, like when she danced in the church procession, or when she wore the cat's mask during the Carnivale, but she wrinkles her nose at me, thinking hard, then shakes her head.

But she does remember Pazienza. She and Nonna talk constantly about her and on the anniversary of Pazienza's death, Nonna, Ginevra and I visit her grave in San Polo. Ginevra takes two sprigs of blossom, one for Pazienza and one for that other Ginevra, who lies nearby in the pauper's pit. I have told her that she was at her mother's funeral too and that she was called Ginevra as well, and she and I were best friends.

Ginevra loves me to tell her about her mother's childhood and the campiello where we grew up. 'You used to dance together, Veronica.' she said, one day. 'Nonna told me. And Alfonso played a whistle. And you used to do the Sun and Moon Dance? I am so lucky. I have two mamma's. How many have you got, Veronica?'

'Just the one,' I say, without even thinking. 'Nonna.'

'She' s my Nonna too, isn't she?'

I nod and she smiles and says. 'You can share one of my mamma's if you like?'

I can hardly credit that I have been a courtesan for four years. Some of my patrons have become friends, one or two, my enemies, and there was a nobili I almost loved. I choose not to have long liaisons. Life is not sweet, but, for a street urchin from the campiello, it is better than most. I no longer roam the streets at night. I have the status of a courtesan to uphold. I still write poetry for my lovers' amusement and secretly create dances to include in my book, but the days are long. I wished for some excitement in my life. I could see my life creeping slowly onwards, until my looks fade and I am pensioned off. I have enough money for Ginevra's dowry and there is the pearly necklace. Maybe there is a Carlo for her somewhere. One day I hope she can come home to me and Nonna and Alfonso and I might be friends once more.

I still dance but have never danced the Sobria again, even though my patrons implore me. When I was young, Ginevra and I had danced for the sheer joy of being alive but now I dance for someone else's pleasure. But thank God there are still times when the dance takes me and I move without thinking, to the music of my soul.

Each time I attend balls and functions with my patrons, there is still a tiny flame of hope that I might see Alfonso and his musicians, but he is never there. When I return home to Nonna, she sees my disappointment and comforts me. She says Alfonso has to work long hours at the traghetto. But I know the truth. He will always hate me.

I miss my childhood days. There was a freedom there that I don't have now. Back then I had envied Mamma her beautiful clothes and exciting life but now I know the truth. Mamma was right, we have to obey the rules. There were still rules on the streets of course, rules of self-preservation, but then I was free to be myself.

The Duke del Vasallo continues to be a thorn in my flesh. He propositions me continually, sending Mamma to plead his case, but I always refuse him. There is some satisfaction in spurning him but how can he think I could ever become his lover after what he did to my friend? What he did to me has hardened me At least I am in a position to rebuff him and I relish ignoring his messages and destroying his gifts.

I had wanted to kill him, and I still might, but I get some malicious gratification from goading him, whenever the opportunity arises. At the last ball I attended with my current patron, the Duke D'Agnio − a jolly man with a mighty sense of humour −, the Duke del Vasallo had the audacity to approach me for a dance. This was totally forbidden in all polite society. I was contracted to the Duke D'Agnio. The Duke del Vasallo came and stood before me, offering me his hand, so I merely turned my back on him, leaving him standing there, with everyone watching. My duke thought it highly amusing and laughed outright, but Vasallo was enraged. All the assembly saw his humiliation. He left shortly afterwards, with Anna trailing after him, her eyes slicing through me like a knife.

The Pestilencia

Life might have gone on like this but for a new outbreak of the pestilencia. There were reported deaths in Cannaregio and San Michele, tales of strange clouds and witches' covens and plagues of flies. That's when I remembered Carlo's 'treasure.'

I found the hidden key and Nonna and I went in search of the small chest in the cellar. The floor was awash with filthy rio water but I tied a kerchief to my nose and held my breath as I dragged the chest up onto a steps. The lock was rusted and wouldn't open. Nonna fetched a hammer and I shattered the lock. Inside there was row upon row of blue lapis lazuli bottles, covered in dust and dead flies. Nonna and I carried them carefully upstairs, cleaned and polished the bottles and then counted them, one by one. There was enough for us all, as well as for Giada and my friends on the Rialto. The remainder could be sold. I blessed my Carlo. He still watched over us still.

I sent a servant with theriac to La Guidecca and the Rialto. Nonna wanted to take the elixir to Alfonso and Ginevra herself but I kept her at home. There was all sorts of mischief abroad and the Inquisition were on the prowl. The pestilencia had not reached La Guidecca yet, so I sent a messenger to Alfonso, warning him to stay away from San Marco. I didn't expect an answer from him, but I knew he would look after our girl.

Word spread of my theriac and I was petitioned by the nobili and patriciates, who offered me huge amounts of money for a bottle of the same elixir, they had once reviled as 'that filth.' I enjoyed turning down some of their requests–Anna del Vasallo for one. She demanded some of the theriac for the Duke, who was ailing. How much pleasure it gave me to turn her away empty-handed. I pray that Pazienza will be avenged.

For a short time it seemed as though my future was secure but I should have known that trouble was never far from me. As with any epidemic of the pestilencia the Church and the authorities sought someone or something to blame. Witches, shroud-eaters, foreigners, Jewes, whores and courtesans, all came under suspicion, and it wasn't long before the rumours began. They said I was a witch and had put a death spell on my husband in order to get control of the theriac. I was sure Anna del Vasall0 was behind these ridiculous lies and laughed them off but she was not a woman to make an enemy of. I should have befriended her as Mamma had. I had made her husband look a fool in public and refused him the theriac. She would never forgive me. However, fortunately for me. my latest duke intervened before I was questioned by the Inquisition.

But she didn't give up that easily. I don't know how she found out, but she discovered I was a Dance Master. Surely my dear Alfonso, would never have betrayed me? To be a female Dance Master was a crime against Our Most Illustrious Republic and Holy Mother Church. It was a sin against men and the power of men. No woman was fit to be a Dance Master.

281

The woman's spies were everywhere, gathering information, spreading their lies. There were 'witnesses' who would swear that I had used my magical powers to entrap the husbands of noble women. It was well known that I wrote poetry and that I championed the destitute women who plied their trade on the Rialto. And now the whole of Venice knew that I was the creator of lewd and ungodly dances that they had all been enjoying, so recently. In other words I was a dangerous woman, and dangerous women have to be silenced.

Nonna and I tried not be frightened but we tip-toed around one another, avoiding each other's eyes and not speaking of it. But despite all of this, or maybe because of it, Nonna still insisted on going to the market each morning. I begged her to send the maid but Nonna insisted that she got better bargains than the silly child. She loved to haggle with the street vendors but she wasn't well and I worried that she was infected. The disease spread quickly in those busy streets, especially amongst the old and frail. I wanted her to take the theriac but she distrusted any potions not of her own making. She looked at me and patted my face. 'There is a time for all of us, Veronica. Maybe it is my time. I am not afraid.'

But there were worse things than the pestilencia. One morning Nonna had gone to the market as usual, but she hadn't been long gone when I heard her outside our door coughing – she always coughed when she hurried. I ran to the door. 'Nonna...' I began, taking her basket from her and meaning to scold her, but then I saw her face. Her skin was white and her eyes stared out at me, as if she'd seen a ghost. She caught hold

282

of my hands, trying to speak, but she couldn't catch her breath. I thought she was going to faint and I caught her in my arms and we sat down together on the doorstep. She pushed me away. 'Run, Veronica,' she gasped, 'You must run...'

'...Shh, shh.. Take a deep breath. Has someone frightened you?'

'No,' she moaned, trying to stand . 'No, it's you. You must leave, now.'

'But why? '

'They're all talking about you. All of them. They know...'

'...Know? What do they know?' I asked, smiling, trying to keep the panic out of my voice.

'You are accused of witchcraft, my Veronica. There's a poster in the market square signed by the Duke del Vasallo and others of The Ten. I saw it. Everyone saw it. They say you roam the streets at night with a cat. You join in ungodly practices. That you have used your powers to harm your enemies. That you create lewd and lascivious dances, that you consort with the devil... You must run, I will help you pack a bag. Please, Veronica. Hurry.'

'Be calm Nonna,' I soothed. 'This is nothing but Anna Vasallo's vicious tongue. None of these charges are true and I have powerful friends who will speak up for me. I promise, it will all blow over.'

I fetched her some water and sat with her while she drank, then I helped her to my room, where she lay on my bed and fell into a fractious sleep.

As I sat beside her, listening to her laboured breathing, I allowed myself the time to prepare for what might lie ahead. With

283

such powerful enemies the likelihood was that I would be taken by the Inquisition. Since my Carlo's death I had no fear of dying, what frightened me was the manner of my death and I couldn't forget the terror on Pazienza's poor ravaged face. She had escaped the public execution but I had seen her, when they had dragged her from the rio. I had watched as they removed the shackles from her poor wasted arms and legs. I had closed her wide terrified eyes and seen to it that she had a dignified burial, but I will never, never forget the look on her face. What horror she must have felt when they threw her in that filthy water. Did she try to hold her breath, or frantically pull at her chains? Was she thinking of her Ginevra? How long did it take?

When I used to roam the streets at night I had felt Death's fetid breath on my neck. I knew that one night I might feel his hand on my shoulder, then I would turn and meet him face to face.

The day they came for me I woke to the sound of splintering wood. Running to the casement I saw four burly men hacking down my street door. They wore the papal insignia. The Inquisition. 'Nonna,' I screamed, 'don't go down.'

She appeared at my side and we clung to each other. The men were inside now and crashing up the stairs. 'Be brave,' Nonna whispered. 'They will not dare to harm you.'

As the men entered my bedroom Nonna pushed me behind her, shielding me from them, but one of them grabbed her by the hair and hurled her onto the floor. They kicked her viciously and she cried out in pain. I leapt at them, scratching and punching but one of them

284

struck me hard and I fell backwards, half dazed. I must have blacked out for a moment because when my eyes opened they were shackling Nonna's legs. 'No,' I shouted, struggling to my feet. 'You've made a mistake. It's me you want. Not her. Leave her alone.'

The man who'd struck me laughed and pushed me away. 'The Inquisition doesn't make mistakes. Now, shut your mouth, or we'll take you too, for protecting this filth.'

'But what's the charge? She's never done anything wrong.'

'The witch finders disagree.'

'Witch? Nonna a witch? Never. You'll be cursed if you hurt her. She fasts three days a week, she attends Mass every morning, no food or water crosses her mouth until the sun sets on Holy Days. Leave her be.' But they ignored me. 'Show me the order.' I demanded, trying to keep my voice steady. 'You have no right. I demand that you show me the order. My patrons will punish you.'

The leader laughed and spat on the floor. 'What? Them? They don't care about the likes of you. Your friends are clearing off, like all the cowards. But we're not going anywhere. The Holy Office of the Inquisition remains and we do its bidding, faithfully and diligently.'

I begged and begged them to leave Nonna with me. 'She's an old woman and has the pestilencia. See? She has the marks. Look, on her face. You will be infected if you touch her.'

'No matter. She'll burn whatever ails her.'

I offered them the money I had.

'Bribing the officers of the Inquisition is a capital offence, whore,' they said, stuffing their pockets with anything they could find.

Nonna cried out to me. 'I go willingly, my Veronica. My time is over and the good Lord waits for me. I am in His hands. Tell the child her Nonna loves her.'

Then they dragged her to the stairs. I tried to stop them but they thrust me back into the room.

'I will come for you, Nonna, I promise.' I shouted after her.

And then she was gone. The last man bent down before he followed the others and tore the top of my night gown, exposing my breasts. He leered at me as he touched me. 'Never fear, whore, we'll be back for you soon enough. Maybe have some fun, eh? We couldn't afford you before, but now...we can do anything we want.'

When I was alone I fell on my knees. 'Please, please, save her. Spare her the torture and let her die quickly, before they take her to the pyre.' I prayed over and over again but I knew it was hopeless. God wouldn't listen to me. Why should He?

I had begged Him in just the same way to save my Carlo. I promised that if He spared him I would make pilgrimages to the Holy Land and crawl on my knees to the Holy Sepulchre, but Carlo died anyway, in terrible agony. Then I bargained with God, when my little baby was born, that if she lived I would never dance again and cloister myself away in a nunnery with my child. But my little darling was taken too, and on that day I vowed I would never believe in God again.

I'm impatient for the Inquisition's return. They know I am here and can choose their moment. They think it frightens me, but I don't care. I want to share my precious gift with them. They would all die, just like me. But they would be so disappointed with God. After all,

286

they are doing God's will, aren't they? The pestilencia is not a nice way to reward your keenest supporters is it? Let them come.

Safe Passage

The same day they took Nonna, Mamma sent word for me to prepare to leave Venice. Her new lover had offered us safe passage, but we had to be ready to leave the next day.

When she burst into my rooms, early the next morning, she was horrified to find me still in bed. She pulled my bed covers back and shook me hard. 'What are you doing? Get up!. We have to leave. '

I turned over and closed my eyes. 'Leave me be, Mamma. I'm not coming.'

She pulled at my arm. 'Do you want to die?'

I shook her off. 'I don't care what happens to me. '

'Is this about that old woman? There's nothing you can do for her now. My informants say she's dead already.'

I sat up and stared at her. 'I don't believe you. She's innocent. They will send her home to me and I will be here, waiting for her.'

'She's guilty.'

'Of what? She gives alms, she fasts, she attends the Mass every day , she's never hurt anyone in her entire life. She's a saint.'

Mamma had found a bag and was throwing my things into it. 'There are witnesses.'

'Witnesses?'

'To her magic.'

I jumped from the bed and grasped her arms tightly, pinning them to her sides. She struggled to get free but I held her fast. 'Tell me what you mean.'

'Let me go, Veronica, you're hurting me.'

She couldn't look me in the eyes and in that moment I knew what she had done. 'No, Mamma. Please, no...'

'...They wanted to take someone connected to us, Veronica – anyone would do, so...'

'...You...you gave her to them?'

'She's old. Her life is over...'

'...You let those fiends take my Nonna? You gave her to the Inquisition? '

'...There was no choice, Veronica, it was you or her. Now, we must leave. My man will carry down your luggage. Hurry. My lord is impatient to be gone. The militia are closing all the bridges and water-ways to Terra ferma. The whole of Venice will soon be quarantined.'

'I'm staying here, Mamma.'

'But you'll die.'

I shrugged. 'You want me to run away to safety while my Nonna lies in chains in The Doge's dungeons?'

'There's no time for this, Veronica. Come. I have begged and coerced so many people to get you out of Venice. You have many enemies. We have to pray the old woman doesn't tell them about your night walks and your dances...your stupid, stupid dances.'

'Too late...much, much too late, Mamma. Goodbye.'

She stared at me. 'You stubborn little fool. What's that ugly, bent old woman to you? Did she carry you in her womb, or pay for your education, or make you into a Lady? She's nothing. Her father sold her to me for a bottle of cognac."

'She's the only mother I've ever known and I love her.'

' Love?' She curled her lip, as though the word was something dirty in her mouth. 'Anyone can love, Veronica, anyone. It's easy to love but it takes a special sort of courage to survive. Where would you be without me? Could that old woman have saved you from the Inquisition?'

'But she did, didn't she Mamma? She gave her life willingly for me. You sent her to her death to save me? Why? It wasn't for me, Mamma. None of this was for me.'

She smoothed down her beautiful fur-trimmed gown and turned towards the door. 'Please, Veronica,' she touched my arm gently. 'Come with me.'

'What's the matter. Frightened of losing your milch cow?'

Her fingers tightened on my arm, pinching into my flesh. 'You will die here, Veronica.'

'Hurry away mother."

I...have no one if you die.'

And I shut the door in her face.

I fell on my knees after Mamma left and cried out to God, to any god, Pagan, Christian or Muslim. I even asked sweet Gobbo di Rialto to take pity on my Nonna.

And my prayers were answered because Nonna did return to me. Maybe they took pity on her or more likely they didn't want a plague victim in their midst. They left her outside my door that night. She was delirious but I think she knew she was home. I picked her up − she was as light as a child, then I carried her to my room, bathed her, dressed her in clean linen and sent the maid for the doctor.

The doctor warned me to protect myself from the contagion. He urged me to have Nonna moved to the island and very soon he stopped coming. At first the serving girl brought food and looked after our needs but then she disappeared too. All the servants fled. I didn't blame them, they needed to be with their families. I hoped they lived. There was some food in our cold store but Nonna ate nothing and I ate stale bread and remnants of cheese.

Nonna never spoke again but I held her hand. I sang some of her old peasant songs to her and danced. I prayed for her death to be swift and it was. I watched as the pestilencia washed through her old limbs like a cresting wave. Soon the swellings came and my beautiful Nonna was covered in the pustules of poison − her soft, skin tainted with livid purple stains. I read prayers from her prayer book and I trust that the gentle, compassionate God, she believed in, heard me, because He was my last hope. She faded away like a small candle that death had leant over and snuffed out. A little death. When it was over I wrapped her gently in the shroud and waited for the men to come. Boats carrying the dead and dying to the plague islands, plied the canals day and night, calling out for families to bring out their dead and dying.

291

After she was taken, all I could do was wait for the contagion to claim me. I felt the city tingling with fear around me and watched as people ran distractedly this way and that, like ants from a destroyed nest, piling their possessions into boats, trying to escape. Food was running out. Clean water was rationed. They said 50,000 Venetians had died, along with my Jacopo and the old Doge. I didn't care about The Doge but my friend was a great loss to me.

I hadn't heard from Alfonso and I couldn't get a message to him, but I had to trust that he, his family and my Ginevra, were still alive.

I wished I had visited my poor friends on the Rialto one more time and distributed the last of my 'treasure'. I had accomplished some of my promises to the women but there was still much to do. The safe houses I had promised were only half built. The council had refused my petition to fund houses where they and their children could live safely, away from the squalor and deprivation. The school was only half built. All the fine words I had spoken, all the promises I had made? I had failed those pathetic creatures, who still sold their bodies for a loaf of bread or wine. They had no protectors, the Magistrati alla Sanita, the nobili and the patriciate turned their backs on them − the despised Meritrica.

I was ready for my death. I didn't deserve to live.

Today

1576

'Lazzaretto Vecchio. Avanti.' The ferryman is calling. His voice is strong, and I drag myself to the window and see the boat. It is already full of people.

'Have you room for one more, Signor?' My voice is weak and cracked but the boatman hears and heads his craft towards my mooring. Once there he looks up to where I stand, shielding his eyes against the sun's glare, then he leaps effortlessly onto the tow path. I had forgotten how the healthy move. He's in the shadows beneath my balcony now and, as he stares up, I see his face clearly.

'Alfonso?' I whisper, not believing my eyes. 'Alfonso? Is it you?'

'Signora Bertrame? My lady,' his voice trembles. 'But they told me you were dead.' Someone is shouting and he glances to where soldiers are dragging huge metal sheets into position on the bridge. One man beckons urgently to Alfonso.

'We must hurry before they close this bridge, my lady."

'Will you come up and help me descend?' I ask. 'I have not the strength.'

293

San Marco's bells toll as I creep down the steps to the canal. I almost fall but Alfonso steadies me, half carrying me down the last few. It surprises me to see his face uncovered and I turn my head away, so as not to spread the contagion. Out on the tow path the canal water laps and I raise the hem of my gown without thinking, so as not to soil the material. Such silly vanity.

'Can you stand?' he asks, 'while I fetch your luggage?'

I shake my head. 'No luggage, Alfonso,' and, taking two rings from my purse I hold them out to him. 'My payment for the ferry.'

'No, grazie, Signora, Magistrati alla Sanita pay me.'

He jumps down into his boat and holds his hands out to me. I almost fall as I attempt to climb over the gunwale but he steadies me, guiding my feet into the craft. I pull the shawl tightly over my head and hold it tight against my mouth. There are several people slumped or crouching where I stand, their faces shrouded, their bodies defeated. There is no sound. Alfonso offers me a small space beside the oarlock. I sink down and he hands me a rough blanket. 'It may be cold on the lagoon, my lady,' he says, as he pushes off from the bank.

His kindness is almost too much to bear. I had thought that there was no kindness left in this savage Venice. The foul canal water is thick and sluggish and sucks at the boat, like a miser clutching at his gold, afraid to lose it. There is no sound, except for the creaking of the oar and the occasional moan or curse from someone, as we move slowly under the bridge. Soldiers line it, ready to lower the metal plates to seal off the bridge, when we are through. Two of the *labourers take off their caps and stand, heads bowed, as we glide beneath them. Turning onto the Big Canal a gentle breeze springs up.*

The figure slumped beside me is wrapped from head to foot in a long cloak. The face is bandaged, except for a slit for the eyes and nose, and a claw-like hand, which clings to the edge of the boat. The other is clamped over the mouth. The patch of skin showing is a mass of vivid purple blotches. My dress and the death pustules, how well we match one another.

The effort of getting into the boat has exhausted me and I sit quietly gathering my strength. It is so good to see Alfonso's sweet familiar face and I keep looking at him, making sure I am not imagining him. If he lives maybe my girl lives too. There are many questions I must put to my friend.

I try to remember how old Alfonso is now. Certainly no longer a boy. He is strong as he steers the boat but he looks gaunt and exhausted.

When I can, I speak. 'Why do you not cover your face from the contagion? You must protect yourself. Venice will have need of people like you, when the city is saved.'

He takes a deep shuddering breath and closes his eyes 'I have no need to protect myself, my Lady. I am cured.'

Hope flares in me. 'The theriac?'

He shrugs. 'The priest says I have been saved for a purpose.' He looks grim. 'The living still have work to do in Venice.'

I didn't understand. Why was he not happy? He was cured, blessed. 'And Ginevra? Is she cured?'

295

He looked away from me. 'She has taken the theriac.''

'And?'

'I had to send her away, my Lady. Giada has her safe.'

'You sent her to the Rialto? You sent her to that place, Alfonso?'

'I had to. The pestilencia? It came to our house. I knew you had the plague here too, San Polo was safer. There was nowhere else to send her. And Giada lives away from the Carampane in the dressmaker's house. Ginevra will be safe.'

'But you are cured, she could have stayed with you.'

'I fell ill with my family, my Lady. I thought I would die.'

I was fighting with myself, trying not to blame him, trying and failing to understand what had made him do such a thing. The one thing I'd asked him to do and he had failed me. 'And your family? Alfonso?' I say quietly, spitefully, unable to stop myself. 'What of your family? Have you taken better care of them? Of your little Sofia and your old father. Are they well? You didn't send them away did you? Are they cured, Alfonso?'

'No, no,' he sobs. 'Tutti familia. All gone... I wrapped them in shrouds and stacked them in the pits, one against one, like bolts of cloth. My mother, father, brother, my little sister... all gone.'

'Oh, no! My poor friend I am so sorry. Forgive me. I didn't know'

'I wanted to die too, Signora, I prayed to God, but I survived. I am not blessed I am cursed.'

'No,' I murmured, reaching out to him. 'You must live, Alfonso.'

296

He was quiet for a moment and then he said. 'May I ask you something, Signora? Are you frightened of dying? How bad is the pain? Do you believe in God?'

He must have seen my face because he let go of the oar, hid his head in his hands and wept. 'Forgive me, I didn't mean to be cruel, I just wanted to know how they felt...how they felt when they....' The boat had stopped moving and, those that could, looked up wearily to see what was wrong.

Taking his hand in mine I raised it to my cheek. My flesh is slippery with sweat but his is strong and cool. 'No, I am not frightened of dying, Alfonso. I will be with my Carlo, my child and Nonna. Live your life, Alfonso.'

'Nonna?'

'Yes,' I say. 'Her too. Find the child, my friend. She will be alive, somewhere. Find her and make a life for yourselves. My house is yours.'

Shifting his body he pulled strongly out into the Canal and I catch a glimpse of something beside his bare feet. It is a lute. He sees me looking and kicks the instrument further under a plank, out of sight. He doesn't speak, but he turns his head and stares at me.

I look into his eyes — his bright, blackbird eyes. 'Alfonso? Do you still play?'

'Not since ...that night...'

'...But you kept your lute?'

'It's the only thing they left, after they looted the farmacia. They came when I was burying my family. They took everything, Sofia's

297

dolls, Mamma's best copper cooking pot. All they left were the rats and the lute. But they broke the strings.'

'You can restring it. You must play, Alfonso."

'Did you still dance for them? The patriciate?' His eyes are challenging but he sees my distress and looks quickly away.

'There was no other way, Alfonso. Believe me, there was no option.'

'I could have helped you.'

'No one could help me. It was just a way of surviving. And they meant nothing to me - less than nothing.'

'But Signor Bertrame? He would have been so sad.'

'Carlo died, Alfonso.' I feel a tear on my cheek. So cool on my hot flesh. I had not meant to cry. I made myself concentrate on the boy. 'You disappeared from my life after...I missed you. There was no one else who loved Carlo as well as you and me.'

Alfonso lifted his face to mine. 'I couldn't...my Lady, I'm sorry. I have worked the canals with my family. Ginevra came too. We often came beneath your windows. She didn't understand why we didn't see you.'

'My Carlo loved you like a son.'

'He was good to me.'

'You are blessed, Alfonso.'

His fist clenches. 'Si, I am blessed' He is quiet for a moment and then he looks at me and I see the horror and misery in his eyes. He reminds me of another boy as he died in my arms, slain by the vipers' venom.

298

'Now, let us go to the Lazzaretto, my friend. Maybe, if God is willing, Veronica Bertrame and these people will be blessed too and one day I will dance again with Ginevra, to your sweet music.' Then I reach into my sleeve and pull out my red book. 'This is for you, all our dances and music are in here. Keep it safe and one day you will become the great dance master Alfonso Ortha. No one will know the dance creations are mine, no one except you and your children and their children's children. Your fame will be mine.'

He shakes his head .'No,' I try to press the book into his hands but he won't take it and my nerveless fingers can't hold onto it. It slips down into the grey bilge water, that laps at our feet. I cry out, as though in pain, and he scoops it up before the foul water destroys my work. Rubbing moisture off the leather he puts the book inside his jerkin. 'I will guard this for you, Signora, until you are well again and we will perform your dances. I am saving every ducat from this ...business and I will look after you and Ginevra and you will never need to be a....'

'...Forget me, Carlo. You could be a great musician. Make me proud of you. And... Alfonso, please don't hate me.'

He looked at me and slowly shook his head, 'I never hated you, my Lady. I was wrong. You did what you had to. But I couldn't bear it. I'm sorry. Forgive me.'

I smiled. 'All this time wasted.'

He nodded. 'All this time.'

Once in the Lagoon the water is clear and turquoise. Small silver fish dart amongst the seaweed-wrapped skeletons of ancient wrecks. I close my aching eyes and try to picture Carlo and me here. We had often visited the islands, and knew them well. I remember the tall-masted brigantines moored off the Lazzaretto Vecchio, waiting for their quarantino to pass, so they could unload their exotic cargoes of spices, food, wine, glass and carpets. Those with the pestilence on board flew black flags before the sailors and merchants were allowed into our city.

All too soon we are entering the small canal which leads to the landing stage on the plague island. Orderlies swathed in long coats and cloaks line the banks awaiting us. Their faces are hidden. Two men stand beside a cart pulled by an old nag. Once Alfonso ties up at our mooring the dead are quickly removed, stacked in the cart and driven away. Several people run after the cart screaming and lamenting. But they cannot keep up and soon sink to the ground, their outstretched arms reaching for their loved ones. The doctors come next, wearing long-nosed masks, stuffed with vinegar infusions to ward off the pestilence. They move amongst us silently, pulling back face coverings, examining arms and legs, assessing each new victim. The stench of their infusions hits the back of my throat. Children cower in terror as the doctors approach them. One doctor has a limp like a carrion crow, his black cape flapping, like battered leathery wings. Many of these people are not infected yet but they will be soon. They have been locked up in their homes with their dead and dying

300

relatives. It will soon be their turn. The almost-dead are carried to the sanatorium on stretchers and the rest shuffle along behind, leaning on sticks, helped by those who can bear their weight.

Alfonso carries me onto the bank and two stretcher- bearers help me lie down. I struggle. 'I can walk, let me walk,' and Alfonso pushes them aside and helps me to stand.

'I will see you again, my lady. Do not despair. May God go with you.'

I take his calloused young hand in mine and feel the warmth of him. Then I open my purse and let the pearl necklace fall into his hands. He backs away, a look of horror on his face, 'No, I can't,' he says, thrusting the necklace back at me.

'No. Please, take it,' I say. 'Find Ginevra and make a new life for yourselves, Alfonso. Promise me?'

His eyes are huge and bright and I turn away. I mustn't see him cry. I stagger forward and an orderly grasps my arm but I shake my head and we follow the line of people shuffling towards the hospital, Alfonso calls after me.

'Signora? We will meet again. When you are cured. You will dance again.'

'Goodbye Alfonso, be happy. And look after our girl? Promise me?' He nods and I walk on, trying not to stumble, not looking back.

'When you are well, write to me, my Lady, at the Magistrati alla Sanita and I will return for you. I will watch your house. Do you hear me? They will let you write to me. Do you hear me, Veronica? I promise, I will come for you.'

301

I raise a weary hand in farewell and his words drift away. Somewhere there is the sound of music, the music of my soul, and I lift my step in time to the sweet sound.

A MESSAGE TO ALFONSO ORTHA

Veronica Maria Bertrame lives

Signed: Magistrati alla Sanita

Republic of Venice. Agosto-1576

Anne Ousby lives on the Northumbrian coast in England.
Her stories have been published in anthologies
and broadcast on Radio 4.
Her stage plays have been performed widely in the North East.
A television drama 'Wait till the Summer Comes,' was broadcast on
ITV.

Novels

'Patterson's Curse ' 2010.

'The Leopard Man.' 2012

'The Last Iceberg' 2014

'Your Friend E'   2015

'The woman who loved to dance' 2019.

21834110R00184

Printed in Great Britain
by Amazon